EDGE LINES

Fallen Messengers # 3

AVA MARIE SALINGER

silver
orb
publishing

COPYRIGHT

Edge Lines (Fallen Messengers #3)
Copyright © 2022 by Ava Marie Salinger
All rights reserved.
Registered with the US Copyright Office.
Hardback edition: 2022

ISBN: 978-1-912834-27-3
www.AMSalinger.com

Edited by Right Ink On The Wall
Cover Design by 17 Studio Book Design

Want to know about Ava's upcoming releases? Sign up to her newsletter for exclusive stories, new release alerts, sneak peeks, giveaways, and more.

WANT A FREE PREQUEL STORY?

Sign up to Ava's newsletter to get Unbound, as well as new release alerts, sneak peeks, giveaways, and more.

FALLEN MESSENGERS
GLOSSARY

Aerial: An angel or demon who can control wind.

Alchemist: A human who can create new matter or
manipulate existing matter into new forms. Emits a scent
of powdered iron.

Aqueous: An angel or demon who can control water.

Argent Lake: Home of the Naiads.

Argonaut Agency: Organization responsible for law and
order in the supernatural and magical communities.
Headquarters in New York. Agents include angels, demons,
and magic users.

Astrea Sea: Home of the Nereids.

Bloodsand: A black tree with red veins that grows in the Nine Hells. Created by warlocks who made pacts with the Underworld after the Fall. Can be used to summon war demons from the Nine Hells.

Blossom Silver: A silver derivative that can heal injuries caused by demonic weapons or black magic. Made by the Naiads.

Cabalista: Demonic organization. Agents include demons only. Headquarters in London.

Dark Blight: A powder black-magic users use in their rituals and which is poisonous to angels and other magic users. Made by Shadow Empire alchemists from the heart of a Dryad.

Demi: The offspring of a God of Heaven/God of the Underworld and a human or a being possessing divine powers. Can take on any appearance.

Electrum: Naturally occurring alloy of gold and silver, as well as copper and other trace elements. Used extensively by Argonaut in their weapons. Combined with steel, titanium, and Rain Silver to make their bullets.

Empyreal: The highest order of angels or demons, with powers equal to those of a Demigod.

Enchanter/Enchantress: A human who uses illusion magic. Emits a scent of cedar.

Fiery: An angel or a demon who can wield Heaven or Hell's Fire.

Fractured Soul: A human's damaged soul core, extracted from the body – a powerful source of magic.

Ghoul: An evil spirit who consumes the flesh of humans. Emits a scent of rotting meat.

Glitterfang: A pale powder white-magic users employ in their rituals and which is poisonous to demons and black-magic users. Made by Nereids.

Hexa: Guild of magic users. Agents include magic users only. Headquarters in Seattle.

Incubus: A male demon who gains power from sleeping with humans and divine entities.

Ivory Peaks: Home of the Dryads.

Khimer: A creature born of the fusion of a Reaper and a living being.

Lucifugous: A heliophobic demon who abhors light and who can control darkness.

Mage: A human who uses an arcane staff to focus their magic powers. Emits a scent of Juniper.

Magic Levels: Classification of magic users based on their

abilities, with Level Six being the weakest and Level One the strongest.

Messengers: Those belonging to the Third Sphere of Heaven and Third Hierarchy of Demons.

Order of Rosen: Religious order affiliated with the Catholic Church. Agents include angels only. Headquarters in Rome.

Rain Silver: A liquid-silver derivative that can injure and kill demons. Made by the Nymphs.

Rain Vale: Home of the Nymphs.

Reaper: A soul collector and guide of the dead. Emits a scent of camphor.

Reaper Seed: A drug that can intoxicate most beings and which is fatal in high doses. Mined by Lucifugous demons in the Shadow Empire. Potent hallucinogen for Lucifugous demons.

Shadow Empire: Home of Ghouls, Lucifugous demons, and Dark Alchemists.

Sorcerer/Sorceress: A human born with powerful soul core magic. Uses the energies around them to manipulate magic. Emits the scent of Valerian.

Soul Core: A living being's life force. Red for demons, white for angels, and dirty gray for humans.

Spirit Realm: Home of Pan, the Gods of the Underworld, and lesser spirits.

Stark Steel: Strongest and most magic-resistant metal on Earth. Found exclusively in the weapons and armor of the Fallen.

Succubus: A female demon who gains power from sleeping with humans and divine entities.

Terrene: An angel or demon who can control earth and its derivative metals.

The Fall: An unexplained event five hundred years ago that resulted in an army of angels and demons falling to Earth.

The Fallen: Angels or demons who fell to Earth.

The Nether: The space between Heaven, Earth, and the Nine Hells.

The Abyss: A forgotten realm beyond the Nether from where there is no escape.

War Demon: Demon soldiers created for battle. Remnants of an ancient war between Heaven and Hell. Banished to the deepest parts of the Hells.

Warlock: A human who draws power from demons and the Hells and converts it to magic. Emits a scent of sulfur.

Wizard/Witch: A human who learns to use magic through spell books, and who utilizes potions and rituals to access their soul-core magic. Emits a scent of Frankincense.

PRELUDE

The wrath of a God can destroy worlds.

The words resonated in Cassius Black's mind as he fought the unearthly powers lashing at him. Ice and snow wreathed the air in a violent storm that sought to sap him of his will and freeze his limbs. Frozen grass crunched under his foot when he took a step forward, the smell of winter a clean, cold scent sharp enough to bite. He gritted his teeth and forged ahead.

To fall now would mean the destruction of this world and the annihilation of countless others.

Light flared on Cassius's flesh and armor as he called upon his demigod powers, the divine energy melting the frost creeping along the metal and piercing the shadows suffocating the space around him. He could sense Morgan King in the distance, the angel's soul core a point of heat that echoed with his own across the thick, white veil separating them. The demigod's black wind and Dryad magic made the air howl as he held back the God screaming at them.

There was another with him. A man Cassius had thought he knew better than most. A demon whose true powers had finally manifested during this battle.

Victor Sloan was more than he had claimed to be, just as Cassius and Morgan were. Whether this was by design or by omission was still unclear.

One thing was certain though.

Whatever twisted fate had connected Cassius and Morgan before the Fall, Victor had played a part in it. Just like that time under the cathedral in San Francisco, when the man who had manipulated Chester Moran into tearing the Nether open had revealed his hatred for them and given them a glimpse of their pasts, but they had only seen a fraction of the truth.

Cassius scowled.

Now's not the time to dwell on that! I need to see this through or there won't be a future left for us to find that bastard and get the answers we need!

A shape finally loomed out of the tempest. It was a giant oak tree, one that soared some two hundred feet above the ground and bore roots that meandered deep into the sacred forest.

A figure stood beneath it.

The demigod glowed with the fury of winter, his eyes cold and unseeing. The radiance emanating from his body and the divine weapon he wielded on his head barely held the darkness swathing him at bay.

Cassius looked up, his preternatural sight piercing the inky squalls shrouding the land in eternal gloom. His heart thumped heavily against his ribs.

The sky rippled far above the frozen branches of the oak tree, the boundary protecting the realm he stood in splintering under the power of the Frost Crown. The ground cracked beneath his feet.

Cassius's alarmed gaze found the comatose demigod once more. He focused on his body, knowing he had only one chance at this. A glimmer emerged, one that flickered in and out of sight.

Let's hope I'm right about this!

A shape loomed out of the storm. It grabbed the frozen figure bearing the Frost Crown before he could react, its colossal arms closing tightly around him.

"Now, Awakener!"

Cassius clenched his jaw, closed the distance to the captive demigod, and stabbed him in the heart with the weapon bequeathed to him. At the far end of the meadow, beyond the angel and the demon restraining him, the Wild God bellowed in rage and despair.

I

ONE WEEK AGO

"Their Majesties, the king and queen of the Dryads, now invite you to grace them with your presence."

Morgan's face tightened as the herald's solemn words echoed across the sumptuous hall leading to the throne room.

"Grace them with our presence?" he grumbled to Cassius under his breath. "We've waited a goddamn week to see them!"

Galliad Fenhorn cleared his throat diplomatically where he stood beside them in formal court attire. The former Head Mage of the Dryad royal family had been assigned the task of being Cassius and Morgan's official guide during their stay in Ivory Peaks.

"It wasn't deliberate," Cassius murmured.

The Dryad guards started pushing open the towering, gilded oak doors before them, the wood creaking loudly as it glided across a pale marble floor.

Morgan ran a finger around the neckline of his silk shirt

12

and kaftan, irate. "Still, I can't wait to get out of these clothes."

"You look good in them," Cassius said.

Surprise flashed across Morgan's handsome face. "I do?"

Cassius clamped his lips together. Morgan looked so pleased he was almost puffing his chest out.

"Those clothes were made by a three-thousand-year-old Dryad who tailors exclusively for our royal family," Regina Bvarvik remarked drily. Gold and silver glittered in the opulent dress of the Dryad court's seer as she shifted, her ash-wood staff thumping the ground with a firm sound. "Few have the privilege of wearing her garments."

Morgan rolled his eyes.

Cassius bit back a sigh. His lover was not one for pomp and ceremony. If Morgan had had his way, they would have left Ivory Peaks several days ago, with Julia and Zach. It was Galliad who had convinced them to stay, the Dryad promising there had to be a valid reason for the king and queen's absence from the capital. Regina's silence on the subject had spoken volumes.

It hadn't taken long for Cassius to pick up on the undercurrent of tension coursing through the palace in the days following their arrival. Even Morgan, who was usually obtuse when it came to such things, had sensed it.

Something was happening. Something grave enough to have taken the rulers of the Dryad kingdom and their first-born heir away from the capital. The third and fourth princes had remained tight-lipped on the subject during the dinners and the tea parties they'd hosted, keeping to neutral topics with the practiced ease of born diplomats.

Cassius had seen traces of their older brother, the second prince Cedric Esteban, in them, though Arfinn and

Tor were more refined and tactful than their sharp-tongued sibling. Cedric hadn't accompanied Cassius, Morgan, and Galliad to Ivory Peaks, preferring instead to stay on Earth to better get to know Eden Monroe, his fiancée and the wielder of the Bloodcursed Devilwood Summoning Staff.

That no one was willing to tell Cassius and Morgan why they'd had to wait a week to meet the Dryad king and queen was not necessarily a bad thing. The two angels had no right to be privy to the private affairs of the Dryad court.

Except that Morgan is one of them.

It had been a month since Morgan had manifested Dryad magic during their battle with Lucille Hartman, the disciple of the man who had manipulated Tania Lancaster and her son Chester Moran from the shadows to achieve his dark goals. Having saved the life of the second prince of the Dryad kingdom, Morgan and Cassius had been invited to Ivory Peaks by the king and queen of the Dryads to receive their thanks.

Though he'd ventured into the Dryads' territory on a few occasions in the past few hundred years during his missions for the agencies that governed the otherwordly on Earth, Cassius had never visited the capital. The people he'd been after would never have dared venture this far, preferring instead to keep to the vast mountain ranges and thick forests that characterized the kingdom. There was also the fact that the only official gateway between Earth and the Dryad realm was under the control of the royal family. The criminals Cassius was usually after used the unstable rifts that had opened between all the realms and Earth following the Fall instead.

And yet, the glittering city perched on the side of the

highest elevation in Ivory Peaks had felt strangely familiar to Cassius from the moment he'd walked out of the portal with Morgan and the others a week ago. He had no doubt the cognizance he felt originated from the demigod he had been before the Fall.

Not for the first time, Cassius cursed the spell Chester and Lucille's secretive master had spoken of, the day Cassius and Morgan had confronted him under the cathedral in San Francisco. The spell that had erased the memories of all the Fallen.

It was because of that spell that Morgan had had nightmares ever since the Fall. It was the reason that the two of them could not recall their past connection as lovers, nor the enemy who had once defeated them.

Finding the truth about who they were and what had caused an army of angels and demons to crash-land on Earth five hundred years ago was now a matter of dire urgency. Because it was clear Chester and Lucille's master was up to something again.

Breaking the magic behind the spell was not an option. The agonizing pain that had threatened to shred Cassius's sanity every time he'd attempted it was proof of this. It was a truth he'd hidden from Morgan, aware the Aerial would be upset that he'd dared put himself at risk in such a futile endeavor.

Instead, seeking those who retained some vestige of knowledge of the events before the Fall was the only recourse he and Morgan now had. Bostrof Orzkal, the former king of the Lucifugous demons and ruler of the Shadow Empire, was among those who still retained faint memories from his past life. It was the Lucifugous who had told Cassius he bore the title Guardian of Light. His wife, the Nymph Lilaia, had similarly advised Morgan that he was once known as the Prince of Night. Both Bostrof and Lilaia had been confident Cassius and Morgan would not find the answers they sought on Earth. The couple had speculated the demigods would likely find someone who could tell them about their pasts in the Spirit Realm.

Considering no one knew the location of any rifts that might have formed between Earth and that dominion, and that none of its Gods or spirits had ventured to Earth since the Fall, Cassius realized his and Morgan's chances of finding the truth from that avenue were slim at best.

The doors to the throne room came to rest with a thunderous boom.

The herald took a few steps inside, stopped, and bowed stiffly at the waist. "Announcing their Majesties' visitors, Cassius Black and Morgan King, along with their companions, the honorable Galliad Fenhorn, former Head Mage of the royal court, and Regina Bvarvik, the royal court seer."

His voice reverberated across the palatial chamber that lay over the threshold.

Surprise jolted Cassius when Morgan clasped his hand, his strong fingers twining firmly with his. He took a deep breath and made to move.

MORGAN FELT CASSIUS STARTLE WHEN HE TOOK HIS
hand. The Empyreal did not resist his touch as they
entered the majestic throne room beyond the gilded doors.
If anything, he shifted closer to Morgan. Guilt tightened
Morgan's chest.

He knew he was being an ill-tempered asshole, but he
couldn't help it.

In their wisdom, the Dryads had assigned him and
Cassius their most splendid guest suite. The lavish rooms
took up the northwest corner of the first floor of the
palace and offered dizzying views of the valley below the
capital and the far-flung mountain ranges framing it. The
suite also looked out onto a private garden guarded twenty-
four-seven by palace guards, the windows and doorways
open to the elements but for trellises heavy with flowers
and ivy; despite the ice and snow-clad peaks above them,
the air in the capital was eternally balmy. Only the bathing
chamber and changing room in the suite offered some

semblance of privacy, the gauzy curtains letting in the light while only hinting at the figures behind them.

All this meant he hadn't made love to Cassius in a week.

The Empyreal had refused to even entertain the notion, claiming their bedroom sessions would be overheard by the palace guards. His look of utter disbelief when Morgan had promised to be quiet had done little to curb the Aerial's frustration.

"You know as well as I do that that's a big fat lie," Cassius had scolded when Morgan had tried to get amorous during their bath two nights ago. He'd ignored Morgan's raging erection and climbed out of the copper tub before turning to face him, hands on his hips and completely disregarding his own stirring cock. "Get it in your thick head. We're not making out until we get back to San Francisco!"

"I might die by then," Morgan had griped.

Cassius's lips had flattened into a thin line before he'd marched out of the bathroom. Morgan had stared hotly at his alluring form and told himself attempting to seduce the Empyreal further would only end with him earning a black eye and likely having to suffer a longer period of enforced abstinence. Though Cassius knew Morgan's sexual drive outdid his own, it didn't mean he was willing to entertain his every desire. The fact that he stood up to Morgan and challenged his hot-blooded behavior was one of the many things Morgan loved about the beguiling Empyreal.

Still, he'd better be prepared. He's not going to be able to walk for days when we get home. Morgan glanced at Cassius. His lover gave him a puzzled look. *Make that a week.*

With that idea firmly in mind, Morgan finally paid heed

to the imposing hall they were navigating. Dazzling sunlight washed across them as they traversed a central concourse, the bright rays filling the opulent space with an almost unearthly radiance. Towering oak pillars framed the wide aisle, the trees twined with boughs laden with foliage and fragrant flowers that twisted and arched to a distant, vaulted ceiling.

Legend had it that the Dryad palace had sprouted from the remains of the first Dryad consort, husband to Atlanteia. Though Morgan didn't exactly cherish the thought of treading the innards of a long-fallen God, he had to admit that the place was something else. Nothing on Earth matched its majestic splendor or the pureness of the air that wafted through its imposing spaces.

Nobles crowded the space around them, their luxurious attire another testament to the prosperity of the Dryad kingdom. A few whispers sounded when they observed Morgan and Cassius's linked hands. Several twisted their mouths in displeasure.

Although homosexuality was universally accepted on Earth and among the Fallen, there were realms that still entertained ancient notions about what constituted an acceptable union in the eyes of the Heavens.

Morgan ignored their murmurs and furrowed brows, his gaze focused on the raised stage ahead. Roald and Hildur Esteban watched them steadily from where they sat on their thrones. Elwyn Fremaine, the Head Mage who had replaced Galliad after he came to Earth, stood to their right, the green robes he wore and the alderwood staff he wielded symbols of his station. Arfinn and Tor were on their parents' left, the princes resplendent in their official royal attire.

There was no sign of Leiv Esteban, the first prince, nor Thalia Fenhorn, Galliad's wife and chief commander of the Dryad kingdom's army.

Disquiet darted through Morgan. *So, their strongest warriors are still missing.*

He and Cassius stopped at the bottom of the steps leading to the thrones, dropped to one knee, and lowered their heads respectfully. Galliad bowed at the waist and Regina curtseyed primly.

Morgan recited the official Dryad greeting he had been taught, his words echoed by Cassius and the two Dryads.

"May Atlanteia's blessing be with thee."

The king and queen spoke. *"We receive her blessing and grant thee the same."*

Roald rose from his seat, Hildur following suit. Clothes swished behind Morgan as the Dryad nobles lowered themselves to their knees in deference to their liege.

Roald's commanding voice resonated across the throne room. "Rise."

Morgan stood up slowly, Cassius at his side. He observed the king and queen with a neutral expression and wondered if his lover had picked up on what he'd just noticed.

The Dryad royals looked exhausted, as did the mage beside them.

From what Arfinn accidentally let slip at breakfast, they came back yesterday, in the dead of night.

"We apologize for keeping you waiting so long," Hildur said graciously. "It was not our intention to ignore you. We have been looking forward to your visit."

Remorse pierced Morgan at the queen's words. He

could tell from Cassius's demeanor that the Empyreal was trying hard not to give him an "I told you so" stare.

"Galliad sent news about the incident concerning the Bloodcursed Devilwood Summoning Staff," Roald said. "We are truly grateful for all that you did to protect our son and the artifact he was guarding."

Hildur sighed. "Although, truth be told, we were surprised to hear about his sudden engagement."

A surprised babble rose around them. Judging from the Dryad nobles' expressions, they had not been made aware of Cedric's betrothal to Eden Monroe.

Arfinn and Tor did their best to keep straight faces.

The two princes had collapsed in undignified fits of laughter when Cassius and Morgan had recounted what Cedric had done to save Eden. They'd wiped their eyes and confessed that they'd always believed the second prince to be an old coot in a young man's body and that they'd feared he was destined for a life of celibacy, so taciturn was he in the presence of the female Dryads who had attempted to court him over the years.

"I gather my future daughter-in-law is a powerful mage," Roald observed drily.

"She is indeed," Cassius said. "She can summon magic from the Nine Hells."

This time, the murmurs rose to a disconcerted brouhaha.

"She will be a much-valued addition to our family and our kingdom, I am sure," Hildur observed, her gaze sweeping the court.

The hubbub died down in the face of her sharp stare.

"I bet she and Brianna will get along like a house on fire," Morgan muttered to Cassius.

Cassius hushed him.

Elwyn stepped forward, his gaze firmly on Morgan. "Although Galliad has told us of your abilities, we would still like to see a demonstration."

An expectant silence fell upon the throne room. The nobles exchanged sidelong glances. Morgan stiffened slightly as all eyes turned to him. It seemed rumors about him had already circulated across the Dryad capital.

He'd been warned by Galliad and Regina that he might have to manifest his demigod and Dryad powers during his audience with Roald and Hildur. According to them, it would be the fastest way for the Dryad king and queen to convince the nobles in attendance of Morgan's royal lineage and foil the hours of debate that would likely follow any other kind of official revelation. He looked over at Cassius.

The Empyreal dipped his chin, his expression encouraging. He stepped away, giving him space. Galliad and Regina followed suit.

Morgan took a shallow breath, conscious of the unblinking stares leveled at him. *Here we go.*

THE FIRST TIME MORGAN HAD UNLOCKED HIS DEMIGOD powers had been during his and Cassius's initial encounter with Chester Moran, when Cassius had called his true name and sent a spark of divine energy to his core, cracking the seal suppressing his abilities and releasing the black wind he had been born to wield.

The second time had been during his cage fight with Bostrof, when his rage had caused another seal to shatter, turning his wings black and allowing him to manifest the Sword of Wind.

The last time had been during their clash with the bloodcursed mage Lucille, when the demigod inside Cassius had broken a third lock stifling Morgan's powers and unleashed his Dryad magic.

In the time since that latest battle, Morgan had learned to access his newly rediscovered gifts on his own.

Heat filled him as he drew on the divine energy and ancient magic permeating his soul core. His wings sprouted from his back with a loud clap, the gray feathers darkening as a black tempest engulfed them and the dark armor that covered his clothes. He rose amidst the growing vortex, the Sword of Wind whooshing into existence in his left hand.

Startled gasps sounded as an emerald light bloomed around him, the ethereal glow dancing prettily within the shadowy currents swirling around his body. Green shoots formed on his dark blade, the weapon taking on a new, thicker form. Creepers snaked up Morgan's arm, twigs and leaves sprouting on them even as they strengthened his hold on the sword.

A crown of oak and black wind formed on his head.

A stunned silence descended inside the throne room as he landed lightly on his feet, the storm around him a controlled, dull hum that made the air quiver.

Roald and Hildur stared, pale-faced.

"It is true," Roald finally murmured. "You are a descendant of Queen Atlanteia. It is the only reason you could manifest that crown."

To Morgan's surprise, the king and queen bowed their heads, along with Elwyn and the two princes. The Head Mage's half smile told Morgan he had exceeded their expectations.

Clothes swished and armor clinked as the entire court and the guards bowed and curtseyed, startling him. Even Cassius bent at the waist, the way he pinched his lips telling Morgan he was finding this situation intensely amusing.

Morgan squinted at Galliad, suspicion bringing a chill to his voice. "Did you know this would happen?"

The mage looked up and scratched his cheek, abashed. "I had an inkling it might."

Morgan blew out a sigh. He retracted his powers and

his wings before addressing the chamber. "Please, every-one. Just...get up."

Roald and Hildur straightened, their court following suit.

A thought hit Morgan.

"I hope no one is about to suggest something inane like me inheriting the Dryad kingdom," he warned.

The look Roald and Hildur exchanged almost had him groaning.

"It is rightly yours," Hildur confessed demurely. "We may be of royal lineage, but we are not direct scions of the first Dryad queen."

Morgan arched an eyebrow. "You would give up your throne so easily?"

Hildur shrugged. "Unlike the human world and the other realms, Dryads do not fight over positions of power. Only those who are born to it wield the title of ruler."

Morgan observed the royals for a moment.

"Look, no offense, but I have no need for a throne," he said bluntly. "Running my team is enough of a pain in my ass. Ruling a kingdom would give me permanent indigestion." He rubbed the back of his neck and made a face. "In fact, if Cedric's attitude is anything to go by, I'd be riddled with ulcers within a month."

Arfinn and Tor stifled snorts. Roald's lips twitched. Regina sighed. Galliad's shoulders shook slightly.

"I can't believe you just said that!" Cassius hissed, eyeing Morgan sharply.

Morgan shrugged, undeterred. "It's the truth. You saw how stubborn that kid is. Imagine having to deal with countless similarly pigheaded Dryads."

"The worst of them is standing right next to me," Cassius scolded.

Hildur smiled at their exchange. It was clear their status as lovers did not bother her or the king.

"Then please know that the throne will be waiting for you if you want to claim it one day." Roald dipped his head respectfully. "Once more, you have our eternal gratitude for saving our son. If there is anything you wish for, anything at all, please let us know."

Morgan hesitated before cutting his eyes to Cassius. The Empyreal nodded encouragingly.

"There *is* something we'd like to ask you," Morgan said quietly. "Two things, actually."

Hildur arched an eyebrow. "Pray, continue."

"You believe me to be a descendant of Atlanteia." Morgan faltered. "Do you know who my parents were?"

Surprise widened Roald and Hildur's eyes. They looked at one another.

"I am afraid we do not," Roald replied reluctantly. "Atlanteia had many children."

Hildur pursed her lips. "But if I had to hazard a guess, I would say it was one of her sons. The black wind and the blade were gifted to you by your mother."

Morgan stared. "Why do you think that?"

"Because your Dryad magic smells distinctively male."

Morgan glanced at Cassius, surprised. "I didn't know that."

"It comes with experience," Hildur said kindly. "Female Dryads have a more refined nose than males, so we sense these things better."

"You said there are two things you want to ask us,"

Roald observed in the silence that followed. "What is the second?"

"Galliad told us there was once a gate between Ivory Peaks and the Spirit Realm," Cassius said. "He mentioned it was severely damaged during the Fall. Is that still true?"

Roald nodded. "I am afraid so. The only way to travel to the Spirit Realm from here would be if someone in that plane opened a doorway to our kingdom."

"I take it from your query that you wish to go there?" Hildur asked curiously.

"Yes," Morgan replied.

"Why?" Regina said in a flat voice.

"Because it may hold answers to our true identities and what caused the Fall," Cassius explained. "The former king of the Shadow Empire believes there are otherwordly there who have retained their memories from before the Nether tore open. They may be able to tell us the identity of the God we think might have been responsible for that disaster and help us stop him before he does it again."

Tension thickened the air inside the throne room. The Dryad nobles exchanged uneasy looks and whispers. Roald and Hildur's expressions hardened.

"You believe a God was responsible for the Fall?" Elwyn said stiffly. "And that he's trying to repeat the same horror from five hundred years ago?"

"We suspect so," Cassius said. "But we're not certain."

"If it weren't for Cassius and Morgan, the Nether would have torn open again in San Francisco," Galliad declared.

A low roar erupted across the chamber.

Roald frowned and raised a hand to quieten his subjects, his gaze on Cassius and Morgan. "I was not made aware that such an incident had taken place on Earth."

"I am sorry, Your Majesty," Galliad said apologetically. "It was only recently that I found this out myself."

"You saw something similar happening in the future, didn't you?" Morgan turned to Regina. "Cedric told us about the vision you had. The one that compelled you to send him and the Bloodcursed Devilwood Summoning Staff to Earth."

Regina hesitated.

"It is true that my second sight showed me glimpses of a formidable battle that will have Earth as its grounds," she said in a stilted voice. "But I am afraid I did not see the enemy nor their goal, so cannot hazard a guess as to which God you may be alluding to." She faltered, her expression thoughtful. "But one thing is for certain. The Bostrof Orzkal I know is not someone who tells lies. If he advised you that the answers you seek may be found in the Spirit Realm, then you must endeavor to—"

The seer froze. A gasp left her.

"Regina?" Elwyn said, alarmed.

Galliad took a step toward the seer.

Regina's eyes turned white from edge to edge. A faint glow emanated from them. The blood drained from her face.

"No," she mumbled numbly, her blind gaze focused on something no one else could see. "It cannot be!"

A commotion outside the throne room had heads turning. The doors opened hastily, the armed guards moving aside to make way for a bloodied figure in armor.

A Dryad soldier staggered inside the chamber and half ran, half stumbled toward the throne.

Dread filled Morgan as the soldier fell to his knees

beside them. He looked over the man's head at Cassius and saw the same foreboding reflected in the Empyreal's eyes.

"Your Majesties!" the soldier cried, his voice shaking. "The First Army has fallen! Prince Leiv and General Fenhorn's forces have been vanquished!"

Hildur inhaled sharply. "What?!"

The queen pressed a trembling hand to her mouth and swayed where she stood. Her husband folded her into his arms, agony and anger darkening his face. Arfinn and Tor rushed to their side.

Dryad magic exploded around Galliad. He took out his wand, the weapon lengthening and thickening into a rune-covered, elmwood staff under the influence of his powers.

A muscle jumped in the mage's cheek as he glared from Regina and Elwyn to the king and queen. "What the devil is going on?!"

The floor shook with a violent tremor before anyone could speak. A crack split the marble near the entrance and raced up the central concourse. Cassius yanked the wounded Dryad soldier out of the way as the ground splintered and gave way, forming a chasm some three feet wide.

The air fluttered with a current of pure corruption.

Morgan swore. Cassius scowled.

They both knew this foul energy.

"*War demons!*" Morgan growled.

4

SCREAMS ECHOED THROUGH THE PALACE AS THEY MADE their way to the terrace outside the throne room. They staggered to a halt before the wide balustrade, the ground shuddering beneath them. More fissures appeared, marble and stone splitting under the forces rattling the city. A giant oak tree cracked open in the royal gardens below, trunk cleaved neatly in half.

Cassius's eyes widened.

"What the—?!" Morgan started, aghast.

Beyond the panicked birds rising to the sky and the trees and buildings toppling across the royal capital, a wall of darkness cleaved Ivory Peaks. The phenomenon extended across the width of the valley and up to the heavens as far as the eye could see, a solid barrier of greasy, writhing shadows that seemed to absorb the light around it. Macabre, winged figures were emerging from it, their shapes deceptively small in the distance.

Cassius's nails dug into his palms. He knew all too well the war demons stood eight feet tall up close and had deadly claws almost as long as their skeletal limbs. The remnants of an ancient war between Heaven and the Nine Hells, war demons had been banished to the darkest depths of the Underworld eons past by the very Gods and demons who had created them, their never-ending thirst for destruction unmatched by any other creature in the known universe and unnerving even their own makers.

Roald and Hildur grasped the stone railing with white-knuckled grips, their grim expressions indicating they'd been dreading this very situation as they gazed at the black rift.

Galliad glanced at Elwyn, horrified. "Is this why you were away?!"

"Yes." The mage swallowed, ashen faced. "We didn't think it would grow so quickly!"

Galliad ground his teeth. "You mean, you let me sit on my ass for a week while you lot were fighting this? Are you insane?!"

"Do not blame Elwyn, Galliad," Roald said. "It was my order that you not be disturbed."

"Is that the Nether?" Morgan asked Cassius, a muscle jumping in his jawline.

Cassius hesitated. "I'm...not sure." He looked over at Roald and Hildur, his mouth dry. "When did this start?!"

"Two weeks ago," the king said darkly. "At the very edges of our realm. It was not as big as this, though."

"We sought to close the dreadful thing with magic, but we failed," Hildur added bitterly. "The war demons who appeared from it finally retreated in the face of our army." The queen's eyes turned flinty. "It seems our victory lulled us into a false sense of security."

Arfinn pointed at something high above the valley. "There!"

Cassius stared.

A giant eagle had appeared from the clouds. It swooped and scattered the war demons, its golden wings bright against the dark wall and its screech echoing across the vale and the mountains. Sunlight glittered on the armor and sword of the man atop the bird as they engaged the monsters who had invaded their realm, the spell bombs blasting from his staff faint, green explosions in the distance.

Other eagles appeared, fluid shapes arrowing effortlessly through the air despite being laden with Dryad soldiers. A muted roar rose from the floor of the valley.

"It seems news of the demise of your army was premature!" Cassius spread his wings and took to the sky, his dagger lengthening into his Stark Steel sword. "Your soldiers are still fighting!"

"Leiv," Hildur mumbled, her gaze on the warrior on the golden eagle. She looked at Roald. "We must help him!"

The king nodded, his expression equally determined. Shadows rushed over them. Cassius braced as a powerful downdraft drove him down a couple of feet.

A flock of giant eagles landed in the gardens, their passage shaking the trees and bushes. The armed guards atop them clung to the leather and vine harnesses around the birds' chests while the creatures settled down amidst the leaves and twigs fluttering to the ground.

The Dryad in charge of palace security jumped off the lead eagle and landed on the grass with a solid thud.

"Your Majesties, we must make haste and take you and

the princes to safety!" he shouted as he stormed toward the steps leading to the terrace.

"I am afraid we cannot do that, Commander Holm," Hildur said grimly.

To Cassius's everlasting surprise, the queen unhooked her cloak, gave it to Regina, and tore the side seams of her dress from the mid-thigh down. The seer winced as pearls and precious stones clattered to the stone floor.

She and Brianna would definitely get along!

Despite being the head of Hexa, Brianna Monroe was not one to shy away from a fight. And by the looks of things, neither was the Dryad queen.

Holm paled. "My Queen, you do not mean to—" He gulped in the face of Hildur's thunderous frown and turned beseechingly to Roald. "My liege, *please!*"

Roald had already gotten rid of his cloak and unleashed his laurel staff.

"We will not abandon our army in their time of need," he said, lifting his chin. "Besides, the Dryad magic the royal family wields is among the strongest in this realm. It would be foolish for us to stay out of this fight!"

"We're coming with you," Tor said adamantly.

Arfinn nodded vigorously. Roald and Hildur hesitated.

"If anything happens to us, Cedric can rule the kingdom," Tor stated, matter of fact. He pointed at Morgan. "Or he can."

Morgan scowled as he joined Cassius in the air, the Sword of Wind in hand.

"You fools better not die out there," he warned. "I swear, I will hound your souls to the ends of the realms and bring you back kicking and screaming if I have to!"

Hildur smiled faintly.

"Go!" Roald indicated the prince and the soldiers atop the eagles diving through the hordes of war demons above the valley. "You will reach them before us!"

Cassius dipped his head and shot across the gardens. Morgan kept pace as they headed for the palace walls. They skimmed the ramparts and soared above the city.

Unease twisted Cassius's stomach when he looked down.

Fires had broken out across the capital, the flames licking dangerously close to the ancient forest that meandered through it. He spotted scores of Dryads putting out the blazes as he and Morgan flew over.

"They'll be okay," Morgan reassured him as they hurtled above the outer city walls and the steep cliffs that dropped sharply to the valley floor. "Dryads are a long-lived race. And their forests will not burn so easily."

Warmth filled Cassius's chest at his lover's words. As always, Morgan had read his mind and said the words that would allay his anxieties.

The aerial battleground grew up ahead as they winged their way toward the dark wall, the corrupt forces it emanated raising goosebumps on Cassius's skin.

Whatever this was, they had to close it and fast.

A host of war demons spotted them emerging from a bank of clouds, white wisps trailing behind them. The monsters screeched a warning to their brethren and twisted around, their thin, leathery wings spread wide.

By the time Cassius and Morgan stormed their midst, the two angels had assumed their armored, demigod forms.

The oak crown atop Morgan's head pulsed with powerful Dryad magic as he swung his greenery-festooned blade, the dark currents around him pushing the enemy back even as the Sword of Wind carved their repugnant forms into pieces.

Cassius's snow-white wings and metal suit crackled with dazzling radiance, the bright maelstrom engulfing his body and pale hair causing the war demons to shield their eyes and fall away.

Light was poison to them and they hated any being gifted with it.

He raised his divine blade and was about to charge the closest war demons when movement caught his gaze.

An armor-clad figure with a blackthorn and alderwood crown had fallen off an eagle some hundred feet to their right. He clung grimly to the creature's leg as the bird fought off the monsters trying to overrun them, giant talons tearing into the war demons raking her head and flanks with their claws. The eagle's motion rocked the Dryad as the latter attempted to climb back onto her.

The figure cursed as he lost his grip. The eagle screeched, alarmed.

"Your Highness!" someone yelled.

A Dryad rider plummeted toward the falling figure atop her own eagle, her expression one of pure fury and concentration beneath her helmet. Emerald magic danced on the elmwood staff and blade she wielded. Her long, black hair fluttered wildly behind her as she slashed at the monsters blocking her path, her destructive spells lighting the air with violent explosions.

Cassius dove after her.

5

WIND WHISTLED IN CASSIUS'S EARS AND WHIPPED AT HIS face as he steered deftly through a group of war demons. He shot past the female Dryad, slipped through a thin blanket of clouds, and swung his sword.

The blade sliced the wings clean off the back of the monster about to sink his claws into the falling figure.

Cassius's heart raced as he picked up speed. He reached the armored Dryad, grabbed his arm, and braced his wings sharply, halting their descent mid-flight. A grunt left the man at the sudden deceleration. He stared at the valley floor thousands of feet beneath his dangling legs before carefully looking up.

Despite his wounds and his precarious position, Leiv Esteban studied Cassius calmly. "You must be Cassius Black."

"Prince Leiv!"

The woman with the elmwood staff rocked to a halt beside them, her eagle thrumming the air with strong beats of his giant wings. They observed Cassius with a mixture of relief and suspicion.

Cassius carried the prince over to them. "Are you Thalia Fenhorn, Galliad's wife?"

The general's eyes widened at his words. "You know my husband?"

"I do. He will be joining the battlefield shortly, if he isn't already here."

Cassius looked down. Reinforcements from the capital swarmed the valley floor, joining the army on the ground and helping fend off the enemy. More appeared from the city, sunlight glinting on the weapons and armor of the aerial troops heading their way atop eagles.

"This man is the visitor I spoke of," Liev told Thalia as he climbed on behind her. "The one who saved Cedric and the Bloodcursed Devilwood Summoning staff from the enemy who attacked our palace."

Thalia stilled. A screech drew their gazes before she could speak.

Leiv paled. "Asteria!"

His eagle dropped several hundred feet, blood dripping from the gashes on her body as she valiantly fought off the war demons swarming her. Cassius tensed.

The demons were herding the eagle toward the dark wall. *What are they——?!*

He stiffened, a chill cooling his body as an eerie sensation washed over him. There was something inside the rift. A presence watching them.

Asteria squawked, a sound of pain.

Cassius extended his wings and shot up toward the struggling beast, Thalia and Leiv following. The war demons scattered as they approached, their loathsome faces wary of Cassius's shining form.

There was no time to fight them one on one.

"Shield your faces!" Cassius warned the two Dryads.

The radiance around him intensified a heartbeat after they obeyed his command, the power pouring out of his soul core and his eyes brightening the landscape with an incandescent flash. The war demons within a one-hundred-foot radius of him shrieked, their ghastly figures disintegrating into ash under Heaven's Light. Asteria's giant form was propelled clear of the rift by the explosive strength of the divine energy pulsing from him.

Cassius's stomach rolled in the next instant. The wall of greasy darkness was throbbing violently in response to his powers.

A giant skeletal hand emerged from the void and closed in on him.

Cassius swore and twisted in mid-air.

"Move!" he yelled at Leiv and Thalia.

The Dryads stared in horror at the ghastly apparition, Thalia's eagle and Asteria similarly frozen.

"*Now, dammit!*" Cassius barked.

They startled and dove toward a wispy bank of clouds. Cassius glanced over his shoulder as they streaked through the air. His eyes rounded.

Black bands of corruption were snaking out from the bony fingers dropping toward them, the threads multiplying exponentially as they accelerated.

Cassius veered around and arrowed toward Thalia's eagle. Alarm widened the prince and the general's eyes as he barreled into the bird, knocking them sharply out of the way of the sinister threads. The spectral cords closed on his left ankle before he could make his escape.

Icy pain bloomed on Cassius's flesh through his armor as the bands latched on with a sibilant hiss. He scowled and slashed at them, blood pounding in his veins. They kept growing back, each one he cut with his holy sword replaced by dozens more.

"*Cassius!*"

A dark storm exploded above the valley as Morgan swooped toward him, his powers amplified by fear and fury.

Cassius gasped, the corrupt threads pulling him inexorably toward the being trying to capture him within the undulating barrier of shadows. Bile burned the back of his throat.

He could sense a bottomless emptiness awaiting him beyond its threshold. A void that would swallow him whole.

A memory flitted through his mind, faint and blurry. It was followed by blinding agony as the spell that had erased his past kicked in, threatening to crush his skull. Cassius ground his teeth and clutched his head, a rictus of pain twisting his features.

A sudden heaviness weighed him down. His consciousness flickered.

Heat flared through his soul core, a bright spark that roused him and caused him to gasp. It had come from Morgan.

The demigod arrived amidst a wrathful tempest, his shout of outrage filling Cassius's ears as he carved through the black chains biting into his leg.

Cassius sagged as the fetters broke, the Sword of Wind

slicing them clean in two. The mantle of darkness threatening to drown him dissipated, clearing his head of the haze clouding his reasoning.

Was that some kind of mind control?!

He had no time to dwell on what had just transpired.

Morgan roared and attacked the skeletal hand, his lightning-fast movements evading the shadowy tendrils trying to latch onto him. Loud explosions thumped against Cassius's eardrums as the Sword of Wind clashed repeatedly against the pale bones, a black and green storm that mimicked the rage of the demigod who wielded it.

A crack appeared in the apparition's thumb. It froze for an instant before slowly withdrawing into the rift.

Cassius's pulse stuttered. More war demons were pouring out of the dark wall that had split Ivory Peaks.

The Dryad army will truly be overwhelmed if we don't do something soon! We have to get rid of these demons and close that thing NOW!

"Bring them to me!" he told Morgan. "The war demons! Bring them all to me!"

Understanding dawned on Morgan's face. His eyes darkened with unease. "Are you sure about this?!"

"We don't have time to debate this, Morgan! Just trust me!"

A muscle twitched in Morgan's cheek. He nodded and moved, quickly spreading the word among the Dryad army in the skies despite his misgivings. Thalia and Leiv dove to the valley floor and did the same.

Hildur appeared atop an eagle a moment later, a blackthorn and alderwood crown on her head. The Dryad queen's staff had transformed into a giant bow brimming with glowing runes. She flexed her fingers, steering the magic weapon floating in front of her with ease. A storm of dazzling arrows left the bow and shot toward the enemy, driving them closer to the demigod.

An immense, green sphere made of Roald's powers enclosed scores of war demons where they fought the troops on the ground. More appeared, Galliad and Elwyn aiding the king to clear the valley floor along with a group of palace mages.

Emerald spell bombs flashed through the air as Arfinn and Tor directed the Dryad aerial forces pushing the war demons in the west toward the dark wall and Cassius. Thalia and Leiv did the same in the east.

Cassius's heart beat heavily in his chest as the enemy was herded toward his position. *I hope this works!*

Morgan joined him. "I'll cover you! In case that skeletal asshole appears again!"

Cassius nodded. He startled as Morgan snaked a hand around his nape and tugged him close. "What are you—?!"

Morgan swallowed the rest of Cassius's protest with his mouth.

6

MORGAN SHUDDERED AS HE KISSED THE EMPYREAL, THE sweet resonance of their soul cores heating his blood. Cassius blinked dazedly when Morgan finally lifted his mouth off his, his cheeks flushed.

"You looked like you could do with the pick-me-up," Morgan said roguishly.

Cassius touched his lips. "You're incorrigible, you know that?!"

Morgan grinned. "And you love me more for it." He sobered as he observed the war demons encircling them. "Time to do your thing, Hot Stuff."

Cassius rolled his eyes at the nickname.

They shifted and placed their backs against one another. Morgan felt Cassius inhale deeply, his ribs moving powerfully with his breath. The Empyreal exhaled and unleashed the demigod powers inside his body.

Heaven's Light bloomed across the valley, so white and pure it threatened to burn the land. It washed across the forests and the mountains, stretching for miles along the dark wall that had cleaved Ivory Peaks.

The divine brightness annihilated the army of war demons that had invaded the Dryad kingdom in a matter of seconds.

Morgan sucked in air. *Bloody hellfire!*

The monsters' dying shrieks echoed across the valley as their bodies disintegrated, wings and flesh blazing brightly before turning to ash. Blood thundered in Morgan's veins when the radiance emanating from his lover finally faded. Cassius twisted around to face him, his expression animated, oblivious to the incredible feat he had just accomplished.

"I think I know how to end this thing!"

"How?" Morgan asked, still lightheaded from what Cassius had just done.

"I felt something when I let my powers loose just now." Cassius jerked his head toward the wall of shadows. "That rift has a weak point. I think the Sword of Wind can shatter it!"

Morgan's pulse spiked. "Are you sure?!"

"Yes."

Morgan hesitated. He trusted Cassius with his life. If the Empyreal thought he could close the barrier, then he would try his damnedest to do so.

"Okay."

Hildur came abreast of them as they headed toward the throbbing rift, her expression reflecting the same stupefaction Morgan could see pasted across the entire Dryad army. "What are you doing?!"

Roald and Galliad appeared beside her, similarly wonderstruck.

"We're going to close the rift," Cassius explained. "It would be best if you moved your troops back."

Hildur stared.

"Alright," she said finally. "We will do as you say."

She dropped away, the king and Galliad following her.

Morgan and Cassius moved toward the wall. Corrupt energy danced across Morgan's flesh as they came to a stop a couple of feet from the barrier.

He could taste evil beyond the rift.

"What do we do?" Morgan asked tensely.

"Follow my move."

Divine power burst into life around Cassius. He lifted his blazing blade, focused on a spot Morgan couldn't see, and pierced it. A thunderous screech boomed across the valley, the wall screaming in rage at the holy wound.

The sound threatened to burst Morgan's ear drums. *Shit! Is this thing alive?!*

"*Now, Ivmir! Right next to my sword!*" Cassius roared.

Morgan clenched his jaw, aware the demigod inside Cassius was the one who had just spoken. He slipped the Sword of Wind alongside Cassius's blade and stabbed the wall.

It resisted his attack, dark tendrils snaking out to grasp the weapon and wrench it from his hands.

Morgan scowled, the creepers around his arm creaking as they held on to the sword. The storm around him intensified as he poured his demigod and Dryad powers into his blade, a vortex of riotous shadows and green light.

The Sword of Wind sank into the barrier inch by slow inch.

"*This land is yours, Ivmir,*" Cassius said. "*So, do your duty and protect it.*"

He placed a hand on Morgan's back and closed his eyes.

Light flared around and through Morgan. Heat detonated inside him. He gasped as a torrent of magic poured out of his soul core.

Awareness filled him. He didn't know what Cassius had just done to him. But he could now sense the energy in the land beneath him and in the forests and creatures that dwelled upon it.

It thrummed strongly, a heartbeat that echoed his own.

Morgan understood what Cassius meant for him to do. He took a deep breath and reached out to the power of the land, emerald radiance blooming around him.

Sparks lit the air as a dazzling, viridescent mist rose from the very bones of Ivory Peaks and its inhabitants, magic in its purest form responding to the will of his blood. Shocked cries echoed throughout the Dryad army as some of the energy within their souls got absorbed into the haze.

The light wrapped around Morgan, bringing with it the force of all Dryads and the realm that was his to command. A thunderous roar worked its way up his throat as he focused the unholy energy into the Sword of Wind and twisted the weapon.

The air above the valley contracted with a violent thump. Morgan braced his wings against the invisible implosion, Cassius grunting as he imitated him. The wall of darkness shrank at a dizzying speed, the shadows converging rapidly toward the tip of Morgan's blade across miles of mountains and valleys.

The rift closed with a boom that reverberated across the very land. Ice cracked on the peaks high above them, triggering mini avalanches that got absorbed by the thick forests draping their flanks.

Cassius released the tremulous breath he'd been holding, the echoes of the snowslides finally dying down. He gasped as Morgan took him in his arms and squeezed him close. Shudders shook Morgan as he clung to him.

Cassius embraced him just as tightly. "Are you okay?"

"Yeah." Morgan took a shaky breath and buried his face in Cassius's neck, his heart hammering against his ribs. He felt drained all of a sudden. "I will be. I just—I need a minute."

Alas, he was not to get a moment's peace.

7

"How in Heaven's name did you do that?!"

They turned.

Hildur and Roald hovered next to them atop an eagle, eyes wide and mouths slack. Galliad appeared next to them, on the back of his wife's eagle.

"We felt you absorb our magic," the mage told Morgan in a strained voice.

Thalia watched the two angels with a probing gaze from where she straddled the giant bird.

"We can talk about that later," Cassius said. "We should get to the city first and put out those fires." He looked out toward the horizon, brow wrinkling. Smoke was spiraling toward the sky from other distant Dryad settlements. "They could do with our help too."

It was late by the time they returned to the palace gardens. The sun had started to sink behind the mountains and the shadows lengthened as twilight encroached upon the valley. Thin, black trails blotted out the sky above the capital, the smell of wet ash and smoke carrying from dying remnants of the blazes that had been put out.

"Well?" Hildur asked briskly as she alighted from her mount.

Roald joined her, along with Galliad, Elwyn, and Regina.

Morgan found himself the subject of a battery of stares. To his relief, most of his energy had returned.

It was Cassius who answered the Dryads' burning question.

"The first ruler of Ivory Peaks left powerful remnants of her magic in the very bones of this world as a last defense before she passed from this realm." He looked at Morgan, his gaze warm. "As Atlanteia's direct heir, Morgan is able to wield that power and that of all those descended from her and this land, be they Dryad, beast, or forest."

A stunned hush followed.

Roald's brow furrowed. "How did you know something even we did not?"

Cassius hesitated. "Because the demigod inside me told me so."

"I—" Galliad stopped and rubbed a hand down his face, too shocked to speak for a moment. "I have never read of such a phenomenon in any of our books."

"Neither have I," Elwyn mumbled.

The mage exchanged a troubled look with Regina.

"That's because it's never been done before," Cassius said.

Morgan startled. "Really?"

Cassius smiled at him. "Really."

Morgan's heart swelled with emotion at the Empyreal's

expression. He closed the distance between them, took Cassius in his arms, and kissed him passionately.

It wasn't until Cassius punched him in the ribs that he finally let go.

Cassius's gray eyes had shrunk to slits. "I'm pretty sure we had an agreement that you would stop doing that in public!"

"We almost died," Morgan protested.

"I doubt that would be an easy feat to accomplish," Roald observed drily.

"He really cannot keep his hands off you," Hildur told Cassius with a hint of sympathy.

"I wish he would," the Empyreal grumbled.

A large shape swooped down from the sky before Morgan could say anything in his defense. It was Leiv, along with Arfinn and Tor, borne by Asteria. The giant bird's wounds had been healed by Dryad mages and her beautiful feathers cleaned of gore.

The princes slipped off the eagle's back and headed for their parents.

Hildur took each of them in her arms and kissed their brows in turn. "You did well. I am proud of you, my sons."

Asteria shifted closer to Cassius. She brought her head down to the angel and peered at him with beady, golden eyes.

"What's she doing?" Cassius asked Leiv nervously.

A soft croon left the eagle. She swept a proprietary wing around Cassius, gathered him close, and rubbed him affectionately with her beak.

Cassius relaxed and laughed. "That tickles."

He stroked the bird's head gently. Asteria squeezed him closer.

"Hey!" Morgan growled. "That angel is mine, you stupid bird!"

"Why do I feel like my wife just cheated on me?" Leiv muttered to his mother.

Hildur smiled.

"I do not even know how to begin to thank you." Roald's solemn gaze swept over Cassius and Morgan. "Not only did you save our son, you've also protected our realm from a fate worse than death." He faltered, his face wan. Hildur clasped his hand. "I doubt we would have won this battle if you had not been here."

"I agree," the queen murmured. "We are truly in your debt."

"I suspect Fate has more to do with this than even I know," Regina remarked.

The seer's gaze pierced the two angels.

A commotion drew their attention before Morgan could ask her what she meant. One of the mages had exited the palace and was headed rapidly toward them.

"Your Majesties!" The Dryad stopped and bowed to the king and queen. "There is a messenger at the gate. A Terrene angel." His voice wavered as he stole a glance at Cassius and Morgan. "She seeks an urgent audience with your guests."

Unease coiled in the pit of Morgan's stomach. *Now what?*

"It must be Julia," Cassius said stiffly.

"Open the gate," Roald ordered.

The portal between Ivory Peaks and Earth was located in a clearing guarded by towering oak trees brimming with magic, south of the palace. The flaming torches lining the glade cast Morgan and Cassius's shadows across the giant trunks as they entered it with the royal family and their entourage.

A pair of ancient, stone columns stood twenty feet apart on a platform in the middle of the clearing. They were protected by the series of concentric rune circles ringing them.

The Dryad mages in charge of the gate undid the spells holding it shut. A green haze filled the air, sending the fresh scent of Dryad magic dancing on a breeze. Light flared between the stone columns. It solidified, forming a shimmering, radiant wall that spanned the space.

Julia Chen stepped through it a moment later. Morgan took one look at her face and knew something was horribly wrong.

"You need to return to San Francisco," Julia said grimly.

8

THE CREVASSE WAS HALF A MILE LONG AND EIGHT FEET wide. It extended along the southern boundary of the Financial District, splitting Market Street all the way from 3rd to the Embarcadero, and stopped just two hundred feet shy of the historic Ferry Building overlooking San Francisco Bay.

Cassius could see the lights of the emergency services vehicles crowding the closed-off street from where he stood in Francis Strickland's office, on the tenth floor of the high rise housing the offices of the San Francisco branch of the Argonaut Agency. A pall of smoke still lingered above the city from the fires that had erupted along the road as a result of the incident eighteen hours ago, casting a twilight-like gloom over most of downtown.

Though night had already fallen when he and Morgan had left Ivory Peaks, it was barely midday here, on the U.S. West Coast.

Cassius turned and frowned at the bureau director seated at the desk. "The seismologists are certain this has nothing to do with the fault line under the San Francisco Peninsula?"

Strickland ran a hand through his hair and sighed. "Yes. I spoke to Dr. Miyahara Misao, the head of the Earthquake Science Center in Menlo Park, last night. Although this phenomenon was accompanied by tremors, she is adamant there were no foreshocks or other precursors to indicate a true quake was imminent." He pressed his lips together. "Besides, the anomaly on Market Street is three hundred feet deep. That's unheard of for a surface crevice."

"No wonder the gas pipes ruptured," Morgan muttered.

He was leafing through the reams of reports Argonaut and the NYPD had gathered where he sat opposite Strickland, lines furrowing his brow.

There was a knock at the door. Adrianne Hogan walked in without preamble, Zach Mooney, Bailey Green, and Charlie Lloyd in tow.

"Another two just appeared in Portugal and Turkmenistan," Adrianne said in a strained voice.

She took the remote from the coffee table and turned on the flatscreen TV on the wall of Strickland's office.

The director didn't reprimand the sorceress. Morgan's crew was leagues above the other Argonaut teams when it came to resolving the difficult cases that came the agency's way. As such, they were given more freedom than the other agents when it came to accessing Strickland's private space.

Cassius swallowed a sigh.

There was also the fact that Adrianne and the others often overlooked etiquette and what they deemed to be gratuitous courtesy. Though some viewed this behavior as arrogance, those who'd worked closely with Morgan's team over the years knew that was far from being the case. The fact that they didn't bother with niceties meant they were more efficient.

It was a fact Cassius had witnessed shortly after his arrival in San Francisco, when he'd inadvertently ventured into a crime scene involving a human sacrifice and had become the focus of a short-lived witch hunt by Argonaut and Morgan's team.

The national news channel the sorceress brought up was full of breaking news about the latest anomalies that had appeared across the world in the last twenty-four hours.

Zach's phone buzzed. The demon took his cell out of his pocket.

His eyebrows drew together when he looked at the screen. "Reuters are reporting tsunamis near the Azores and in the Sea of Japan."

A chill danced down Cassius's spine. *This is getting out of control.*

It had been a handful of hours since he and Morgan had returned to Earth from Ivory Peaks with Julia, the Dryad portal delivering them to Yosemite National Park shortly after sunrise that morning. Since the state of emergency the state had declared meant all otherwordly had been given permission to use their full powers, they'd flown back to San Francisco using their own wings, making the return trip in less than half the time it would have taken them to get there by conventional means.

The Fallen were normally prohibited from using their abilities except under exceptional circumstances or unless they were in active danger. Working for Argonaut and the other agencies who employed the angels and demons who had crashed to Earth five hundred years ago meant the latter was a daily hazard.

They'd only had time to wash up and change before they'd had to leave Cassius's apartment. Loki, the demon cat Cassius had adopted a couple of months back, had protested their abrupt departure with loud yowls. Since Adrianne and Charlie had taken turns looking after the imp while Cassius and Morgan had been away in Ivory Peaks, Cassius hadn't felt too guilty about leaving him again so soon.

"Hexa is positive no magic has been detected at any of these sites, black or otherwise?" Morgan asked persistently, his gaze on the TV screen.

A map of the world filled the monitor. The areas affected by the fracture lines were being highlighted with red dots.

"If there is magic behind this, then it's a spell no one has ever seen before," Adrianne replied somberly. "I sincerely hope that isn't the case. Even our little bloodcursed mage might have a hard time dealing with it."

"I suspect Brianna will want to keep Eden as far away from this situation as possible," Strickland said with a grunt. "She already has the magic guild on her case about her daughter."

Fearing for Eden's life, Brianna had bound her daughter's bloodcursed magic hours after her birth. Her uncle, the then head of Hexa, had assisted her, as well as several formidable mages. Bloodcursed magic was an anomaly thought to have arisen after the Fall, a mutation in the inherent magic inside humans. Alas, despite the incredible abilities it bestowed upon the person who could wield it, it was more a curse than a gift. The few bloodcursed magic users the world had known since the Fall had all died when they were still children, their soul cores consumed by a power they could not control.

Eden was the only bloodcursed magic user who had lived to see her teens. Now that she was bonded to the summoning staff Lucille Hartman and her master had been after, her soul core was stable and she was no longer in danger of dying as a result of her powers.

Cassius stared at the screen as more dots populated the map. His breath caught. A pattern was starting to emerge. A knock came at the door before he could voice what he'd just grasped.

Julia came in.

Morgan visibly stiffened when he saw the tall, blond man who walked in behind her. Cassius stilled, his heart now thumping for a whole other reason.

A warm smile split Strickland's mouth. "Victor."

The director rose and came around the desk to shake hands with the demon who now headed Cabalista, the demonic organization with its headquarters in London.

Victor Sloan pulled Strickland in for a quick bear hug before letting him go, an answering smile curving his sculptured lips.

The demon and the mage had been firm friends ever since their joint mission to take down Tania Lancaster and her black magic sect thirty years ago. It was Cassius who had eventually put an end to Tania's life, not that the world knew about it; he'd insisted Victor take the credit so as to hide his Empyreal abilities.

It was shortly after that incident that Victor had first asked Cassius out.

Victor sobered as he gazed at Cassius, his blue eyes calm. "Hi, Cassius."

It was the first time Cassius had seen Victor since they'd broken up and he'd left England for the States. Although they'd parted ways amicably, Cassius had been dreading seeing his former lover again. He knew all too well the reason why.

Guilt.

Victor had made it crystal clear how much he cared for Cassius early on in their relationship. Though Cassius had reciprocated many of the feelings the Fiery demon held for him, he had never been able to surrender his heart fully to him. That fact had eaten at Cassius for years before he'd finally let go and done the right thing.

Victor deserved a hell of a lot more than an angel with a damaged soul who was unable to say three simple words.

Yet, instead of the awkward tension he'd expected to fill the space between them, Cassius was surprised to experience only relief and the strangest sense of melancholy. Whatever amorous feelings he'd once had for the demon had faded in the face of his current affection for Morgan.

Cassius gave his former lover a genuinely pleased smile. "Hi, Victor. It's great to see you again."

Victor's face relaxed in an answering smile. "It's good to see you too." He grimaced as he looked at the TV screen. "Though I wish it were under better circumstances."

"Is England still free of fracture lines?" Strickland asked.

"Yes. As is most of Europe."

Lines wrinkled Victor's brow as he studied the map.

Cassius's pulse quickened. "Do you see it?"

"I do."

The demon sounded as troubled as Cassius felt.

Adrianne's puzzled stare swung between them. "See what?"

Understanding washed across Julia's face. "Oh, shit."

Morgan rose and came to stand by Cassius, filling the gap between the Empyreal and Victor. "What is it?"

Cassius swallowed a heavy sigh. He could practically feel the jealous vibes radiating off the Aerial.

He took a marker pen from Strickland's stationery holder, paused the live feed on the TV, and drew a line across the screen connecting the red points indicating where fracture lines had been appearing.

"My God." Strickland's face went slack. "They're practically all on the same latitude!"

"It's not just any latitude," Cassius said grimly. "That's a ley line."

9

It was late by the time Morgan felt Cassius drawing close, the warmth dancing through his belly a sign of the angel's proximity. It was yet another consequence of the strengthening bond between their soul cores. It had thrilled Morgan to no end the first time he'd sensed it, after their battle with Lucille Hartman.

Right now, he was too pissed to appreciate the connection.

Loki jumped out of his arms where he sat outside brooding on a deck chair, in the dark. The cat dashed across the terrace and slipped through the open sliding doors. A reproachful meow left him when Cassius walked into the apartment seconds later.

"There, there," the Empyreal crooned. "I know. I missed you too."

Loki's remonstrations turned into a satisfied rumble when Cassius picked him up and petted him. Cassius stepped outside. Morgan narrowed his eyes at the imp.

Traitor.

Loki blinked at him innocently.

Cassius's face tightened when he observed the cigarette in Morgan's hand. "I thought you'd quit smoking."

"I needed the distraction," Morgan grunted, knowing he sounded churlish and not really caring.

He put out the cigarette with a small burst of wind. It was his first in two months and had tasted even worse than he'd thought it would.

Cassius sighed and came over to sit next to him. "Are you going to be like this every time he's in town?"

The anger that been bubbling inside Morgan all evening exploded in a flurry of furious words.

"You mean, am I gonna be pissed every time my lover gets invited to dinner by his ex and the conniving bastard insists it just be the two of them?! Why, yes. I would have to be fucking dead not to react to that, Cassius!" He glared at the Empyreal. "We spent the whole afternoon trying to work out the reason for those cracks appearing along that ley line. Then you two just waltzed out together at the end of the day as if it were the most natural thing in the world to do!"

Loki leapt down from Cassius's hold. The demon cat cast an irate glance at them before slinking inside the apartment, tail stiff.

Cassius had weathered Morgan's outburst with a calm expression.

"Victor knew it would be awkward for me if you joined us." He hesitated before laying a placatory hand on Morgan's arm, his tone turning gentle. "It was just dinner between two friends, Morgan. We ate, chatted, had coffee. Nothing more. Victor was a perfect gentleman throughout."

Instead of calming his ruffled feathers, Cassius's words only inflamed Morgan more. "He still *wants* you! It's as clear as day to everyone, except you, apparently!"

Cassius's mouth flattened into a thin line.

"Even if that's true, that doesn't mean I reciprocate his feelings," he said sharply. "Do you think I'd cheat on you?"

Morgan stared at him hotly.

Cassius went still. "Fuck. You think I'd cheat on you, don't you?"

Morgan's chest grew tight.

"I never said that," he protested.

Cassius swallowed hard. "You didn't have to. Your face said it."

He rose stiffly and headed back inside, the hurt in his eyes making Morgan feel like an utter bastard. He froze when Morgan came up behind him and looped strong arms around his waist, stopping him halfway across the living room.

Morgan pressed his body against Cassius's back and buried his face in his hair, his throat thick with emotion. "I'm sorry. I know you won't cheat on me." He took a deep breath and closed his eyes. "But I'm also certain Victor won't give up trying to claim you again."

Cassius's heart thumped heavily under his hands where he held him. The Empyreal inhaled shakily. "I can't control Victor's emotions, Morgan."

"I know." Morgan turned him around and cradled his face. "I know that. But I can't help this—this feeling!" He touched his forehead to Cassius's, their breaths mingling hotly in the space between them. "Look, I won't deny that I'm a possessive bastard."

Cassius smirked at that.

Morgan groaned. "Yeah, it's not exactly my most charming personality trait. But every time I think of Victor, every single time I imagine the two of you making love, it tears me to pieces!"

He lifted Cassius's hand and placed it atop his thundering heart. "It's more than jealousy or just wanting all of you for myself." A burning sensation filled Morgan's chest. "I feel like something inside me will break if I lose you again!"

A storm of emotions clouded Cassius's face at Morgan's ragged confession. He kissed Morgan softly before burrowing his face against his shoulder.

"I owe Victor, Morgan."

Morgan stiffened, not liking where this was going. "Why?"

"Because he's the first one who accepted me for who I am."

Cassius's words pierced Morgan's heart and conscience.

Regret knotted his belly. He couldn't deny that he'd hurt the Empyreal the first time they'd met. He hadn't been able to control his intense reaction to Cassius and had ended up almost suffocating him. He clenched his jaw so tight it ached.

It seemed Victor's behavior had been the exact opposite.

"He was the first true friend I made after the Fall," Cassius continued in a low voice. "For that, I will be forever grateful." He drew back a little and met Morgan's eyes squarely. "But it doesn't mean I'll date him again just out of gratitude. You're the one I'm in a relationship with right now. And I can't see that changing for a long, long time. Not unless you break up with me first."

Morgan squeezed his eyes shut briefly, relief making him almost lightheaded. "That's never going to happen!"

A light chuckle left Cassius. "I'm glad to hear it."

Silence fell between them as they gazed at one another.

"I'm sorry," Morgan murmured.

"For what?"

"For being an asshole."

Cassius stroked his face lightly. "Apology accepted. And FYI, you're *my* asshole."

Morgan turned his head and kissed Cassius's fingers, liking the possessive light in the Empyreal's eyes.

Cassius's pupils flared. His gaze grew heavy-lidded as it dropped to Morgan's mouth. His tongue darted out to touch his lips. The air between them sparked, desire lighting their blood in a heartbeat.

Cassius stepped out of Morgan's hold and took his hand, a flush staining his cheeks. "Let's go to bed."

By the time they reached the bedroom, Morgan had stripped them both of their clothes.

"Shower first," Morgan growled. "I want to wash his scent off you."

Cassius gasped as Morgan lifted him in a fireman hold and strode inside the bathroom. "I can walk!"

Morgan ignored his protest, turned the shower on, and stepped under the steaming spray. He slid Cassius down his body, every delicious inch of the Empyreal's toned flesh gliding hotly against his own as he placed him on his feet. He crowded the angel against the wall and took his mouth demandingly.

Cassius responded with equal fervor, his lips opening easily under Morgan's tongue, his hungry hands clasping Morgan's shoulders and ass like he never wanted to let go.

Their erections touched tantalizingly while their tongues mated.

Blood pounded heavily in Morgan's head as he reluctantly ended the kiss. He was so turned on all he wanted to do was turn Cassius around, spread him open, and take him there and then.

He knew Cassius wouldn't mind. The Empyreal loved the mind-blowing orgasms Morgan brought him to when they had rough sex.

But it wasn't rough sex they both needed tonight.

10

MORGAN GRABBED THE BODY WASH AND POURED A generous amount into his hands, doing his best to curb his raging desire. Cassius shuddered and panted as Morgan cleaned him thoroughly from his head to his toes, precum pearling prettily on the tip of his straining cock. By the time Morgan finished washing up and sank to his knees in front of Cassius, the Empyreal was dripping wet.

Morgan worshipped Cassius with his fingers and lips before taking him in his mouth, the salty evidence of Cassius's pleasure a hot balm that warmed his tongue and stoked his lust. Cassius braced his legs and sank his fingers into Morgan's hair as he finally gave in to his instincts, fucking Morgan's mouth with powerful thrusts. His gasps and moans echoed sweetly in Morgan's ears as he tipped his head back and rolled his hips, chasing his pleasure.

A guttural shout escaped Cassius a moment later. He stiffened and rose on his toes as he came, his cock pulsing violently on Morgan's tongue as he ejaculated. Morgan swallowed it all greedily.

It wasn't until Cassius sagged against the wall that Morgan finally let him go and rose to his feet.

Cassius bit his lip, his expression sultry as he observed Morgan's erection. He touched Morgan lightly, his fingers scorching his stiff flesh.

"I want you inside me!"

Morgan cursed at the wanton words. He tugged Cassius out of the shower, dried them off briskly, and led the Empyreal into the bedroom, his cock so hard he could barely think. Loki vacated his spot on the end of the bed as they tumbled onto the sheets, the cat streaking toward the living room.

Morgan grabbed lube from the nightstand, lay on his back, and positioned Cassius above him. Cassius shivered as he found himself braced on all fours, his cock and ass hovering over Morgan's face while Morgan's dick probed his jaw.

"Suck me," Morgan commanded.

Cassius obliged him greedily, his pretty lips parting to engulf Morgan inside the intoxicating depths of his mouth. Morgan hissed, almost coming there and then. He uncapped the bottle, warmed a generous amount of lube between his hands, and parted Cassius's butt cheeks.

Cassius's hole contracted when Morgan's breath tickled his opening. A long, low sound hummed out of him as Morgan spread him open with his thumbs and flicked his tongue against his rim, the vibration of his jaw causing Morgan's hips to jerk off the bed.

Heat resonated between their soul cores as they pleasured one another, Cassius taking Morgan inside his throat over and over again as he blew him hard and deep, his cheeks bulging with Morgan's thick shaft. Morgan rimmed

Cassius with his tongue and thrust his lubed-up fingers inside him to soften and stretch his passage, his mouth turning to Cassius's cock where it danced above his face.

Tension wound through Morgan's spine as Cassius brought him closer and closer to his orgasm, his skin prickling and tingling.

"Wait!" He tried to tug his swollen organ from Cassius's hungry lips and groaned when the angel resisted. "I want to come inside you!"

Cassius let him go with a wet pop and stared at him hotly over his shoulder. "Hurry!"

He dropped a hand to his groin and started rubbing himself briskly, his fingers slick with cum and spit and his mouth open on shuddering breaths.

Fuck!

Morgan maneuvered Cassius down the bed and knelt behind him. Cassius sucked in air as Morgan spread him wide and nudged his hole with his erection.

Morgan snaked his hands up Cassius's belly and torso and pulled him down onto him as he sat back on his heels. He sank his teeth into Cassius's shoulder and pressed the head of his cock against his entrance.

"Take me in, Cassius."

Cassius's heart pounded violently against Morgan's palms, the breathy little sounds he made telling Morgan exactly how he felt about that command and the intruder about to impale his passage. He grabbed his ass and carefully lowered himself onto Morgan's dick, a hiss of pleasure falling from his lips.

Morgan almost climaxed as he experienced the intoxicating sight and feel of Cassius's body swallowing him one hot inch at a time, Cassius's passage stretching deliciously as Morgan stuffed him hard and good. It wasn't until Cassius was seated fully on Morgan's groin that the Empyreal finally let out the breath he'd been holding.

"Morgan!" Cassius gasped.

Morgan pressed tender kisses against the Empyreal's sweat-slicked spine and squeezed his hips. "Yeah?"

He nipped at Cassius's skin when Cassius tightened hungrily around him.

"*Ah!*" Cassius's throaty cry echoed around the bedroom. "Please!"

Morgan nuzzled and kissed Cassius's nape. "Please what?"

He knew he was being mean but he couldn't help it. Nothing got Cassius off faster than this little game they were playing.

"Fuck me!" Cassius pleaded feverishly, his head drooping forward. "*Now!*"

Morgan obeyed with a growl, hips drawing back before ramming up with enough force to lift Cassius up.

Cassius cried out and came, his cum splashing hotly on Morgan's thighs where he straddled him.

Morgan thrust through his convulsions, his own climax racing down his spine and tightening his belly as he plunged his aching shaft in and out of Cassius, their soul cores resonating and amplifying their pleasure.

Cassius whimpered as Morgan exploded inside him a moment later, flooding his insides with the scalding evidence of his orgasm.

The Empyreal stiffened in surprise. "Oh!"

Morgan carried on pumping his hips, still hard despite the dizzying climax he'd just experienced. He grabbed hold of Cassius's jaw and turned his head sideways, desire overwhelming him all over again.

Cassius gasped, Morgan taking his mouth in a kiss full of fire, his eyes a molten gray.

"I'm gonna fuck you till my balls are dry!" Morgan growled against his lips, his gaze burning.

The way Cassius's pupils dilated and his passage clenched around Morgan's steely length told him he loved that proposition. Morgan ended the kiss and bit down gently on Cassius's shoulder, one hand dropping to rub Cassius's trembling cock while the other squeezed his stiff nipples.

They made love into the early hours of the morning, all the pent-up desire they hadn't been able to fulfill while they were in Ivory Peaks erupting like a deluge that threatened to drown them. By the time they collapsed into each other's arms and fell into a deep sleep, the sky was lightening to the east.

11

THE TREMORS JOLTED THEM AWAKE AT SEVEN FORTY-SIX a.m. Cassius bolted upright, the sheets sliding to his hips, an unnamed dread making his stomach roll. Morgan swore and jumped off the bed stark naked.

The floor and walls shuddered and groaned around them, the morning light oddly distorted as it streamed through the rattling windows. The clock on the wall tilted precariously. Something shattered in the living room.

A black shape dashed inside the bedroom amidst the plaster dust sifting down from the ceiling. Loki leapt into Cassius's arms.

The imp was trembling, fur on end and yellow pupils so wide they almost filled his eyes. Cassius hugged the cat to his chest.

"Is it an earthquake?" Morgan said in a clipped tone.

He was staring at the lights. They were flickering alarmingly.

Cassius shook his head and climbed out of bed, flinching as something else smashed in the apartment. "I don't think so. Loki wouldn't be this scared if it were a simple quake!"

He got dressed hastily, Loki protesting when he put him down for a moment. Morgan followed suit. They grabbed their cellphones and headed out onto the terrace, the cat firmly ensconced in Cassius's arms once more.

Cassius looked north. His belly twisted.

A dark haze was forming across downtown. It rose and extended rapidly toward the skies before widening sideways, splitting the city in a northeast to southwest direction. The foreboding Cassius was experiencing solidified into a cold certainty.

He was positive the phenomenon was centered over the crevasse on Market Street.

"Morgan?"

"Yeah?"

"I think this is what happened in Ivory Peaks," Cassius said hoarsely, his heart knocking rapidly against his ribs.

Morgan traded a worried glance with him. The Aerial stiffened in the next instant. There was no mistaking the stench of corruption drifting south on the wind. Morgan cursed as the haze thickened to a solid, black wall.

The air trembled as it grew.

The rift sliced clean through the Embarcadero and Ferry Building, the iconic, white clock tower toppling with false grace as the structure caved in on itself. It cut across the ferry terminal and carved apart the dark waters of San Francisco Bay, the sheer momentum of its progress churning the estuary's surface violently as it raced parallel to Bay Bridge.

"No!" Cassius mumbled numbly.

He raised a hand helplessly, knowing he was too far

away to do anything about the disaster about to unfold before their very eyes.

The wall smashed into the causeway connecting Treasure Island to Yerba Buena Island with a thunderous boom. It destroyed the embankment in the blink of an eye and tore through the marina beyond as if it were made of matchsticks.

Bile burned Cassius's throat as he watched scores of boats and yachts fly up some hundred feet in the air before smashing down amidst turbulent waves. Many disappeared beneath the roiling waters.

"Fuck!" Morgan lifted his phone in a white-knuckled grip and hit a number on speed dial. It connected after a single ring. "Francis! Are you seeing this?!"

Debris drifted to the surface of Treasure Isle harbor in the wake of the attack. Cassius clenched his jaw and went to grab their guns and blades. By the time he returned to the terrace, Morgan had the other agencies' directors on a conference call.

"Cassius and I forgot to tell you guys something yesterday," the Aerial was explaining grimly. "With everything that's happened on Earth since we got back, it kinda slipped our mind. Whatever this—thing is, we witnessed something similar in Ivory Peaks. It nearly tore that realm in half."

"What?" Strickland barked. "And you didn't think to report this to me?!"

"Like I said, I was pre-occupied!" Morgan snapped.

Guilt stabbed Cassius. He was pretty certain Morgan's distraction had to do with a certain blond, six-foot-two demon.

I can't exactly blame him. Victor's visit surprised all of us.

"What the hell is it anyway?" Jasper Cobb asked.

The Terrene demon in charge of the San Francisco branch of Cabalista sounded as irate as usual.

"It's some kind of rift. But not one any of us had seen before Ivory Peaks, including the Dryads." Morgan looked over at Cassius, his brow wrinkling. "But one fact we know for certain. It'll start spitting out hordes of war demons soon. It took an entire Dryad army to hold them off before Cassius destroyed them and I closed it."

"War demons?" Strickland repeated, horrified. "Are you certain?"

"Very." A muscle jumped in Morgan's jawline. "And I'm talking hundreds of them."

Cassius's nails dug into his palms. An oily sheen was spreading across the dark barrier.

It really is the same!

"You and Cassius managed to close this thing?" Reuben Fletcher said sharply.

The head of the local Order of Rosen bureau was Jasper's lover and an Aerial angel like Morgan.

"Yes," Morgan confessed reluctantly.

"How?" Reuben asked, his tone flat.

Morgan hesitated. Cassius frowned.

The only ones who knew of his Dryad lineage were their team, Strickland, and Brianna. Strickland had made the Aerial promise not to reveal his newly rediscovered powers to the rest of the world yet. Though Morgan and Cassius had fought alongside Reuben and Jasper in the past, they weren't exactly close friends. Jasper, in particular, seemed ready to provoke them at a moment's notice and Reuben was quick to come to his lover's defense.

Cassius reached a decision.

Time was running out. And this was not the moment for secrets.

"Morgan is descended from the first Dryad Goddess, Atlanteia."

He ignored Brianna's gasp and Strickland's curse. Morgan stared at him, equally shocked.

"It's okay," Cassius said grimly. "They need to hear this."

"This is not the time for jokes!" Jasper snapped.

"It's not a joke, Jasper," Strickland grated out.

"Francis is right," Brianna admitted tensely. "I saw it with my own eyes. Morgan can wield Dryad magic."

"I need to have a word with you two when this is over," Strickland added darkly for Cassius and Morgan's benefit.

Another tremor raced across the city. Bay Bridge swayed and buckled. The rift started to throb, the pulsations visible even from their distance.

"We're gonna have to talk about this later!" Morgan said urgently. "Get everyone who can fight downtown, now!"

He ended the call with Strickland and the other directors mid-protest. The distant blare of car alarms tore the air as Cassius lowered Loki to the ground.

"Stay!" he ordered.

Loki yowled and shivered, tail and ears drooping.

Cassius squatted, picked the imp up, and looked him dead in the eyes. "You'll be safer here than over there with me, you dumb cat."

Loki stopped shaking. His ears perked up. He stared unblinkingly at Cassius before pressing a paw to his chest. Cassius inhaled sharply.

The place where Loki touched him was growing warm.

A golden glow erupted over the cat's belly. His eyes

flashed crimson. He gagged and regurgitated the Eternity Key.

"What the—?!" Morgan exclaimed.

Cassius stared at the golden dagger at his feet, his heart racing. It was pulsing with divine power.

He blinked slowly at Loki. "You want me to take it?"

Loki meowed, placed both paws on Cassius's chest, and leaned in to lick his face. The cat's gaze swung to the throbbing wall of darkness carving through the city and San Francisco Bay.

Cassius stared from the barrier to the imp, his stomach knotting. "I need it for the rift?"

Loki growled his assent.

Cassius hesitated. "Okay."

He put the cat down, changed into his Empyreal form, and slipped the Eternity Key inside his left gauntlet. Though he didn't know how the artifact would help him, he trusted the imp.

Wind swept across the terrace as Morgan transformed, black currents swirling with Dryad magic dancing around him in a controlled roar. "Let's go."

They took flight just as the sun was swallowed by storm clouds. Loki's forlorn cry faded rapidly behind them. Twilight fell across San Francisco as they shot toward Mission Bay.

With it came the war demons.

By the time Cassius and Morgan neared downtown, screams were echoing across the city and smoke from dozens of fresh fires blanketed the air.

The rift had opened amidst heavy morning traffic. Though Market Street remained closed, hundreds of cars and pedestrians had been caught out by the tremors that had ripped through the surrounding neighborhoods. Abandoned vehicles lay haphazardly where the roads had heaved and sunk, headlights flashing and alarms wailing. Power lines dangled from shifted poles, the cables sparking dangerously where they touched debris. The smell of leaking gas soured the air.

Cassius's stomach rolled as he stared at the large area of devastation beneath them and the panicked figures milling about on the ground.

These people are sitting ducks if those war demons attack now!

He looked up, trepidation quickening his pulse. For a reason he couldn't fathom, the monsters had taken position high up in the sky above San Francisco. It was as if they were waiting for something.

The wind picked up. Rain started to fall across the city, a drizzle that cooled his overheated skin.

A shocking truth struck Cassius then. "*Shit!*"

Morgan looked at him, alarmed. "What?!"

"Francis and the others! They were trying to tell us something before you cut them off!" Cassius's chest grew heavy with dread. "They can't help us if they're on the other side of the wall!"

All four agencies that governed the otherworldly and magic users in the city were located in downtown. Which meant the directors and agents already at their bureaus were currently north of the barrier, while they and the war demons were south of it.

Morgan cursed. He tapped the earpiece he'd put on before they'd left the apartment. His eyes turned flinty.

"I can't get through to Francis. This thing must be blocking phone signals!"

The air grew heavy. Lightning cracked overhead.

"Try our team," Cassius said tensely as the distant rumble of thunder boomed across the city. "All of them bar Charlie live south of Market Street."

Julia and Zach answered immediately, their raised voices coming through Cassius's own earpiece.

"Are you guys okay?" Julia shouted.

"What the hell is that thing?!" Zach snarled.

"We're fine. It's a rift of some sort." Morgan glanced at Cassius. "The two of us faced something similar in Ivory Peaks, yesterday. We didn't have time to tell you guys about it."

"Great," Julia grated out. "Are those war demons?"

"Yeah." Cassius observed the silent army above them with a frown. "I don't know why they haven't attacked us yet."

"I can't get through to Adrianne and Bailey," Morgan said.

"They were planning to go in early today," Julia said. "They're probably already at Argonaut."

"Which means they're stuck on the other side of that thing," Zach said bitterly.

"Where are you?" Morgan asked.

"We're half a mile southwest of your location," Julia said.

"You can see us?" Morgan said, surprised.

"Cassius looks like a second sun against that wall," Zach replied tartly. "All of us are converging on your position."

Cassius startled. *All of us?*

He looked behind them.

The sky was full of gray wings and glinting armor, the angels and demons south of the divide arrowing swiftly toward them through the thunderstorm. From his rough calculation, they made up about half of the otherworldly working for the agencies.

Relief flooded him. It was short-lived.

The war demons were stirring.

"We need to clear this area of civilians," Cassius told Julia and Zach urgently. "Meet us on Market Street!"

He closed his wings and dropped, Morgan on his heels.

A chill danced across Cassius's skin as he streaked through clouds of smoke. He stared at the wall of throbbing darkness to his left.

Morgan scowled beside him. "You feel that too?"

"Yeah," Cassius said tightly.

He could sense a sinister presence behind the veil, just like he'd experienced in Ivory Peaks. *It must be that skeletal figure! That's who the war demons were waiting for to order the attack!*

Cassius tucked that piece of information at the back of his mind.

A detonation erupted at the intersection of Front and Freemont just as he and Morgan prepared to land. Cassius's eyes widened at the sight of an armored figure surrounded by war demons.

"Victor!"

He shot up the road. Morgan swore and followed.

Cassius's grip tightened on his Stark Steel blade. The monsters were creeping out of a wide split in the crevasse.

Victor was holding them at bay, his gaze crimson with power and Hell Fire sizzling on his sword and his Stark Steel suit. He blasted the closest war demon with an explosive fireball, ducked beneath another's talons, and cut a third monster down.

Cassius smashed into the creatures converging on Victor and unleashed Heaven's Light. The war demons screeched and shielded their faces and bodies with their leathery wings, to no avail. They burst into flames with Cassius's next heartbeat, too close to escape his divine radiance.

Victor lowered his arm from where he'd covered his eyes. He stared at the dying embers that were all that remained of the enemy as they floated down around him.

Cassius closed the distance to Victor, his anxious gaze roaming the demon's figure for injuries. "Are you okay?"

"Yeah, I'm good." A faint smile stretched Victor's

mouth as he studied Cassius's dazzling form. "It's been a long time since I've seen you like this."

His expression softened. He reached out to touch Cassius's face.

A storm exploded above them, powerful currents whipping at their hair and armor. They looked up, Cassius startling guiltily.

Victor's mouth flattened to a thin line.

Morgan dropped down next to them in a flurry of dark wind and Dryad magic.

"What are you doing here?" he asked Victor roughly.

"My hotel is downtown." Victor narrowed his eyes at the oak crown on the Aerial's head and the emerald light twined with the black currents engulfing him. "That's new."

He glanced at Cassius, his look faintly accusing. An impatient sigh escaped Cassius as the Aerial and the demon watched each other coolly.

I really don't need this bullshit right now!

"We'll explain later," he told Victor tersely. "We need to get these people out of here first and close that rift."

He glanced at the injured and panic-stricken pedestrians stumbling blindly past them, clothes drenched and hair plastered to their scalps.

Victor's tone turned steely. "You know what this thing is?"

Cassius dipped his chin. "Something that looked exactly like this appeared in Ivory Peaks while we were there. Morgan and I fought the war demons alongside the Dryad army and managed to close it."

"Hey, are you guys with Argonaut?!" someone shouted to their right.

They turned.

A witch was approaching rapidly from the direction of Fremont Street, the faint scent of Frankincense she emitted telling Cassius she was a Level Two magic user. A sorceress and a mage were hot on her heels, their Valerian and Juniper scents signaling them to be Level Three at best.

Recognition flashed across their faces when they clocked Victor's Fiery demon appearance. They slowed when they saw Cassius's Empyreal form, their expressions growing wary.

The sight of Morgan had them flinching to an abrupt halt.

"What the—?" the mage mumbled, his knuckles whitening on his staff.

A shadow swooped over them.

Cassius's eyes widened. "Watch out!"

He dashed toward the trio, Victor and Morgan at his side.

Julia and Zach reached the plunging war demon first. They crashed into the monster before he could tear into the magic users with his long, curved claws and carried him toward the frontage of a building. Concrete and glass detonated around them as they smashed straight through the lobby, teeth bared and scents full of bloodlust.

War demons were their enemy of old.

Cassius watched the shadowy maw of the foyer, his mouth dry. Julia and Zach emerged from the wreckage a moment later, their swords dripping with dark blood. They stared at the sky, faces tight.

"One down, several hundred to go, huh?" Zach muttered as he observed the army above them.

"Thank—thank you!" the witch mumbled shakily.

Her companions murmured their thanks, faces equally pale.

More angels and demons dropped down around them, armor and swords clinking. Scores of magic users followed on foot. Everyone grouped around Cassius, Morgan, and Victor, clearly looking at them for direction.

Victor turned to the two demigods.

"This is your rodeo," he said in a hard voice. "You fought this thing once before. Lead us."

Surprise flashed in Morgan's eyes. Victor's status meant he should be the one in charge.

Cassius, on the other hand, had expected no less from his ex-lover. One of the things he'd always admired about the demon was his ability to look beyond power and prestige and choose the best person for the situation.

In the case of Tania Lancaster, that had been Cassius. In this scenario, the demon had again selected the right people to guide them into this battle. Cassius's chest swelled at the Fiery's implicit trust in his and Morgan's abilities.

He took a deep breath. "Level Four to Six magic users, clear the area of civilians. Get to the closest subway entrances and go as deep as you can."

Murmurs broke out among the magic users. They exchanged uneasy glances.

"What about the rest of us?" the Level Two witch Julia and Zach had saved asked.

"Find cover in those buildings." Cassius indicated the high rises spanning the width of Market Street. "Make sure they're stable before you enter them. You are to watch our backs and protect the people on the ground. A few war demons came up through that crevasse. There may be more." He studied the troops of armored angels and demons with a heavy frown. "As for us, we take this battle to the sky. Do not let those monsters reach the city."

13

"DAMMIT!" JULIA FUMED FIFTY FEET TO MORGAN'S right. "There's no end to them!"

Her nostrils flared where she hovered back-to-back with Zach, the gore dripping off their blades soon washed clean by the pounding rain. The Aqueous demon wiped flecks of blood from his face, his breaths heavy and his expression deadly.

Morgan spun around on himself, the Sword of Wind and his Stark Steel blade singing in his grip. The weapons carved through the war demons converging on him, felling them in one swoop. He looked beyond their falling corpses to the aerial battlefield above San Francisco, his stomach knotting.

They'd been fighting the enemy for over two hours.

Though angels and demons were known for their supernatural strength and stamina, this prolonged a skirmish against such a powerful enemy was slowly sapping them of their strength.

It didn't help that a group of them had had to divert

the news helicopters that had taken to the sky to report on the ungodly phenomenon that had devastated the city. Now that the news crews had been grounded, the only things in the air apart from the angels and demons were the fighter planes the U.S. Air Force had deployed.

The jets hovered some two miles south of the rift, their engines distorting the air with streams of supersonic heat that evaporated the water drenching the atmosphere into thin trails of vapor. Having failed to make a dent in the wall with their missiles, they'd fallen back to a safe distance.

Morgan clenched his jaw as he observed the tiring angels and demons. *We need to do something! Soon!*

Light blossomed overhead.

Unease gnawed at Morgan's insides as he looked to where Cassius fought a horde of war demons some two hundred feet away, Heaven's Light obliterating them almost as quickly as his divine blade.

He can't keep this up forever!

Victor's flames lit the shadows below, distracting him.

It had become clear pretty early on during their fight that the only ones who could truly hold their own against the war demons were the three of them. As such, Cassius had devised a strategy that would best maximize their offense and stop their enemy from reaching the city.

The Empyreal had taken the highest position on the battlefield and was attempting to force the monsters back into the rift along with a large troop of angels and demons. Beneath them, Morgan and the next battalion carved through the creatures who'd escaped the first line of defense. At the bottom, shielding the city with the final legion of angels and demons, was Victor.

It was a brilliant scheme and one that was working, albeit too slowly for Morgan's liking.

He suspected Cassius had been thinking of doing what he'd accomplished in Ivory Peaks, when he'd destroyed the army of war demons with a single, incandescent explosion of his powers. The fact that he hadn't done so was because the enemy's strategy had changed.

Having learned from their defeat in the other realm, the war demons were avoiding being herded en masse toward Cassius's position.

In a twisted sense, Morgan couldn't help but be glad of this. He didn't know how much more Cassius's soul core could bear releasing divine power on such a prodigious level, especially since there were almost twice as many war demons here than they'd faced in the Dryad kingdom.

A wave of corruption made the air throb unpleasantly. It came again, scattering the haze of smoke overshadowing the city and shoving him and everyone else back some hundred feet from the wall. His skin prickled.

Alarmed shouts sounded above.

Morgan's head snapped up. He froze.

A giant skeletal hand was emerging from the barrier. It closed in on Cassius where he hovered, a dazzling, lone figure at the forefront of the battle. Evil black threads shot out from the bones and latched onto the Empyreal's armor in the blink of an eye.

"*Cassius!*" Victor roared.

The demon rose in a blaze of flames, Morgan ahead of him.

A dark globe swallowed Cassius a second before the hand closed around him. Fear squeezed Morgan's heart.

"*NOOOO!*"

COLDNESS ENGULFED CASSIUS.

Dammit! This thing is moving faster than it did in Ivory Peaks!

His breath fogged faintly in front of his face before the sphere sealed him in suffocating blackness. Blood thrummed heavily in his ears, dread leaving a bitter after-taste in his mouth.

He couldn't sense Morgan's soul core.

Icy tendrils of evil slithered over his armor, trying to sink beneath it and into his flesh. Cassius blinked, surprised. Unlike the time before, when they'd caused him pain even through the Stark Steel plates protecting his body, he could only feel mild discomfort.

Something was resisting the darkness.

A faint glow lit the gloom. He stared at his left gauntlet.

The Eternity Key!

Heaviness filled his head before he could reach for the weapon, just like it had done in the Dryad realm. He gritted his teeth and released a burst of light, fighting the darkness trying to numb his mind. The sphere reacted violently, the air pulsing and tossing him around in a storm of shadows and brightness.

The shadows won. Panic choked Cassius's breath as sight and sound disappeared.

No!

Morgan's face rose before his eyes. With it came an agony that threatened to tear him apart. A memory flitted through his mind, faint and blurry. The emotions of the demigod he had once been pierced his soul, a hurricane that threatened to rip away the spell that had robbed him of his past.

I can't...I can't lose him...not again!

"*Ivmir!*" Cassius whispered brokenly.

A voice reached him before he could give in to the despair tightening his chest, a low hiss that seeped into his very consciousness and jolted him out of the terror threatening him to eat him alive.

HELP...US...

Cassius froze before looking around frantically. His preternatural sight failed to detect anything but the inky void that had imprisoned him.

"Who's there?!"

For a moment, nothing happened. Then, the voice came again, low and strained.

DEATH...

Cassius's eyes rounded.

DO YOUR DUTY...AWAKENER...FREE THE WILD GOD...BEFORE ALL IS LOST...

Heat bloomed inside Cassius before he could make sense of the words the presence had uttered. It filled his veins and his very blood, lifting the veil suffocating his reason. Light exploded from within his gauntlet.

Cassius finally grasped the Eternity Key. He stared at it numbly as it extended into a golden broadsword brimming with Heaven's Light.

Wait! This thing is a weapon too?!

There was no more time to think. The shadows around him were pressing in, trying to crush him.

Cassius took a ragged breath, closed his eyes, and reached to the very heart of his powers. Divine energy overflowed from his core, a deluge that burst through the dams that always held it contained. The weapons he grasped throbbed in his grip, his Stark Steel blade and the Eternity Key pulsing with the same force that was making his teeth rattle. He opened his eyes and carved through the darkness, a roar leaving his throat.

The shadows exploded into nothingness, revealing the bones that had contained them. Warmth flared in Cassius's belly, his soul core resonating sweetly once more with that of the demigod who loved him.

Dark wind wreathed with Dryad magic fluttered weakly between tiny slits in his skeletal prison. Hell Fire sizzled through another gap. Morgan and Victor's voices reached Cassius dimly as they pummeled the solid shield separating them from him, their tones shrill with rage and fear.

GO...AWAKENER...YOU ARE THE ONLY ONE... WHO CAN...LIBERATE...US...

The skeletal hand opened slightly, digits creaking under the tension. It was clear the being it belonged to was fighting a power stronger than itself. Death's voice came again, a warning that shook Cassius's skull.

NOW...

An opening appeared. An arm wrapped in a dark tempest reached through it.

"*Cassius!*" Morgan yelled.

Cassius grabbed Morgan's hand. Their cores connected with a violence that rocked his entire being. He gasped, the Eternity Key growing hot in his grasp. Divine radiance detonated around him, forcing the skeletal fingers apart.

Cassius's soul went super nova, locking his breath in his lungs.

14

It felt like a lifetime before he regained some semblance of control over his powers and his consciousness. Awareness slowly returned. Cassius exhaled shakily and dimmed Heaven's Light before exiting his prison, only to fall into Morgan's waiting arms.

Morgan squeezed him close, shudders racking his powerful frame. His heart pounded violently against Cassius's chest as he gripped him tight.

"I thought—" He stopped and swallowed, his hands trembling on Cassius's back. "I thought I'd lost you!"

Cassius closed his eyes and hugged Morgan back just as fiercely.

Heat washed across them. Cassius opened his eyes and saw Hell Fire pierce the storm of wind and magic cocooning him and Morgan. He looked over at Victor and reached a hand out to the demon. Victor flinched. He swallowed before grasping his fingers, his flames dancing harmlessly across Cassius's armor.

Cassius's stomach twisted with sorrow and regret. He

had never seen the men who loved him look as devastated as they did in that moment.

"It's okay," he mumbled with a weak smile. "I'm alright, really."

The angel who held him and the demon who looked like he never intended to let him go watched him for a wordless moment. It was then that Cassius registered the silence around them. It throbbed in his ears, shocking in its suddenness.

The war demons were gone. In their place was a veil of embers and ash.

The angels and demons who'd fought alongside the three of them hovered a short distance away, their faces filled with equal wonder and apprehension as they watched Cassius through the fading haze. The clouds above were rolling back in from where something had torn them asunder, bringing forth a light drizzle.

"Did I—" Cassius stopped and swallowed, his stunned gaze finding Morgan and Victor. "Did I do that?!"

"Yeah," Morgan murmured.

"Just now," Victor said with a dip of his head. "I'm pretty sure they saw that light in the next state over."

Cassius's pulse stuttered. He stared dizzily from the Eternity Key to the wall.

The skeletal hand had disappeared, though he could still feel its presence beyond the rift. He was certain the voice he had heard while he was inside his prison of shadows and bones had belonged to its owner.

I wonder if that was what it was trying to do in Ivory Peaks!

He recalled the words the entity had spoken.

"I think I know how to close this thing!" Cassius told

Morgan and Victor urgently. "But there's something I must do first!"

He shot up some thousand feet in the air. Morgan and Victor joined him seconds later.

"What are you doing?" Morgan asked, confused.

Cassius frowned at the city spread out beneath him. "Give me a minute."

Victor followed his gaze, understanding dawning. "Who are you looking for?"

"A God."

Victor and Morgan exchanged a startled glance.

Cassius shut them out and focused. Millions of soul cores appeared in his mind's eye. He clenched his teeth and filtered rapidly through them, frantically looking for the one that didn't belong. He was beginning to wonder if he'd been wrong when he finally spotted it.

His mouth went dry. He opened his eyes.

"There!" Cassius pointed at an area north of Bay Bridge. "I need to get to the bay!"

He tucked his wings and dove.

Morgan's shout followed. "What are you talking about?"

The Aerial came after him.

Victor appeared on Cassius's left. "What do you need?"

"Get every Aqueous demon and angel here and follow me to the water!" Cassius barked.

Victor stared before dipping his head and angling away.

Cassius maneuvered through the legion of otherwordly hovering above the city, his pulse thrumming rapidly in his veins. From what he'd just detected, the God was nearly at his limits.

We don't have much time!

He found the two figures he was looking for and rocked up beside them. "Come with me!"

Julia and Zach traded a surprised look. They obeyed him wordlessly.

Wind whistled in Cassius's ears as they headed for the surface of the estuary, Morgan and Victor bringing some dozen angels and demons in their wake.

The godly soul core Cassius had sensed flickered weakly in his mind's eye. Cold fingers wrapped around his heart. He fisted his hands, his divine sword and the Eternity Key whining in resonance with his will.

Hang on, whoever you are!

Cassius stopped some twenty feet above the bay, the waves surging beneath him under the force of his deceleration. He looked at Zach as the demon dropped beside him.

"I need you to create a funnel down to the bottom!"

The demon blinked slowly. "Okay."

He retracted his blade, sheathed the weapon, and brought his hands together.

Water churned as he began to force it apart. It became a spinning whirlpool, the center dropping slowly. The motion accelerated when the other Aqueous angels and demons joined them and combined their powers with his.

Cassius watched impatiently while a thirty-foot-wide, vertical channel formed below them.

Faster!

Julia swore when the bottom finally appeared. "What the hell is that?!"

Cassius narrowed his eyes at what was anchored to the floor of San Francisco Bay. "A God in trouble!" His gaze darted to Julia and Morgan. "Follow me!"

Cassius dove inside the tunnel, the angels at his side.

Victor watched them leave with a worried frown.

Currents roared around Cassius as he descended into the artificial channel, a cold, damp mist soaking into his hair and face from the waters spinning around them. The light faded, the gloom deepening the farther they dropped.

Divine brilliance pierced the shadows below in faint flickers, the God trapped within the black orb fighting the evil holding him captive. The corruption choking the air grew as they neared the bottom of the bay.

Cassius indicated the shadowy bands fixing the sphere to the floor of the bay. "Morgan, carve him free!"

Morgan landed in the sludge and started slicing through the dark cords with the Sword of Wind. It took him almost a minute to separate them from the orb.

"Don't bother trying to break through that wall with your sword," Cassius warned Morgan as the demigod prepared to do just that. "You won't be able to cut through it in time!"

Morgan frowned heavily.

"Can't you use that?!" Julia shouted, indicating the Eternity Key.

Cassius shook his head. "Not down here I can't! The resulting tsunami would destroy the cities around the bay! I need you to bring him up instead!"

Understanding dawned on Julia's face. She scowled, put away her blade, and flexed her fingers. A pillar of rock grew under the orb. It rose, lifting the sphere up the funnel.

They kept abreast of it and cleared the surface seconds later.

Victor joined them, his face pale as he stared at the throbbing globe of darkness atop the rocky projection that now towered some twelve feet above the bay. "What is that?"

"A prison." Cassius tightened his hold on his divine blade and the Eternity Key. "Stand back, all of you!"

Morgan and the others fell away, the funnel closing with a roar beneath them as the Aqueous angels and demons retracted their powers.

Cassius rose some fifteen feet, unleashed Heaven's Light, and brought the swords down on the dark orb. The impact made his bones and teeth clatter. A thin crack appeared in the surface of the sphere.

Cassius repeated the attack a second then a third time, the reverberations booming across the bay and rattling the suspension bridge to the south.

It took another three strikes to shatter the sphere.

Dazzling brilliance exploded beneath Cassius. The radiance fluttered before shrinking around the God who was emitting it. The entity threw his head back and bellowed, the unholy roar shaking the city and raising waves across the estuary.

Fear seized Cassius, the sensation locking onto the most primitive part of his brain with a deadly accuracy that left him frozen in place. He could see the same terror draining blood from the faces of the angels and demons around him. Even Morgan and Victor flinched and blanched.

Cassius swallowed and curled his fingers into fists. He knew what they were experiencing was a direct result of the God's scream of rage. He forced his body to move and dropped down before the glowing figure.

"*STOP!*"

The God jerked at his voice. The light faded.

Cassius's eyes rounded. So did those of the enormous, naked, horned man with the lower body of a goat.

Shit. Is that who I think it is?!

"*Awakener!*" Pan growled, baring his teeth.

Cassius blinked rapidly. *That's what Death said too!*

He startled as Pan shot toward him, murder in his eyes.

Morgan and Victor blocked the God's path, the angel and the demon no longer in the grip of the terror that had paralyzed them. Pan rocked to a stop, sending waves surging beneath him. His lips curled as he glared at the three of them. His furious gaze turned to the dark rift that still split the city.

"*You better close that first!*" he spat at Cassius over Morgan and Victor's shoulders.

"I was hoping you'd tell me how," Cassius confessed, his heart in his throat.

Pan clicked his tongue. "*Are your eyes for show?! That is the Eternity Key in your hand, you damn fool!*"

Cassius stared at the golden broadsword, understanding blossoming in his mind. "Is there a specific place I need to use it?!"

"*No,*" the God admitted with a grunt. "*For you and that key, anywhere will do.*"

Cassius dipped his head in gratitude. He shot across the bay, the waters churning in the wake of his passage. Morgan and Victor followed, Pan trailing behind them. They stopped a short distance from him, watching him rock to a halt in front of the throbbing barrier.

Cassius put away his Stark Steel blade, gripped the Eternity Key in both hands, and closed his eyes. He took a deep breath, his throat aching with tension.

Please, let this work!

His grip tightened on the weapon. He opened his eyes and stabbed the holy artifact into the rift.

The barrier screeched, the sound it made threatening to burst Cassius's ear drums. He gritted his teeth and twisted the Eternity Key, a roar leaving him.

Divine radiance exploded around the wound he made, so forceful it shook the broadsword and his very bones. The wall quaked violently and started to disintegrate outward from the dazzling point of light, its outraged protest fading.

It whooshed into nothingness in less than a minute, the six-mile-long barrier vanishing as if it never was.

The clouds parted. Sunlight swept across the city, a rainbow blooming as the drizzle died. It lit up the God glaring at Cassius.

"*You and I have unfinished business, Awakener!*" Pan hissed.

His eyes flashed gold. He curled his fingers into claws and arrowed toward him, his intent all too clear. Cassius choked as the God's hands locked around his throat.

Victor punched the deity in the face at the same time Morgan kicked him viciously in his exposed balls.

15

"*There was no need to kick me in the testicles,*" Pan grumbled.

His brow knotted heavily as he studied Morgan and Victor from where he sat on Strickland's couch, an ice pack on his cheek and a second one held gingerly to his groin under the blanket protecting his false modesty.

The angel and the demon watched him without an iota of remorse where they stood with their arms crossed on either side of Strickland's desk.

It had been an hour since Cassius had obliterated the war demons with Heaven's Light and the Eternity Key, released Pan from his underwater prison of darkness, and closed the rift that had cleaved San Francisco in half. The crevasse in Market Street had also been sealed in the process, an unexpected side effect of the demigod's prodigious actions. Only a faint crack remained where the fracture line had once been.

The news channels and the internet were already teeming with videos of the battle that had been fought in the air and on the ground by the otherwordly and human magic users south of the rift. All were being hailed as heroes. But the ones the city truly considered their saviors were Cassius, Morgan, and Victor.

The phones in the Argonaut bullpen hadn't stopped ringing since the rift had been obliterated, everyone who was anyone wanting to interview the two angels and the demon.

"Are you sure that's a God?" Adrianne murmured suspiciously to Julia from across the room. "He just looks like an unkempt guy in some kind of goat cosplay to me."

"*The word is faun, you impertinent human!*" Pan ground out.

"Shouldn't his wounds have healed by now if he were a true God?" Bailey asked Zach sotto voce.

Strickland pressed his lips together.

Morgan bit back a sigh. *Cassius is right. These guys really do need to learn some etiquette.*

He decided to ignore the fact that the person who required those lessons the most was himself.

The windows rattled as the irritated deity let loose a wave of divine energy. "*I am not in full possession of my powers, you insects! Once I am, I will show these insolent pups what I am capable of!*"

He pointed an ice pack at Morgan and Victor.

"Whoa." Julia grimaced as the blanket settled back down over Pan's enormous member. "We did *not* need to see that."

"Speak for yourself," Adrianne muttered. "Some of us haven't seen any action in that department for nearly a year."

Bailey opened his mouth, his expression brightening. Zach stepped on the wizard's foot.

"I think that jerk just called us dogs," Victor told Morgan coldly.

"That's rich coming from a goat," Morgan scoffed.

Strickland flashed a pained look their way.

"Sorry," Victor said, contrite. "He didn't exactly ingratiate himself with us when we met."

The door opened. Brianna stormed in, Malik Garcia following in her wake. The Hexa agent and sorcerer was Brianna's chief bodyguard and, judging from the content of Eden's text messages to Adrianne and Julia, her current beau.

The witch rocked to a stop. Her face went slack as she took in Pan's horns and hooves. "What the hell is that?!"

"This is why I loathe Earth," Pan muttered to himself. *"You have no respect for Gods."*

Morgan rubbed the back of his neck. *He's not wrong.* He grimaced. *Then again, that's what he gets for attacking Cassius.*

Brianna cut her eyes to Strickland. "He's a God?"

The Argonaut bureau director dipped his head, his face stern.

Jasper and Reuben marched in behind Brianna and Malik, Charlie trailing behind them.

Morgan frowned. *Why is Charlie with them?*

Jasper startled when he saw Victor. Morgan caught the faint frown Reuben directed at his lover.

Cassius had told Morgan the reason Jasper loathed him so was because the Terrene demon was once in love with Victor. The fact that the Fiery had picked Cassius out of all the otherwordly to be his long-term lover had enraged Jasper no end. Judging from Reuben's expression, he wasn't relishing having his boyfriend in the same room as the demon the latter used to desire.

Morgan stole a shrewd look at Victor. *So, he didn't tell Jasper he was coming to San Francisco, huh?*

Charlie's brow furrowed as he looked at Jasper and Reuben. Morgan scowled, a suspicion igniting in his head. Julia and Zach were appraising the trio with a thoughtful stare.

The only members of Morgan's team who seemed oblivious to the intimate vibe between the enchanter and the two otherworldly framing him were Adrianne and Bailey.

Reuben and Jasper went deathly still when they registered Pan's presence. They evidently recognized the God. Reuben finally looked away from the frowning deity.

"What the hell happened out there?" he asked Victor and Morgan grimly. "That light. Was that Cassius?"

The divine radiance the demigod had unleashed in the penultimate moments of the battle had pierced the rift briefly and been seen north of the barrier.

"Yes," Victor replied.

Jasper's jaw jutted out. "Did he really destroy all those war demons with Heaven's Light?"

"It wasn't just Heaven's Light," Morgan said grudgingly. "He used the Eternity Key too."

"What?!" Brianna drew back. "I thought the cat was guarding the artifact!"

Morgan made a face. "He spat it out and gave it to Cassius."

Pan's eyes turned flinty. *"The imp is here?"*

Morgan straightened. He could feel the God's icy wrath even from where he stood. Victor grew similarly alert.

"Yes," Strickland said, ignoring the palpable tension flooding the room. "He came to Earth a while ago. The God who we think might have caused the Fall and who's been exploiting human magic users to do his dirty deeds was after him. Loki was injured when Cassius found him." The director paused. "That God intended to use the Eternity Key to open the Nether. Were it not for Cassius and Morgan, this city wouldn't be here right now."

Gold flashed in the depths of Pan's pupils.

"*The God you think caused the Fall?*" he said in a dull voice.

"He spoke to us through a warlock he was controlling," Morgan explained. "He told us we all lost our memories because of some kind of spell. And that he'd manipulated Cassius in the past."

A tense hush followed. It was broken by a sound Morgan hadn't expected.

Pan chuckled. His sounds of mirth grew until he bent over, tears of laughter streaming down his face while he gasped for air.

Morgan scowled.

"Did I punch him too hard?" Victor muttered darkly.

"This guy's creeping me out," Adrianne mumbled to Julia.

"*Ah.*" Pan finally stopped cackling and wiped his cheeks. "*It has been years since I have laughed this much. Thank you for the entertainment.*"

Morgan's jaw tightened. "Are you done being an asshole? If you know something, then spit it out!"

Pan sobered. "*Why should I?*"

The God became the subject of a battery of stunned stares.

"Isn't it in all our interests to stop whoever caused the

Fall?" Victor said stiffly in the shocked silence. "That God is trying to do the same thing again. What happened here today is likely another scheme of his!"

Pan watched them impassively. "*I have no doubt that the one you speak of was behind the machinations that caused the Nether to tear open the first time. I also believe he is responsible for all the subsequent attempts to repeat that horror and for imprisoning me in that rift. But he did not directly cause the Fall. He does not possess that kind of power.*"

Morgan's eyes shrank to slits. "But you know who does!" He closed the distance to Pan and towered threateningly over the God. "You know his name and that of the one who tore the Nether open! So, why won't you tell us, you stubborn, goat-headed bastard?!"

"*Because I want you to do something for me first.*"

Morgan blinked slowly, too dumbfounded to speak.

The God looked past him to Victor and the rest of the room, his expression cold and calculating. "*If you help me, then I will tell you what I know.*"

16

CASSIUS CLASPED A SQUIRMING LOKI TO HIS CHEST AS HE
landed on the rooftop of the high rise where the Argonaut
offices were located, in downtown. He folded his wings,
sighed, and lifted the imp until they were eye to eye.

"Will you stop fighting me?"

Loki stilled and sulked.

"It's thanks to you that we managed to close the rift."
Cassius held the cat in the crook of his arm and scratched
his head. "I think you should be here for this. Besides,
being cooped up in the apartment all the time isn't good
for you. You should get out more."

Loki grew limp in Cassius's hold, the imp accepting his
defeat gracelessly.

The Eternity Key pulsed warmly where Cassius had
slipped it into the back pocket of his jeans. He was
debating returning it to its keeper when the sound of
rotors distracted him.

The news helicopter that had followed them from the
apartment building was closing in on their location.

"Shit. I thought I'd lost them!"

Loki hissed at the approaching helicopter as Cassius hurried to the rooftop door. It slammed behind him, swallowing them in gloom. The angel descended the stairs to the tenth floor and headed through a fire exit, still frowning.

He'd gotten used to being the center of attention. After all, he'd been singled out for centuries, for all the wrong reasons. Being suddenly shoved into the limelight as a hero wasn't proving to be any better.

How the hell does Victor deal with this constant scrutiny?!

A dull roar rose in the distance as he negotiated the corridors leading to the main Argonaut offices. The noise grew when he approached the bullpen, the blare of dozens of phones piercing the air shrilly.

Zakir Singh jumped up from his desk when he saw him. "Hey, Cassius!" The Argonaut agent waved the phone receiver in his hand, his expression harried. "The mayor's office has been calling for you every five minutes for the last half hour!"

"Tell them I'm busy."

Cassius walked past the bullpen briskly, Loki peering curiously out of his arms.

Singh scowled. "Is that a cat?"

The imp tensed as Cassius approached Strickland's office. He jumped and balanced himself on Cassius's shoulders when they entered the room, startling him.

"*Where the devil is that Awakener?*" Pan was griping where he sat on the couch. "*I still have a bone to pick with him.*"

Victor glowered at the God. "If that bone involves

trying to strangle him again, it's not just your face and your balls we'll be hitting next time."

"You took the words right out of my mouth!" Morgan snapped.

Cassius stared at the angel and the demon. *Are those two actually getting along?*

Strickland drew a sharp breath. "Wait. He tried to kill Cassius?!"

The news crews and bystanders who'd been close to the scene of the battle hadn't been able to capture much of what had happened following the annihilation of the war demons by Heaven's Light, the divine radiance frying most of their cameras and the storm making getting a visual hard. No one had witnessed Cassius saving Pan or what had ensued bar the angels and demons who had been there to see it with their own eyes.

"Yes," Victor said grimly. "And after Cassius freed him, too, the ungrateful bastard."

Pan glared at them.

Loki's hackles rose and his eyes flashed crimson. He hissed and spat at the God, his ire all too clear. Pan jumped to his feet at the sight of the imp, the ice packs he'd been holding and the blanket covering him tumbling to the floor.

"*You stupid Keeper!*" the God roared. "*Where have you been?! I've been looking for you everywhere!*"

Cassius froze as Loki sprung to the floor and transformed into a small, horned imp with rich black fur, red eyes, leathery wings, and a long, sinuous tail with an arrowhead-shaped tip.

"I cannot believe you tried to kill Cassius!" Loki trilled, not paying attention to anybody but the angry deity towering over him. "Also, the last time I checked, I was banished to the Seventh Hell by a bunch of selfish Gods who told me to—wait, let me think." He glared at Pan, his pointed ears quivering and his sing-song voice at odds with his rage. "Ah, yes! If I recall correctly, their exact words were '*Guard the Eternity Key with your life or else you shall be thrown into the Abyss!*'"

Pan spluttered incoherently.

"*You—you had one job, Keeper!*" he finally barked.

"Oh really?" Loki sneered. "Well, you and your job can kiss my furry bottom!"

He stabbed his tail at the God to punctuate his words.

Cassius gaped. Brianna rubbed a hand down her face.

"Look, could you do us a favor?" the witch said in a strained voice.

"*What?!*" Loki and Pan snapped, rounding on her.

"Could you put some clothes on?" Brianna indicated their naked bodies with a vague hand, unfazed by their tones. "I don't know how things are done in the other realms, but we prefer to cover our...intimate parts, here on Earth."

Malik bobbed his head in agreement, his expression pinched as he glanced at Pan's larger-than-life anatomy.

Loki looked down at himself. "Imps do not wear clothes." His gaze found Morgan, his expression turning mildly disapproving. "Also, your statement does not quite match the evidence of my eyes. Morgan spends most of his time in this state when he is at home. And he is constantly using his intimate part to ravish poor Cassius."

Cassius groaned, his face growing hot. Morgan scowled.

Victor's face darkened.

"*Judging from the scent of that human, he has spent the last few hours naked and has had the intimate parts of both the demon and the angel inside him.*" Pan indicated Charlie, Jacob, and Reuben with an accusing expression. "*So, your statement is full of goat shit, woman!*"

"Oh God," Brianna mumbled.

Adrianne's eyes bulged. "*Whaaattt?!*" She grabbed Julia's arm and shook her violently. "Say it isn't so! Please tell me our baby wasn't violated by those two beasts?!"

Jasper bristled. "Hey, watch it!"

"I hate to give you the bad news, but our 'baby' looks like he enjoyed it," Julia said drily as Charlie flushed.

"I'm twenty-five!" the enchanter protested. "I can sleep with anyone I choose!"

Zach cocked a thumb at Jasper and Reuben, his tone dull. "I wouldn't have put you down as the type who'd want to play hide the salami with those two, though."

"Jesus," Strickland said in a disgusted voice. "Can we bring this conversation back on point?"

His request was ignored.

Charlie glared accusingly at Jacob and Reuben. "I told you someone would pick up on things if we came here together!"

"It doesn't matter," Reuben said.

"Yeah," Jasper grunted. "We were planning to make things official anyway."

Surprise widened Charlie's eyes. "You were?"

"I know you wanted more time to think about it, but it's clear to us where you belong," Reuben said. "You're ours."

The enchanter went beetroot red at the possessive light in Reuben and Jasper's eyes.

"I am *not* happy about this," Morgan grumbled.

Jasper crossed his arms and tilted his chin. "I honestly couldn't give a crap. Charlie is in a relationship with the two of us. The faster your obnoxious ass accepts this, the better."

"Jasper," Charlie murmured, pleased.

Cassius turned his attention to Loki. He couldn't help but feel somewhat betrayed by the imp.

"How long have you been able to take on this form?"

Guilt darted in Loki's eyes at Cassius's pained look. "After the wounds I got under the church healed." His ears and tail drooped. "I cannot use it often. It takes a lot of energy to maintain my true form in this realm, so I much prefer my demon cat shape. But this is the only body I can talk in." He blinked his large eyes at Cassius, his expression miserable. "Are you terribly upset?"

Cassius sighed, the tightness in his chest fading. Loki in his imp form was just as adorable as Loki in his cat form.

"I just wished you'd told me the truth sooner."

"I am sorry," Loki murmured, shoulders hunched and wings sagging. He peered at Cassius from under his long lashes. "Can I still stay with you?"

Cassius smiled ruefully. "Of course."

Loki brightened. "Good. Because I like living with you." He glanced at Morgan. "And him too, despite the way he constantly manhandles you."

Cassius bit his lip hard. Julia muffled a snort.

"And you will still—" Loki paused and fidgeted, voice dropping to a low mumble and the tips of his ears and tail turning red, "cuddle me and scratch my head and stuff, right?"

"Christ," Jasper muttered.

"Oh." Cassius blinked at the imp, nonplussed. "Sure."

He glanced at Morgan and almost winced at the latter's murderous expression. "Er, when you're in your feline form."

Loki beamed, crimson lighting his pupils. "Great."

Air poofed around him as he transformed back into a black cat. He leapt into Cassius's arms and butted his chest lovingly with his head, happy rumbles quivering out of his belly.

The look on Morgan's face grew worse.

Pan's horns and hooves retracted. A pristine, snowy suit whooshed into existence as his godly form shrank to that of a deceptively ordinary-looking human. A red rose boutonnière blossomed on the lapel of his expensive jacket, the color matching his white and crimson brogues.

"*What?*" the God said defensively at their expressions.

"You look like a gangster," Julia said dully.

"The kind that didn't make the cut at gangster school," Adrianne added helpfully.

17

"THREE WEEKS AGO, MY LOVER DEMETRIUS DISAPPEARED from the Spirit Realm. At the time, I thought he had departed for his homeland of Hyperborea." A pained look washed across Pan's face. *"That is where he sometimes goes when we have had a fight."*

Loki hissed at that. The cat lay coiled on Cassius's lap, body language still hostile. Cassius suppressed a sigh. It was evident Loki and Pan were not on good terms. Considering it appeared that the imp never volunteered to be the Keeper of the Eternity Key, Cassius got why he was so aggrieved.

Upon their questioning, Loki had confessed that he did not recall much about the Fall or what had caused it, nor did he recollect Cassius or Morgan's true identities. The spell that had erased the memories of the Fallen had reached nearly all the realms, including the Hells, where he had been at the time. The only thing he knew for certain was that the Eternity Key was an important artifact that should never be allowed to fall into the wrong hands.

"It was only after your return from Ivory Peaks that I became convinced you could wield it," the imp had admitted to Cassius.

Cassius observed Pan pensively. The God, on the other hand, had retained many of his memories from before the Fall, like Bostrof had inferred. He furrowed his brow.

I wonder how he managed to do that. Not that it's going to be much help right now. He's made it clear he isn't willing to give us any of that information for free.

"*When I went to Hyperborea to find Demetrius, he was not there. Not only that, the Kingdom of the God of Winter had been almost entirely destroyed.*" Pan frowned. "*By what, I do not know.*"

Cassius straightened in his seat. "The God of Winter?" A name came to him then. One that had not crossed his mind in hundreds of years. "You mean, Boreas?!"

"*Yes.*"

Victor narrowed his eyes. "Something destroyed Hyperborea?"

"Ten bucks says it was a rift," Morgan muttered.

Pan hesitated. "*Demetrius is the son of Zephyrus and a demigod of Spring. Boreas is his uncle. Not many know this.*"

Cassius exchanged a startled look with Morgan and Victor.

Pan grimaced. "*Dem is not one for the limelight. He prefers his identity be kept a secret.*" The God sobered. "*Boreas was also nowhere to be found. More importantly, the Frost Crown is gone.*"

Loki stiffened on Cassius's lap. He transformed back into an imp and jumped to the ground.

"What do you mean, gone?!" he said shrilly.

Cassius's pulse quickened, his gaze swinging between

the tense imp and the God. He was getting a bad feeling about this.

"The Frost Crown?" Brianna repeated blankly.

"*It is an artifact. A weapon similar to the Eternity Key.*" Pan's eyebrows drew together. "*Boreas was its Keeper.*"

Shocked murmurs erupted across the office.

"Was it also used to lock Chaos in the Abyss?" Morgan asked stiffly.

Pan dipped his head. "*Yes.*"

Loki fisted his hands, voice rising and wings quivering. "How could you lose an artifact?!"

However much he may have protested about being the unwilling Keeper of the Eternity Key, it was evident he'd taken the duty assigned to him by the Gods seriously.

Pan's expression soured. "*It is not as if it was done deliberately, you impertinent fiend.*" His jaw set in a hard line as he observed the rest of them. "*The deities who sealed Chaos used many such weapons to secure his prison. They were deliberately scattered throughout the realms and the Nine Hells afterward, so as to confound anyone who ever wished to free the Primordial God from his eternal slumber.*"

Cassius's heart thumped heavily against his ribs.

"Is that what he wants?" He held Pan's hooded gaze, dread pooling in the pit of his stomach. "The God who wants to tear the Nether open again. Does he want to return Chaos to our worlds?"

"*Ultimately, yes.*" Pan observed him broodingly. "*But he equally wishes to destroy all those who could overturn his Machiavellian plans.*"

Cassius couldn't help but feel that Pan had included him in that statement. He stared at the floor while he digested this troubling information, his mind racing.

Everything was starting to make sense. The Fall. The Eternity Key. The incident with Eden Monroe.

Cassius looked up and leveled a piercing stare at the God. "Are the Bloodcursed Devilwood Summoning Staff and Morgan's Sword of Wind keys too?"

Strickland paled. "Morgan's sword?!"

The rest of their team traded nervous glances.

Unease shadowed Brianna's face. Galliad had told them Eden's staff was likely a weapon that had been used to seal Chaos in the Abyss.

Pan's eyes bulged. *"The Bloodcursed Devilwood Summoning Staff is also here, on Earth?!"*

"Yes. It has claimed a human girl as its mage." Cassius's gaze shifted from the shocked God to Morgan. "As for the Sword of Wind, we've suspected it for a while. Lucille Hartman seemed to recognize the blade the first time she saw it. And it's the only thing that can destroy the black magic that the God's followers use."

A muscle jumped in Pan's jawline. He looked decidedly unhappy.

"For three of the keys to be here, on Earth, can only mean one thing," he finally said in a deadly voice.

Cassius held the deity's cool gaze. "This world will be the final stand."

"What?" Strickland froze. "What do you mean by that?!"

The director rose to his feet and pressed his hands on his desk, his horror reflected on everyone else's faces.

Cassius rubbed the back of his neck, feeling tired all of a sudden. Their encounter with the war demons in Ivory Peaks felt like a lifetime ago.

"Regina, the Dryad court seer, reaffirmed what Cedric

told us," Morgan said bitterly. "She has foreseen glimpses of a war that will have Earth as its battleground."

Brianna sat down heavily on the chair next to Cassius. "We need to tell the world about this." The witch's voice trembled. "We have to warn—"

"No." Victor shook his head, his tone adamant. "We cannot do that. Not yet."

Strickland clenched his fists and swallowed. "Victor is right, Brianna. There would be mass panic if this were to be known."

"I agree." Reuben rubbed his chin. "We can help the governments of the world prepare for what is to come, but it has to remain a secret for now." Lines wrinkled his brow. "We need more information."

Pan clenched his jaw and directed a cold stare at Cassius. "*It looks like we shall have to settle our grievances much later than I would have liked, Awakener.*"

Cassius stiffened. "What do you mean by that word? Death said the same thing to me. He called me Awakener when we spoke."

Morgan blinked slowly. "Death?"

Victor went still.

"That giant skeletal hand? That was Death." Cassius's stomach knotted. "I think he was trying to talk to me in Ivory Peaks too. From what I gathered, he's being controlled by whoever is behind these rifts. The only time he managed to communicate with me was when he held me inside his hand. He told me to help Pan." He hesitated. "And he used that word too. Awakener."

"*Death?*" Pan's eyes turned dull. "*You mean to say the Reaper God was here, in this realm?!*"

Cassius's scalp prickled. "The Reaper God?"

Morgan turned the TV on and put it on mute.

All the news channels were broadcasting replays of the epic battle that had played out across the city that morning. A close-up of the bony hand that had emerged from the rift and entrapped Cassius materialized seconds later. Morgan paused the playback.

Pan jumped to his feet, gold flashing in his eyes.

"*That son of a whore!*" he snarled.

The windows cracked under the wave of divine power that pulsed from him.

❦

MORGAN HAD THE SWORD OF WIND OUT IN A heartbeat. Hell Fire blazed on the Stark Steel blade Victor unleashed. They both jumped in front of Cassius, Loki at their side.

Pan inhaled raggedly and closed his eyes, nostrils flaring. His powers dimmed.

"*Put those weapons away,*" he growled at the Aerial and the Fiery. He opened his eyes, his pupils dark once more. "*I have no intention of harming your precious Awakener.*"

The God sat down, a vein throbbing in his temple.

"That's the Reaper God?" Cassius said numbly, staring at the frozen, skeletal hand on the screen.

"*You did not know?*" Pan asked.

Cassius shook his head dazedly.

Pan propped his elbows on his knees and dropped his chin on his interlocked fists, his brow furrowed and his gaze lost in the distance. "*This changes everything. If he has gained control of the Reaper God himself, then all is almost lost.*"

A somber mood descended on the room in the wake of his funereal words.

Pan's eyebrows drew together. He directed a probing stare at Cassius and Morgan. *"What happened in Ivory Peaks?"*

Morgan and Cassius filled the God in on the battle they had fought in the kingdom of the Dryads. Pan listened attentively.

"So, that old coot Roald is doing well?" he said with a grunt after they'd finished.

"Yes," Cassius said. "The whole royal family was pretty amazing, to be honest."

Pan sat back and tsk-tsked. *"Shame. I thought I might finally have a chance with Hildur."*

Morgan snorted in disgust.

"I thought you had a lover," Victor told Pan coolly.

Pan waved a dismissive hand. *"My race is all about polyamory."* He sniffed. *"Although, Demetrius is more than enough to keep me busy these days."*

"You still haven't told us what an Awakener is," Cassius said in a strained voice.

Disquiet swirled through Morgan as he observed his lover. He could tell the lack of memories was gnawing at the Empyreal.

"It is a divine being who can rouse the latent abilities of others. An augmenter of Heaven or Hell's powers, one might say." Pan sighed heavily at their blank expressions. *"The strength deities possess is often too devastating and dangerous to sustain continuously. Some can even destroy worlds. As such, Heaven and the Hells made it so that many have their abilities suppressed until such a time their powers are needed, upon which an Awakener releases*

their divine strength from its prison. The process of suppression and liberation happens voluntarily in almost all cases." He narrowed his eyes at Cassius. *"In all the eons that I can recall, there has never been more than one Awakener at any one time in history. And that person has always been the strongest Guardian."*

Cassius recoiled, blood draining from his face.

A ringing sounded in Morgan's ears. *Is that how my powers were unlocked? Because Cassius is an Awakener?!*

Strickland studied the Empyreal with dull eyes, his stunned expression indicating he was thinking the exact same thing.

"Guardian of Light." Cassius swallowed convulsively. His voice shook when he spoke again. "That's what Bostrof Orzkal and the Lucifugous demons call me. I thought it was just a term to describe Heaven's Light!"

Morgan closed the distance between them and laid a hand on his shoulder, his stomach heavy. Cassius clasped his fingers blindly, his soul core pulsing out weakly in his distress.

Pan went still. *"The king of the Shadow Empire resides here, on Earth?"*

"Former king," Morgan muttered. "One of his subordinates now sits on his throne."

Pan sneered. *"That Reaper Seed addicted fool? Bostrof should have reclaimed his birthright from that false king centuries ago. His realm is full of corrupted souls who would make easy prey for our enemy."* He hunched his shoulders and rubbed his chin. *"But at least now we have a chance."*

Victor's lips pressed into a thin line. "What do you mean?"

Morgan could tell the Fiery demon was as upset with the God as he was. He gritted his teeth. However badly he begrudged the demon his status as Cassius's former lover and his ongoing interest in the Empyreal, there was no denying how much he cared for him.

"*We need to track down Boreas and find out what happened to Demetrius and the Frost Crown. I think all three have something to do with the rifts that are appearing in all the realms.*" Pan looked at his hands, his expression turning haunted for a moment. "*I managed to cast the spirits who live in the land free from the one that materialized in my kingdom before it entrapped me.*" A muscle twitched in his cheek. "*The Reaper God must have teleported me out of that place of darkness when the rift opened here. Which means he knew I needed to be on Earth. And that you and your allies would be able to help me.*" He leveled a brooding stare at Cassius. "*The king of the Shadow Empire may very well hold the key to our troubles.*"

18

"Hell no!" Bostrof snarled.

Cassius's cell almost fell out of his hand. He traded a startled look with Morgan. The latter sat behind the wheel of their SUV.

They were on their way to Nob Hill, where Bostrof's main fight club was located.

"Why not?" Cassius asked Bostrof hesitantly.

"Ask that goat-headed bastard!" the Lucifugous fumed before ending the call.

Cassius stared at his phone for a moment. He looked over his shoulder and squinted at the God slouched on the back seat. "What did you do to him?"

Pan crossed his arms and sniffed. *"That demon takes things far too seriously."*

Victor rolled his eyes where he sat beside the God.

Morgan glowered at Pan in the rear-view mirror. "You didn't answer the question."

Loki made a mocking sound. The imp was back in his cat form, his tail swinging languidly where he sat on

Cassius's lap. Judging from Morgan's pinched expression and hot glances, the Aerial did not approve of the Keeper's current location.

Pan smirked. *"Hey, Awakener. I think the imp wants to mate with you."*

Cassius sucked in air.

"Jesus," Victor muttered in disgust.

Loki transformed with a poof of air. Morgan cursed and almost lost control of the vehicle, narrowly avoiding a car in the opposite lane. Pan swore as he slammed shoulder first into the door.

Angry honking rose behind them.

"Do you want me to drive?" Victor snapped.

The demon had braced his hands reflexively on the roof.

"No!" Morgan ground out.

Loki huffed and puffed where he sat on Cassius's lap, too flustered to speak for a moment.

"I do *not* want to mate with him!" the imp finally squealed, color flooding his ears. "Cassius is like a brother to me!"

"Oh, yeah?" Morgan scowled at Loki. "Then put your dick away!"

"For fuck's sake," Victor whispered.

"You know the history of the Gods," Pan scoffed. His lips curled contemptuously as he gazed at Loki. *"Since when did blood relations ever stop us from fornicating with one another?"*

Morgan's cell buzzed before the imp could come up with a riposte.

He stabbed the answer button on the digital dashboard. "What?!"

"Is everything okay?" Julia asked. "You almost crashed back there."

"Everything is peachy!" Morgan growled.

By the time they turned into the alleyway that led to *Ohomgath* and parked behind a row of dumpsters, Loki was back in his cat form and Morgan was sulking.

Cassius cast a quick look heavenward as they climbed out of the vehicle. *Give me strength.*

Guilt tightened his chest when he caught Victor's troubled look. He knew the Fiery was still brooding about what Pan had said about his Awakener status, back in Strickland's office.

Julia and the rest of their team got out of the second SUV. Brianna, Jasper, and Reuben had returned to their respective agencies after what Pan had revealed to them at Argonaut. There was still a lot to do in the aftermath of the battle that had rocked San Francisco that morning. This included taking care of their injured agents and helping city officials deal with the destruction the rift had caused. Strickland had gone ahead of them to a meeting at the mayor's office.

He'd asked Cassius, Morgan, and Victor to keep all four directors in the loop concerning their meeting with Bostrof.

Adrianne clocked Loki's raised hackles and Morgan's irate expression as she and the others approached.

"What's wrong with them?" she asked Cassius.

"Nothing some timeout wouldn't solve," the Empyreal said flintily.

Morgan's face darkened. Loki uttered a shocked meow. Pan sniggered.

They headed for a metal door covered in graffiti at the

far-left end of the passage, steam from the vents and air-conditioning units populating the towering walls on either side swirling above their heads. There weren't many seedy places in Nob Hill, yet Bostrof had managed to find one such location in the upper-class district. It was a perfect front for his fight club and one that he'd emulated with his other branches across the city.

The door led them into a shadowy warehouse. An industrial-sized, bird-cage elevator stood at the far end, beyond the carcasses of abandoned machinery and burnt-out cars. They entered the rickety compartment and emerged some hundred feet underground. The service stairs that led off the shadowy lobby brought them out into *Ohomgath* a moment later.

"Looks like the rift didn't damage this place," Julia remarked as she examined the shadowy auditorium.

Cassius followed her gaze. The club had fared pretty well compared to the roads and buildings they'd passed on the drive here, the only sign of the tremors that had shaken the city in the wake of the rift's opening the fine layer of dust covering the stands around them.

The cavernous space beyond was wreathed in gloom. Since Lucifugous demons did not tolerate brightness, Bostrof had fitted the place with colored spotlights and fluorescent tubing which turned the club crimson at night-time. A solitary yellow bulb currently shone down on the wired, steel-framed cage in the center of the hundred-foot-deep pit.

A powerfully built Lucifugous was sweeping it clean. The demon stiffened when he registered their presence. He looked up, squinting.

His face brightened the next instant. "Oh, hi guys."

"Hey, Crusher," Cassius said while Morgan and the rest of their team greeted Bostrof's champion fighter. "Is your boss in his office?"

"Yeah." Crusher shifted from one foot to the other. "I'd come back if I were you. He sounds like he's in a bad mood."

Morgan side-eyed Pan. "Seriously, what the fuck did you do to the guy?"

The God remained mute.

They headed down the galleries and entered a crimson-lit corridor leading off the ground floor. Two of Bostrof's guards stood to attention in front of the black, leather-padded and metal-studded door at the end, the demons almost bursting out of the seams of their slick suits.

"I wouldn't go in there," Vorzof warned.

"I've not seen the boss this livid in decades," Goran added with a grunt.

Cassius cut his eyes to the source of Bostrof's anger before looking up at the camera at the top of the door. "We're coming in, Bostrof."

Vorzof and Goran grumbled under their breaths and reluctantly let him pass, the others following in his wake. Cassius's status as the Guardian of Light meant most Lucifugous demons revered him.

Bostrof's office was large and lavishly decorated with crystal chandeliers, leather and glass furniture, and fur rugs. The place even boasted a bar. It was a space not so much designed to flaunt the wealth of its owner as it was a calculated move to awe his associates and his competition.

This was the setting where Bostrof chose to do most of his business dealings. And it was currently clouded with feathers and down.

Powerful muscle and sinew strained under Bostrof's expensive, custom-tailored shirt where he stood in the middle of the floor amidst the pale fillings drifting around him. At eight feet tall and almost half as wide, the demon was a beast among the Lucifugous. Which made the pretty, velvet cushion he was holding mid-tear look even more incongruous in his enormous hands.

Cassius pursed his lips as he studied the remains of the other furnishings on the floor. It looked like a bomb had detonated in the room.

The Lucifugous's eyes flashed crimson when he saw Pan.

"*You!*" he spat. "What the hell are you doing on Earth?!"

He made to move.

Cassius winced and pointed. "Isn't that one of Lilaia's favorite bolster pillows?"

Bostrof froze. He looked down guiltily at the cushion he'd started to rip apart. A scowl darkened his face as he registered the sea of others he'd already destroyed in his blind rage.

"*Shit!*"

Cassius's mouth fell open. "He did what?!"

"He tried to seduce Lilaia," Bostrof fumed, nostrils flaring. "It was shortly after we got married too."

The glass in his hand cracked. He downed his whiskey and slammed it down on the side table next to him. Everyone looked accusingly at Pan.

The God shrugged where he slouched on a leather chair, legs crossed nonchalantly. "*I cannot help it. It is in my nature to want to have sex with beautiful creatures.*"

Morgan could feel a headache starting between his temples. Cassius rubbed a hand over his eyes and muttered something under his breath.

It was with great reluctance that Bostrof had finally agreed to listen to them. Now that they were here, Morgan wasn't sure this was such a great idea. The animosity between the former king of the Shadow Empire and the Wild God was even more acrimonious than that between Pan and Loki. He had a feeling it wasn't just Lilaia's cushions that were in danger of being shred to pieces.

Bostrof grunted irritably before studying Loki where the latter lay curled up on Cassius's lap. "So, that's the Keeper of the Key, huh?"

Cassius stroked the demon cat's head, an indulgent expression flashing across his face. "Yeah."

A happy rumble left Loki. The imp stole a look at Morgan and smirked.

Morgan scowled. *That cocky little shrimp!*

"I saw the news." Bostrof watched Cassius closely. "That was quite some light show."

"It wasn't meant to be," Cassius murmured. "And you forget. I wasn't the only one there."

Bostrof glanced at Morgan and Victor. "Still, I am certain you are the one who closed that rift." The Lucifugous wrinkled his brow. "So, why exactly are you here? I mean, apart from bringing this arrogant asshole to my doorstep." He shot a hot glare at Pan. "I would have thought you guys would be busy sorting out the mess in the city."

Cassius's face hardened. "We need your help, Bostrof."

The Lucifugous grew still while Cassius described what had transpired while he and Morgan were in Ivory Peaks. Victor briefed the demon about their theory concerning ley lines and the cracks that had appeared on Earth, before expanding on the details of the battle that hadn't been captured on camera that morning. Pan pitched in at the end to relate the events he'd uncovered in his realm and that of the God of Winter.

Bostrof's eyebrows rose. "An Awakener?"

Cassius made a face. "Yeah."

Bostrof pursed his lips. "Boreas is missing?"

"*Yes. As are Demetrius and the Frost Crown.*" Pan glanced

irritably at Cassius. *"From what the Awakener witnessed, the Reaper God is also a victim of the machinations of the deity behind all these rifts."*

Bostrof stroked his chin broodingly in the stilted hush that ensued.

"That is terrible news indeed," he finally murmured. "Not just about the artifact and Demetrius and Boreas." He locked eyes with Pan, his own troubled. "Death is one of the Primordials."

"Primordials?" Adrianne repeated blankly.

"He came into existence at the same time as Chaos," Julia murmured.

Bostrof held Pan's gaze. "The Reaper God is not a being who can fall easily."

The God bobbed his head, his face grim.

"He's being controlled," Cassius said. "How, we don't yet know."

Bostrof sat back and rubbed his nape. "I wonder if this has anything to do with what's been happening in the Hells."

Victor straightened. "Why? What's been happening in the Hells?"

Bostrof eyed Victor with a neutral expression. Morgan could tell the Lucifugous was wondering why the head of Cabalista was in San Francisco.

"From what my spies have reported in the last few months, there has been unusual movement among the ghouls and the Dark Alchemists who took refuge in the Shadow Empire after the Hundred Year War. They've also heard of war demons being sighted in several of the Hells." The Lucifugous's pupils flared crimson for a second. "It's almost as if—"

"An army is being mobilized," Cassius interrupted in a strained voice.

Bostrof dipped his chin. "Exactly."

Pan leaned forward, his elbows on his knees and his expression deadly. "*We need you to look for Boreas.*"

Bostrof narrowed his eyes. "What makes you think I can locate him? And something puzzles me. Don't the Gods of the Underworld live the Spirit Realm? Why didn't they fight beside you?"

Pan sneered. "*Those pussies slinked off to the Hells ages ago. They kept muttering about a great cataclysm and the end of everything.*" The Wild God paused. "*In hindsight, I think they probably saw this coming. As for Boreas, it is simple logic. If he is not being kept a prisoner in the other godly dominions, then he must be somewhere in the Hells. And no one has quite the same reach as you when it comes to finding out the goings-on in those realms.*"

Bostrof stayed silent for a moment.

"If he is in the Hells, he will be closely guarded," the demon muttered. "And his location is likely to be an absolute secret."

Pan arched an eyebrow. "*Since when has that ever stopped you?*"

A hard smile stretched Bostrof's mouth.

Morgan caught a sense of the deep friendship that still underscored the relationship between the Lucifugous king and the God despite their overt animosity.

Bostrof's smile disappeared. "I still don't want to help you."

"I think the matter at hand is more serious than some petty past squabble between the two of you regarding a one-time attempt to seduce your wife," Victor said sharply.

"It wasn't just the one time." Bostrof jerked his head at

Pan, lips curling. "This bastard tried to seduce Lilaia for a whole century!"

Julia and Adrianne sucked in air.

Bailey shot a dull look at Pan. "Dude."

"*My sex drive is unparalleled in all the realms,*" Pan stated without an iota of shame. "*It must be satisfied in order for me to be able to function coherently.*"

Morgan pressed his lips together. *This guy is a total douchebag.*

Cassius shot a glance his way.

"What?"

"Nothing," the Empyreal murmured.

Loki smirked. Understanding dawned.

"Hey, I'm hardly as bad as that bastard," Morgan protested, pointing at Pan. "At least I'm not in a permanent state of rut!"

Cassius's expression made it clear he begged to differ.

Voices rose outside the office before Morgan could object further.

"Look, it's been a long day. I'm not in the mood to argue. Getting back here took three hours after that damn thing ripped the city in half! So, why don't you do me a favor and get out of my way so I can see my husband?!"

The door opened on a waft of rich soil and the fresh smell of an untouched forest.

The Nymph who entered the room froze on the threshold. The shopping bags she held fell limply from her hands. Akamon, the Lucifugous demon Cassius had befriended in the sewers during the Chester Moran affair, shuffled in behind her, his arms equally laden with designer carrier bags.

Vorzof and Goran peered around the pair.

"Sorry, boss," Vorzof mumbled, contrite. "We tried to stop her."

"*You!*" Lilaia roared at Pan.

Her pupils flashed gold. She stormed across the office, the floor exploding in a sea of greenery ahead of her. Vines shot out from the ground and snared Pan's ankles and wrists where he sat in his armchair, the creepers responding to the Goddess's wrath.

Pan transformed, divine radiance exploding around him.

Bostrof locked his arms around his wife and lifted her off her feet. "Stop, my love!"

Lilaia struggled in his hold, practically spitting.

"Wow," Adrianne mumbled to Julia. "I don't think I've ever seen her pissed before."

Morgan had to concur. The River Spirit was normally gentle and sedate. He recalled the tale Lilaia had told them a while back, about her first meeting with Bostrof.

Damn. She's so nice most of the time, it's easy to forget she used to command of an army.

The Nymph finally sagged in Bostrof's arms. She let out a frustrated sigh. "Put me down, husband."

Bostrof hesitated and carefully let her go. He hovered protectively close, his posture rigid. The creepers holding Pan prisoner loosened and slithered to the floor.

The Wild God shrank back into his human form and arched an eyebrow. "*Not that I would have harmed you, but should you really be acting so recklessly in your condition?*"

Lilaia drew a sharp breath.

Bostrof frowned. "What condition?"

"Oh," Cassius mumbled.

The Empyreal was staring at Lilaia's belly.

Surprise jolted Morgan. *Wait. Is she—?!*

"*Ah.*" An awkward grimace twisted Pan's mouth. "*Was it meant to be a secret?*"

Everyone ignored the God.

"Wait." Bostrof swayed where he stood, the color draining from his face as he finally grasped what Pan meant. "Are you—are we *pregnant?!*"

Lilaia took his hands and steadied him, her face brimming with emotion. "Yes, my love. I am with child."

She kissed him softly.

Bostrof faltered before taking her gingerly in his arms, as if he were afraid to hurt her. "After all these years—" He stopped and swallowed convulsively. "I thought it would never happen!"

Lilaia rose on her tiptoes and pressed her lips to the demon's brow, tears glittering in her eyes. "I thought the same."

Vorzof and Goran sniffled by the door. Akamon blubbered and rubbed snot on his sleeve.

Adrianne wiped her eyes surreptitiously. "Aw shucks."

Cassius flushed, his face radiant with happiness.

Lilaia stepped out of Bostrof's arms, still beaming. "Excuse me for a moment, my love."

She turned, closed the distance to Pan, and punched the God in the face.

"Thanks for ruining my surprise, your horny bastard!" she berated the stunned deity.

"You totally deserved that," Victor muttered.

20

A CONTENTED SIGH WHOOSHED OUT OF CASSIUS. "I can't believe they're going to have a baby."

Morgan stole a look at the Empyreal as they rode the elevator to the top floor of their apartment building. Loki was asleep in Cassius's arms, the cat looking impossibly snug where the angel cradled him.

Lucky bastard.

Evening had fallen across San Francisco, nightfall finally bringing the tumultuous events of the day to a close. Most of the power grid had come back online. The only areas of darkness now punctuating the city centered along where the rift had opened. Emergency services were still on the ground helping clear debris and find missing persons.

Agents from all four bureaus were assisting them, many working off the clock; the otherwordly and magic users were much faster at moving unstable loads and shifting through wreckage than the heavy-duty vehicles that had turned up on site to deal with the aftermath of the disaster.

To everyone's surprise, the fatalities identified to date

numbered in the low double digits, a miracle that the mayor attributed to the fast response of the agents who'd been first to arrive on the scene.

Morgan had caught a replay of the press conference the man had given with Strickland and the other three agency directors that afternoon, before they'd left *Ohomgath*. Having listened impatiently to the mayor's statement, the media had immediately clamored for an interview with the two angels and the demon whom everyone believed had saved the city. It was Strickland who'd taken the lead in answering them, much to the mayor's relief.

"I'm afraid they are currently unavailable for interviews," the Argonaut director had stated with the succinctness that was his trademark.

"We hear Cassius Black has been secretly working as an Argonaut agent for the last two months. Is that true?" a reporter had asked Strickland animatedly.

Strickland had frowned. "It isn't a secret. Black's status as an Argonaut agent is public information." He'd arched an eyebrow. "We didn't shout it from the rooftop, for reasons I am sure all of you know."

Murmurs had broken out among the conference attendees, many of them looking awkward. They would have been the first to besmirch Cassius's reputation in the past.

"Where is Black right now?" another reporter had shouted above the brouhaha.

"This rift may open at other locations around the world where fracture lines have appeared," Strickland had said somberly. "Black, King, and Sloan are among the team currently investigating the anomalies to try to stop the same thing from happening again."

His reply had caused an even louder furor than before.

With everything that had taken place in San Francisco that morning, many had forgotten about the cracks that had opened in other cities around the planet.

Morgan wasn't the only one who felt sick to his stomach at the thought of what would happen if rifts did open at all those locations at once. It wasn't as if every city had an Empyreal among their ranks of otherwordly. And Cassius wouldn't be able to fly across the world and get to every rift before untold damage was wrought and millions died.

He frowned. *Not that I would want him to. He might be an Awakener, but he must have limits too.* The fact that the very people who had rejected Cassius in the past were now relying on the Empyreal to save them left a bitter aftertaste in Morgan's mouth. *They don't deserve his kindness.*

"Hey." Cassius touched his arm as the elevator stopped on their floor, his eyebrows drawing together. "What's wrong?"

Morgan forced his jaw to relax. "Nothing. Just brooding on stuff." They stepped out into the corridor leading to their apartments. "You look even happier now than you did at Bostrof's place." He paused, his tone turning dry. "You realize it's *their* baby, right?"

Cassius laughed lightly. "I know. It's just—any new life is worth celebrating, even more so when it comes to a couple like Bostrof and Lilaia. They deserve this blessing more than most."

A sudden longing ignited inside Morgan at Cassius's radiant expression. "Did you ever want one?"

Cassius blinked rapidly, his smile fading. "What?"

Morgan took his hand and pressed a kiss to his knuckles. "Did you ever want a baby?"

Cassius's pupils flared. The craving twisting Morgan's belly intensified at what he read in the gray eyes opposite him. A fervent prayer blazed through his mind.

What I wouldn't give to have a child who would bear both our blood.

Cassius's fingers spasmed around his, the faint color staining his cheeks telling Morgan he'd just had the same thought.

A snort sounded behind them. Morgan stiffened. He looked over his shoulder and glared at Pan.

The God was smirking. "*I am sorry, but you seem to be forgetting that the Awakener does not possess a womb.*"

Morgan clenched his teeth. "Why is this asshole with us again?"

Cassius blew out a sigh. "You know full well he doesn't have anywhere to go. And Bostrof categorically refused to have him within a five-hundred-foot radius of Lilaia."

Morgan grunted. "He can sleep in the sewers for all I care."

"Unfortunately, we're stuck with him until this is over." Cassius raised his eyebrows at Pan as they slowed to a stop in front of his apartment. "And you, would it hurt to be more polite? We're letting you stay at our place. The least you can do is be grateful about it."

Pan sneered as Cassius opened the door and headed inside. Morgan followed, turned, and blocked the God.

Pan narrowed his eyes. "*What are you doing?*"

Morgan dropped his apartment key in Pan's hand. "My place is one door down. Don't wreck it."

He started to close the door.

Pan stuck his foot in the gap, face crunching up. "*Hey!*"

"I thought we were going to put him in my spare room?" Cassius said.

"Like hell I'm letting this bastard anywhere near you after what he did this morning," Morgan ground out. He shoved Pan out and slammed the door shut. A thought came to him. He opened the door and scowled at the God storming grumpily toward his place. "You better not do anything sexual in my bed either!"

Pan flipped him the middle finger over his shoulder.

Cassius switched the lights on, rousing Loki. The imp meowed, jumped languidly to the ground, and padded over to the couch. He climbed up, curled into a ball, and went to sleep again.

Cassius leaned on the backrest and ran his knuckle lightly between the demon cat's ears, his expression tender. "He must be exhausted."

A happy rumble left Loki even as he slumbered.

Morgan grimaced. "He hardly did a thing."

He opened the refrigerator and grabbed a couple of beers.

Cassius accepted the bottle Morgan handed him gratefully. "He did say taking his imp form is taxing."

A knock came at the terrace door. A figure glowing with divine light was staring in at them. Morgan swore and stormed across the living room.

He yanked the sliding door open and glowered at Pan. "What do you want?!"

The God grimaced. *"What is there to eat around here? This body grows famished."*

They ended up ordering Chinese takeout. The delivery guy gawped when he saw Morgan and shyly asked for his autograph. Loki woke up halfway through the meal and hissed in alarm when he saw Pan sitting on the couch next to him. The imp bolted into Cassius's arms and climbed onto his shoulder, still spitting.

"*You better get used to me being around, Keeper,*" Pan scoffed.

He shoveled his sweet and sour beef into his mouth and munched with open relish. Cassius sighed and gave Loki some of his Kung Pao chicken.

Four beers later and three food servings later and the God looked like he'd taken root in Cassius's living room. He watched Morgan and Cassius broodingly while they cleared the coffee table.

"*You guys smell like you are about to mate.*"

Cassius nearly dropped a beer bottle.

"Seriously, leave if you're done!" Morgan growled.

Pan ignored him. A smirk curved his mouth. "*Can I watch?*"

Black wind exploded around Morgan.

Cassius laid a hand on his arm. "Calm down. He's just trying to goad you."

Pan rolled his eyes and rose. "*You guys are no fun. And FYI, I meant it. Guardians are notoriously ascetic. I am intrigued to see how one would look during sex.*"

Cassius stilled. The God headed for the terrace.

Morgan frowned. *Guardians?*

"Wait." Cassius took a step after Pan, his face strained. "You mean, there are more beings like me?!"

The God paused and looked over his shoulder, his expression growing cool. "*That information will stay under wraps until you fulfill your part of our agreement, Awakener.*"

CASSIUS OPENED HIS EYES. THE CLOCK ON THE nightstand read 2 a.m.

He'd been wide awake since he and Morgan had gone to bed.

Considering how worn out he'd been when they were driving back to the apartment building, he'd thought he'd be out like a light the moment his head hit the pillow.

Morgan's arm tightened around his waist. "Can't sleep?"

Cassius stiffened slightly before relaxing. He sighed and rolled over so he was face to face with Morgan.

"No. You can't either, it seems."

Morgan's eyes glittered in the gloom. He rose up on one elbow, stretched out behind him, and switched on the lamp on the nightstand. Though they could both use their seraphic powers to see in the dark, they preferred to talk with the light on. He settled back down, took Cassius in his arms, and slipped one leg between his knees.

Cassius burrowed his face in Morgan's chest, his hands

clenching on Morgan's shirt. This was their favorite sleeping position and the one he found the most soothing.

"What's bugging you?" Morgan murmured in his hair.

A mirthless chuckle left Cassius. "Where do I start?"

Morgan's hands found his back. He rubbed his tense flesh in slow, comforting strokes.

"Whatever it is, it'll be okay."

Cassius's jaw tightened. "You don't know that!"

His protest hung hotly between them. Morgan squeezed him closer. Cassius swallowed the sudden lump in his throat.

"I'm sorry," he mumbled into the Aerial's chest. "I didn't mean to sound so harsh."

Morgan stayed quiet, waiting for him to say what was truly on his mind. It was their unwritten rule, one that Cassius had gotten used to as he'd opened up to Morgan in the short time they'd been together.

"I'm afraid," Cassius finally said, worry and frustration lending an edge to his voice.

"What are you afraid of?"

Cassius shuddered and closed his eyes, the fear that had been gnawing at him all day twisting his belly into knots. "Of what Pan will reveal to us if we meet his demands."

Morgan's fingers clenched on his back.

"Nothing he says will change how we feel about you," he said gruffly. "How *I* feel about you."

Cassius felt his lips in his hair. An ache filled his chest.

It was an echo of the sorrow of the being he had once been, the one whose gut-wrenching misery he had experienced when Chester Moran's master had revealed a glimpse of his and Morgan's past under the cathedral. The demigod whom Morgan had fallen to Earth with amidst a sea of ash and blood.

"To have a God that angry with me must mean I did something unforgivable in my past life." Cassius opened his eyes and looked up at Morgan, pain squeezing his heart. "Something even you might not be able to disregard."

Morgan watched him for a moment, his expression inscrutable. "Do you remember when we first met?"

Cassius blinked. "Yeah." He made a face. "How can I forget?"

"I'm sorry." Morgan kissed his brow and hugged him to his chest, his expression repentant. "I resented you when that happened. More than I'd ever resented anyone in living memory since the Fall. I know now that what I experienced in those seconds when I attacked you were Ivmir's emotions."

Cassius's pulse thrummed rapidly, his heartbeat as fast as Morgan's where it thudded against his cheek.

"But it wasn't just rage and fear and pain that I felt at the time. There was longing too. And love." Morgan cradled Cassius's face and took his mouth in a sweet kiss. "My past self and the man I am today have already absolved you of your sins."

Emotion choked Cassius's throat. Tears filled his eyes. Morgan gently brushed away the salty tracks with his lips as they ran down his face.

Heat flashed between their soul cores.

Desire sparked in Cassius's veins. He clung to the man holding him, a different kind of ache welling up inside him.

Fire blazed in Morgan's eyes. He flipped Cassius onto his back and pressed his thigh against Cassius's hardening cock, his breathing quickening.

Cassius twitched and arched, his gasp lost in the mouth of the man who'd taken his lips in a scorching kiss. His grip tightened on Morgan's shoulders. Only the Aerial could assuage the hunger burning his flesh.

The air trembled with a sudden shockwave, freezing them both. Windows rattled and furniture shook. The acrid taint of sulfur suffused the air.

Cassius's stomach rolled. *This doesn't feel like a rift!*

A crash came from the living room just as he and Morgan leapt out of bed and grabbed their weapons. Loki bolted into the bedroom, fur on end and yellow eyes vivid in the half-light. The cat cowered at Cassius's feet.

"What is it?" Cassius asked him in a strained voice.

Loki shook himself out into his imp form. "I—I don't know! Something just—exploded out of nowhere!" He grabbed onto Cassius's shirt, tail rigid and fur on end. "It smells of the Hells."

The fact that neither he nor Morgan had detected an impending attack this close up made Cassius's blood grow cold.

Morgan's face hardened, the Sword of Wind flaring into life in his left hand. "Are you sensing anything?"

Cassius focused. His eyes rounded. "Yes!"

He headed rapidly for the door, Loki stumbling along beside him. Morgan hissed out a curse and followed.

The scent of camphor Cassius had just picked up on grew, filling his nostrils. He entered the living room, flicked on the lights, and flinched.

"*Benjamin?!*"

The Reaper was crouched in the middle of the living room floor. He slowly straightened, scythe in hand and hooded head grazing the ceiling. Smoke was fading from the explosive circle that had scorched the floor and walls of the apartment, the stench of the Nine Hells vanishing along with the fumes.

"What the—?!" Morgan muttered next to Cassius.

Cassius's heart thundered in his chest as he looked upon the anthropomorphic apparition wreathed in shadows. Although Reapers could travel between the realms at will, they rarely put in an appearance before living souls. As for summoning one, the process usually involved complex runes made from blood and a spell few mages could perform. Since opening a doorway between the Earth and the Nine Hells was deemed illegal, the act of calling forth a Reaper was only ever authorized under exceptional circumstances by the agencies that governed the otherwordly and magic users.

Few knew that Cassius could do so using Rain Silver and Heaven's Light.

Cassius's gaze dropped to the cowled figure Benjamin was supporting around the waist. The man's robe throbbed weakly where he sagged in Benjamin's hold, the Reaper's nine-foot frame towering over him.

Benjamin's aura fluttered with a wave of distress. "Help me."

Cassius's stomach lurched. Blood was dripping from Benjamin's skeletal fingers where they poked out of his sleeve of darkness. It was coming from the barely conscious figure he was propping up.

He and Morgan were halfway across the room when the front door of the apartment exploded.

Pan stormed in amidst the wreckage, the divine radiance bathing him pulsing like a second sun. *"What was that?!"*

Morgan scowled. "Knock next time!"

The God's brows lowered when he saw Benjamin.

He transformed into a human once more. "*What is a Reaper doing here?*"

Loki shrunk into his demon cat form and slinked toward Benjamin, a hesitant meow leaving him. He and the Reaper had become friendly during the Chester Moran affair.

Cassius and Morgan took the wounded figure from Benjamin's arms and sat him down carefully on the couch. The guy's hood fell back. Cassius drew a sharp breath. Morgan stared.

The man beneath it was half Reaper, half human. His left eyelid twitched open, revealing a bright blue iris. Crimson flared in the depths of his right orbit.

"*Mas...ter...*"

His eyes rolled back in his head. He slumped, comatose.

Cassius shot a stiff look at Benjamin. "Who is he?"

Benjamin's pupils flashed. "His name is Mortis. He is the Right Hand of the Reaper God."

Cold fingers skittered down Cassius's spine. Pan narrowed his eyes.

Morgan observed the gaping wound in the apparition's abdomen with a grim expression. "We need a healer."

22

SWEAT BEADED LUCY WALTERS'S BROW WHEN SHE finally lifted her hands off Mortis's body, the bright glow of magic fading from her fingers and staff along with the scent of Juniper.

"This is the best I can do." The Argonaut medical mage side-eyed Benjamin nervously. "I'm afraid I don't know much about Reaper anatomy. I could only fix the injury on his human half."

Redness bloomed in the depths of Benjamin's orbits. "That is more than enough, mage. You have my sincere gratitude. I shall remember the smell of your soul."

Morgan grimaced. Victor sighed. Alarm widened Lucy's eyes.

"Er, why?" she quavered with a sickly expression.

"So we can make your passage to the afterworld the best ride of your life," Benjamin declared, deadpan.

His words fell in a silent void of awkwardness.

Lucy made a choking noise.

"I think he's yanking your chain," Julia reassured the mage.

Benjamin's pupils blinked off and on. "Oh. Was it not apparent?" The Reaper frowned and rubbed his jaw. "Dammit. I need to work on my punchline."

Lucy sat down heavily on the armrest. "Please do. I almost crapped my pants."

Guilt shot through Morgan as he studied the dark circles under her eyes. Despite the lateness of the hour and the fact that she'd spent most of yesterday helping heal the victims of the rift, the mage had responded to his call for help straightaway. He'd messaged Strickland while Cassius had called Victor and the rest of their team.

It was clear Benjamin's presence in San Francisco had something to do with the Reaper God and the rifts.

Victor had arrived first, the demon flying straight from where he was staying at the Cabalista bureau. The San Francisco branch boasted a luxurious penthouse on the rooftop of its building. It was there that the Fiery had relocated when his hotel was damaged after the rift opened.

Morgan had frowned heavily when he'd seen the demon land on the terrace.

"Why didn't he just stay there in the first place?" he'd muttered.

"Because he doesn't like the attention," Cassius had said, the soft expression that had flashed across his face causing Morgan's chest to burn.

"Hey, this guy is half Reaper, half human, right?" Bailey murmured to Zach presently.

"It would seem so," the demon said warily.

"How does that work?" The wizard pursed his lips. "Did a male Reaper sleep with a woman or did a man sleep with a female Reaper? I mean, how does a Reaper mama carry a baby? Wouldn't the kid just fall out of her—"

He stopped in the face of Adrianne's scowl.

"That's what you're curious about right now?"

Bailey shrugged. "It's a valid question."

"He has a point," Charlie murmured.

"*He is a Khimer.*"

Morgan's scalp prickled at Pan's words. A vague recollection welled up from the depths of his subconscious, the ancient knowledge he carried with him from his past life unaffected by the memory spell afflicting the Fallen.

Zach frowned. "A Khimer? I thought that was just a myth."

"*I wish it were*," the God said, his eyes tight.

Adrianne's irate gaze shifted between Pan and Benjamin. "What's a Khimer?"

"It is a creature born of the fusion of a Reaper and a living being," Benjamin said. "A God. A demon. A Dryad. A Nymph." He shrugged as the blood drained from Adrianne's face. "It matters not, as long as the soul is strong. Of all the Khimers, the human ones are the beings the Reaper God cherishes the most."

Bailey's eyes bulged. He stared at Mortis. "Wait. You mean this guy is some kind of—living-dead chimera?! Like—"

"A zombie with a scythe," Charlie mumbled, looking sick.

"That's one way to put it," Julia said in a hard voice.

The Terrene angel looked about as excited at the prospect of Khimers as Pan did. To Morgan's utter lack of surprise, Cassius was the only one who didn't appear openly averse to the idea.

Then again, it's not like I expect anything less from him. He's always been a sucker for the weak and the oppressed.

Adrianne gulped. "Why are, er, human Khimers the Reaper God's favorites?"

"Because he has always wanted to know what it is to be a human." Pan grunted. *"The souls Reapers ferry to the afterlife mostly belong to your kind,"* he explained at the sorceress's startled look. *"The Reaper God eventually grew curious. And that curiosity soon turned into an obsession. That is why he started to make Khimers and invariably chooses a human one as his Right Hand."*

Adrianne glanced at Mortis and cleared her throat. "What—what does a Right Hand do anyway?"

"The Right Hand oversees the domain of the Reaper God and looks after his affairs when he is away," Benjamin said. "He is also his closest companion. In theory, the Right Hand can wield the power of the Reaper God."

"Away?" A mirthless chuckle escaped the sorceress. She looked about ten seconds away from some kind of meltdown. "You mean, Death goes on holidays and stuff?"

Julia made a face. "I believe he means when the God is busy with Heavenly or Hellish affairs."

Benjamin bobbed his head. "Scrabble."

This earned him a battery of perplexed stares.

Cassius grimaced and rubbed the back of his neck. "Do you mean Bingo?"

The Reaper sagged. "Darn it all to heck. Yes. Bingo."

Motion on the couch drew their gazes.

Mortis was stirring. His eyes blinked open, one blue, one red. He studied the ceiling for a few blank seconds.

"Where—?" The Khimer stopped and groaned, one hand lifting shakily to clutch his forehead. "Where am I?"

"Don't." Lucy pressed a hand on Mortis's shoulder when he tried to sit up. "Your wound will re-open."

She froze for an instant before carefully lifting her fingers off. Morgan could tell from her glassy expression that she'd just grabbed bare bones.

Benjamin squatted next to Mortis. "Do not fear. We are among friends."

Mortis stared at the Reaper. His right orbit bloomed scarlet. He bolted upright, panic flooding his face.

"Benjamin! Why—why are you here?!"

Lucy swore. Mortis looked at her guiltily before settling back down.

Benjamin frowned. "You do not remember? I came across you in the Third Hell. All you kept mumbling before you passed out was that you needed to find the angel with black and red wings and something about an awakening."

Morgan's pulse spiked. *An awakening?!*

Cassius's eyebrows drew together, the same thought evidently crossing his mind.

"I—" Mortis shook his head and swallowed convulsively. "No! The last thing I remember is—" He went deathly still. The glow of his right eye dimmed in shock and horror. "Master. *Someone captured Master!*"

23

DREAD POOLED IN THE PIT OF CASSIUS'S STOMACH, A weight that threatened to drag him to dark depths. A grim foreboding was starting to grow inside him.

"Calm down, Mortis," Benjamin told the Khimer, his aura flaring with disquiet. "Tell us what happened from the beginning."

Mortis hunched his shoulders, his hands trembling where he gripped his robe. "Someone came to our domain. A God of Darkness with an army of war demons. He—" The Khimer faltered and squeezed his eyes shut for a moment, his fingers fisting with a bony creak. "He fought Master and took him prisoner!"

Cassius met Morgan's wide-eyed stare. *A God of Darkness?!*

"*How?*" Pan asked in the stilted silence. The God's face had grown flinty. "*How could someone achieve such a feat against a Primordial?*"

Benjamin's robe danced agitatedly around him. "Why did the Reapers not hear of this?"

Cassius's nails bit into his palms. The disquiet he was feeling was reflected in Morgan and Victor's eyes. Something had gone horribly wrong in the realm of the Reapers.

"The God—the God made it so that no one who was there that night left the domain alive," Mortis said numbly, his voice ending in a miserable whisper.

Cassius's blood turned to ice.

Benjamin stared. His orbits burst with redness as the truth finally sank in. Cassius tensed, the shadows wrapped around the Reaper exploding in a wrathful storm that shook the air and made the lights flicker.

"*You mean to say this God killed all the Reapers who were in our domain at the time?!*" the Reaper roared.

Darkness filled the corners of the apartment.

Loki yelped and bolted under the couch, back arching and fur on end. A startled sound left Charlie as inky strands brushed his ankle. Zach yanked the enchanter and Lucy out of the way of the sinister manifestation encroaching upon the room and raised a barrier of water.

Morgan caught Cassius's intent a heartbeat before he moved. "Cassius, no!"

Cassius ignored Morgan's warning and headed across the floor. Black tendrils washed angrily against his skin as he braved the howling tempest enveloping Benjamin.

He caught a glimpse of Victor's Hell Fire out of the corner of his eye, clenched his teeth, and leaned into the storm, closing the distance to the Reaper. "Calm down! You're going to wreck the building and hurt people at this rate!"

He grabbed Benjamin's arm. Cold bone chilled his fingers. Cassius ignored it and released a pulse of power.

Divine light bathed the room. The Reaper shuddered.

The shadows fluttered violently as they fought the dazzling radiance Cassius was emitting. They slowly settled back down, the inky currents shrinking until they took the form of his robe once more.

The gloom swallowing the apartment receded. Everyone released the breath they'd been holding. Cassius withdrew his seraphic energy, his heart racing.

Zach sagged where he stood braced near the kitchen counter, his face pale. "Shit."

Lines furrowed Julia's brow as she maintained a defensive stance in front of Adrianne and Bailey, her knuckles loosening a fraction on her Stark Steel blade.

The demon and the angel had reason to be uneasy. Reapers were not warriors by nature, the roles assigned to them by Heaven and the Hells those of silent ferrymen and guardians of souls. It did not mean they could not fight. And theirs was a power that belonged to the darkest, oldest elements of the known universe. No magic could defeat it and few otherworldly could withstand its wrath.

Mortis's mouth quavered, his blue eye full of tears as he gazed beseechingly at the Reaper. "I am sorry."

Benjamin's shoulders drooped. His pupils dimmed.

"You have nothing to apologize for," he said dolefully. "I doubt you could have done anything to stop what happened." The Reaper turned to Cassius, his tone contrite. "Thank you, my friend. My rage overwhelmed me for a moment."

Cassius dipped his head wordlessly.

Mortis's gaze shifted to Pan. "As for how that monster gained control over Master, I did not witness the full details. The devastation wrought by their battle was such that I and the other Reapers were cast a long distance from where they fought." He gripped his hands together, his voice fraught. "But I managed to crawl back to Master before he disappeared. That was when I heard his last order and saw it."

Pan's brows lowered. "*Saw what?*"

"There was something inside his chest. Something sharp and—shiny." Mortis faltered. "It was like nothing I had ever seen before. Master—Master seemed to be in pain from it."

A somber hush fell in the wake of the Khimer's revelation.

"Was there anything else?" Cassius's jaw ached with tension. "Anything you noticed? Even the most minor detail might help us."

Mortis's eyes grew unfocused. He stiffened a moment later. "Yes. There was something else."

Cassius's pulse stuttered.

"*What was it?*" Pan said in a flat voice.

"A smell."

Victor narrowed his eyes. "A smell?"

Mortis nodded. "A clean, cold scent. Like winter."

He pressed his hands on the couch and tried to move up, oblivious to the startled glance Cassius exchanged with the others.

Blood thumped heavily in Cassius's skull. *Winter? Does this have something to do with Boreas?!*

Lucy gently assisted the Khimer into a sitting position.

"Thank you." Mortis panted for a bit before squaring his shoulders and meeting Cassius's eyes, his jaw set in a determined line. "I must fulfill my mission. Master told me to find you so I could give you this."

The Khimer stuck a bony finger down his throat. He gagged and heaved. Something felt into his hand.

It was a ring of bones and black flames.

Cassius's breath froze in his lungs. A buzzing filled his ears.

"He did not tell me more," Mortis added. "I am not sure what you are meant to—"

"Cassius?" Morgan interrupted with a frown.

Scores of memories flitted before Cassius's eyes, too fast for him to make any sense of them. Blinding pain gripped his skull as the spell that afflicted the Fallen kicked in with a vengeance.

Cassius wasn't aware of crying out and falling to his knees. The next thing he knew, he was on the floor, convulsing. Morgan and Victor's figures swam before his eyes, their alarmed shouts reaching him as if through thick fog. His vision dimmed. The last thing he heard before darkness cocooned him in a sea of shadows was the Reaper God's voice.

It came from the ring.

USE...ME...TO...FREE...US...AWAKENER...

24

Cassius opened his eyes. Something blurred above him. He blinked.

A crisp, cerulean sky came into focus, the expanse dotted with a handful of cotton-candy clouds. His chest tightened. He bolted upright.

The sight that met his eyes rendered him weak.

He was lying on top of an elevation overlooking a sprawling city. A dark sea shimmered in the distance beyond and to the left of it, the pale sails of the squared-rigged galleons and carracks scattered across the calm waters a sharp contrast to the rich reds of galleys and fishing boats. Giant, defensive ramparts rose all around the metropolis, the complex fortifications protecting it from land and sea on all sides even as they enclosed the magnificent landscape of palaces, gleaming domes, and towers gracing its seven hills and the gentle valleys connecting them. The smoky scent of cooking fires wafted on a faint breeze, along with the dull roar of a busy capital.

Cassius climbed unsteadily to his feet, his heart

knocking against his ribs. He knew this scenery. Would know it by sound and smell even if he were blinded.

Something fell from his limp hand and clattered at his feet. He looked down. His sword lay in the dirt where he'd dropped it.

Cassius froze.

The blade was coated with fresh blood.

His stomach rolled as he realized he was wearing his Stark Steel armor, the bright plates similarly tainted with crimson stains and gore. Cassius looked jerkily over his shoulder. His breath locked in his throat.

His wings were a pale gray. The same gray as all angels and demons. Yet he was not in his demigod form.

"You are awake."

Cassius flinched. His head swiveled slowly to the left, his neck so tight it ached.

Someone was standing next to him. An angel in shining armor identical to his in every aspect but for its slate-blue color. He was achingly beautiful, his long, dark hair falling past his waist and his arresting, sapphire eyes glittering in his refined face. He was looking out over the city below, his expression calm.

"It is almost time."

Cassius swallowed, his mouth so dry his tongue felt like parchment.

"Who—who are you?" he stammered hoarsely. "And what do you mean, it's almost time?"

The angel did not reply. His head tilted up. Cassius followed his gaze to the sky.

Something was happening to it. Something impossible. Something that should never have been.

Horror wrenched a whimper from Cassius when he

realized what was about to unfold. He stumbled back a step.

"No. Please, God, no!"

His denial was lost in a sound that boomed across the land. The earth and the sea shuddered, the air rippling violently above them. A crack tore apart the sky. It throbbed, edges pulsing with darkness.

Clouds formed where none had been, the atmosphere cooling rapidly under the effect of the phenomenon. Lightning flashed as they darkened and twisted into a fierce maelstrom, the billows spinning in a wind that came from another dimension.

Cassius fell to his knees, his strength leaving him. Bile burned his throat as he stared unblinkingly at the sky, unable to tear his panicked gaze away. The agony squeezing his heart was so fierce he feared it would explode.

The tear extended, a jagged line that cleaved the heavens all the way to the horizon. The storm grew. Darkness fell across the land and the ocean. With it came an expectant hush, the tumult of the teeming metropolis dying as its citizens registered the irregularity above them.

"Run," Cassius mumbled. He rose on shaky legs. "Run!"

His warning was lost amidst distant shouts of horror, the residents of the capital finally realizing that this, whatever it was, was an anomaly that would destroy them.

Cassius yelled until his throat turned raw. But he knew, deep down inside. He knew that there would be no escaping the calamity about to befall Constantinople and hundreds of other cities across the world.

The Nether opened with a thunderous roar.

Smoke and screams filled the firmament.

Winged figures in armor fell from the yawning void where a desperate war had been fought.

Tears dripped down Cassius's cheeks, his low sobs drowned by the terrified clamor raised by the Fallen and the shrieks of the humans whose capital they destroyed. Palaces and temples caved and exploded under the impact of the celestial beings that struck them, the debris filling the air so thick the city was soon engulfed in a pale haze. Inky smoke thickened it further as fires broke out across the city, the poisonous fumes suffocating those who tried to escape the cataclysm.

Something bright lit the shadows high above the land. A shape fell from the roiling chasm that now connected Earth to the Nether, a dazzling figure bathed in light. The brilliance surrounding it flickered and died.

Cassius watched the demigod he had once been crash into a palace, face slack and body numb.

"They tried, you know."

Cassius looked jerkily at the angel beside him. He recoiled, an abject moan rising in his throat.

The left side of the angel's face and trunk were missing. The divine light in his right pupil faded as he met Cassius's horrified stare. A bloodied tear bloomed in his eye. It coursed down his pale cheek, a silent accusation that ripped through Cassius's soul.

"Our brothers. They tried to find us." A smile trembled on the angel's lips. "But they could not retrieve my remains. For there was little left of me to recover."

Cassius's nails scored his palms until he felt the hot sting of blood, a scream of denial choking his throat. The angel closed the distance between them, his magnificent form darkening and crumbling to ash as he disintegrated before Cassius's eyes.

"I'm sorry," Cassius whispered brokenly. "I did—I didn't know! I never intended—"

The angel leaned down, cradled his face, and pressed a gentle kiss to his brow. Cassius's words froze on his tongue, his supplication fading under the love pouring out of the angel's dying soul.

"I know, brother. I know your heart and all that it contains. For it is my heart too." The angel's smile widened. "Which is why you must die."

Heat pierced Cassius's chest. Blood burst from his lips and dripped down his chin, scorching hot. He blinked dazedly and lowered his gaze, his head moving mechanically.

A spear of light was embedded in his heart.

"You must die, Awakener, so that He may rise," the angel hissed, his voice deepening to a growl that did not belong to him.

He twisted the spear and pushed it straight through Cassius's body. Cassius grunted and gasped as the weapon tore out his back. His pulse thudded dully in his ears, his heart shuddering and slowing. Air rattled in his lungs as he took a raspy breath.

He could feel something happening to his wings. They were growing hot and heavy. He blinked and stole a petrified look sideways, his head so heavy it felt like it would tumble from his neck at any given moment. Horror squeezed his chest.

Blood and ash were coating his feathers, turning them crimson and black.

"That is your punishment, Awakener," the being who

had stabbed him crowed. "It is the curse your brothers visited upon you after you killed the South Star!"

The accusation tore through Cassius, the truth behind it resonating deeply inside him. He raised his head, numb to his core.

Darkness filled the apparition's right eye, the seraphic glow that had lit the pupil of the angel whose form he had copied swallowed by evil. His body quivered and flourished once more, his figure taking on the shape of another. One who loathed Cassius with every fiber of his being.

Cassius recoiled.

The monster sneered, a savage grimace full of madness. "Die, Son of Light! Die—!"

A roar filled Cassius's world, drowning out the name the God bellowed.

25

"*NOOOO!*"

Cassius's scream jolted Morgan awake. He jumped to his feet from where he'd been sitting next to the bed, black wind and Dryad magic bursting into life around him. Loki bolted from his spot beside Cassius and dashed under his chair, tail stiff and pupils round with shock.

Rapid footsteps rose from the direction of the living room. Victor rushed into the bedroom. He staggered to a stop when he saw Cassius.

"I'll call you back, Jasper!" he snapped into his cell.

He ended the call, his knuckles white where he gripped the phone. Morgan ignored the demon and observed the ashen-faced angel sitting up in the bed, his heart racing.

He swallowed and took a step forward. "Cassius?"

Cassius flinched. Morgan froze, pain twisting his insides. Cassius was looking at him blindly, as if he didn't know who he was.

Victor cast a faint frown at Morgan. "Take it easy. He's still in shock."

The demon approached the bed carefully and sat on the edge. Morgan fisted his hands and did the same on the other side.

Cassius blinked slowly as the springs squeaked. Awareness returned to his face. His gray eyes lost their dullness.

"Morgan?" he mumbled weakly.

"I'm here."

Morgan reached out and brushed the back of Cassius's hand where he gripped the covers, too scared to do more than that.

Cassius's shoulders sagged at his touch. He turned his palm over and clasped Morgan's hand tightly, his flesh chilly under Morgan's fingers. Heat sparked between their soul cores.

The familiar resonance had Morgan trembling with relief.

The hours during which Cassius had been unresponsive had been the most agonizing of his life. Not just because of how powerless he'd felt in the face of the unknown. But because he'd stopped being able to sense Cassius's soul for a while.

Cassius's face brightened when he looked to his left. "Victor."

He reached out to the demon. Victor hesitated before taking his hand, eyes dark with worry.

Morgan clenched his jaw and ignored the hot feeling in the pit of his stomach. Though he resented the demon's presence in their private space, he could not deny that Cassius needed him right now. Needed them both.

Cassius took a ragged breath and looked out of the window. He stilled, brow furrowing. The light was fading outside.

"How long was I out for?"

"The whole day," Morgan murmured.

"Shit."

Cassius winced and pressed a hand to his chest.

Victor's fingers spasmed where they now lay empty on the covers. "Are you okay?"

Cassius bobbed his head. "Yeah. I think so. It's just... the nightmare I had. It felt so real." His eyes rounded when he met their gazes, some of the color leeching from his face. "The ring!"

Morgan's lips thinned. "Mortis has it."

Cassius bit his lip. "Don't be upset with him. I doubt he knew that was going to happen."

"What *did* happen?" Victor asked in a low voice.

Cassius froze mid throwing the covers off his legs. He went quiet for a moment, his gaze lost somewhere neither Morgan nor Victor could see.

"I heard the Reaper God's voice before I passed out," he finally confessed. He climbed out of bed, not quite meeting their eyes. "And I saw the Fall happen. I think the ring triggered some of my memories." The Empyreal's expression grew flinty. "That God of Darkness was there too. And...there was someone else." He pressed a spot over his heart, a pained look flashing in his gaze. "Someone who looked and smelled just like me."

Coldness spread through Morgan's chest. *What does he mean, someone like him?!*

Cassius walked out of the bedroom before he or Victor could utter another word. Morgan exchanged a troubled glance with the demon as they followed. For once, the two of them appeared to be thinking the same thing.

Whatever had happened to Cassius in the hours he'd

been unconscious had changed something inside him. And not necessarily for the better.

Benjamin and Mortis looked up when they entered the living room. The Reapers were sitting on the couch, the TV playing on mute.

"Where did everyone go?" Cassius said curiously.

"I sent them home," Morgan muttered. "As for Pan, he went back to my—"

The terrace door opened. Pan walked in, a faint glow lighting him up. He met their stares and stopped.

"*I felt the Awakener rise.*" The God shrugged. "*Besides, your door is out of service.*"

He pointed at said absent door.

"And whose fault is that, exactly?" Morgan snapped.

Cassius ignored their exchange and walked over to Mortis, jaw set in a hard line. "Give me the ring, Mortis."

Victor's eyebrows gathered in a thunderous expression. "What?!"

A sick feeling surged through Morgan. He couldn't believe Cassius wanted to go through that again. Let alone what it had done to the rest of them to see him that way.

What it had done to *him*.

Guilt darkened Cassius's eyes when he saw their expressions. "It'll be okay. I think I know what to do now."

Heat filled Morgan's face, his frustration finally giving way to anger. "You had a fit the first time you saw the damn thing! And you've been unconscious for hours! I am not letting you touch it again!"

Mortis flinched.

"He is right." Benjamin studied Cassius with a probing stare. "Your friends were quite irate about what happened earlier. Doubly so your lovers."

Morgan clenched his teeth so tight his jaw ached.

Mortis blinked rapidly. "Oh." His gaze darted from Cassius to Morgan and Victor. "I did not realize the three of you were—"

"We are not!" Victor snarled, barely masking his distaste. "And you." He scowled at Cassius. "Are you really sure you should be doing this?"

"I'll be fine. The Reaper God intends for me to use that ring."

Cassius's statement made Morgan's stomach lurch.

"He does?!" Mortis mumbled.

Cassius dipped his chin. "He told me so."

Mortis opened and closed his mouth soundlessly.

"You heard Master?!" he blurted out.

"I did." Cassius's face grew gentle. "The ring, Mortis. Please?"

Mortis faltered before slipping his hand inside his robe. He removed the ring of bone and black flames and held it out on his palm.

"I cleaned it," the Khimer murmured guiltily. "Lucy said it was unhygienic to vomit it up."

Loki sauntered out of the bedroom.

Morgan narrowed his eyes at the demon cat. "She's not wrong."

Loki assumed an air of supreme innocence and coiled around Cassius's legs, his tail flicking lazily.

Cassius took the ring from Mortis. The fire engulfing the bare bones flared when it touched his skin. Black flames swallowed his hand.

The hairs rose on Morgan's nape. Victor cursed and took a step forward, as if to wrench the thing from Cassius's grasp.

Pan grabbed his arm and stopped him. *"Let him be. It is not hurting him."* The God's pupils bloomed gold. *"Besides, I want to see this."*

Cassius studied the band for a moment before slipping it onto his left ring finger. He flexed his hand a couple of times and closed his eyes.

A high-pitched whine rose from the ring. The sound put Morgan's teeth on edge and made glass hum around the apartment.

The black flames thickened and extended.

Ice filled Morgan's veins as they started to take on a familiar form. Victor drew a sharp breath.

"Son of a—!" Pan swore. *"I knew it!"*

Cassius opened his eyes and frowned at the eight-foot-tall scythe of pure darkness in his hand.

Morgan's heart pounded heavily against his ribs. "What is that thing?"

Benjamin's pupils blinked off and on. "The Ring of Death."

The Reaper's tone was low and reverential.

"It is the weapon of the Reaper God," Pan growled.

Mortis brought a trembling hand to his mouth. "I—I have only ever heard of it before!"

"That is because it has been several millennia since he has had to wield it." Redness brightened Benjamin's orbits as he watched Cassius. "I did not know it could adjust its length to that of its user."

Pan clenched his fists. *"I long suspected only the Reaper God could wield that weapon. It appears I was wrong."*

Cassius flourished the scythe. It sliced the air with trails of hissing darkness that made Morgan's stomach churn. A satisfied light brightened the Empyreal's eyes, the angel seemingly oblivious to their unease.

"He has only lent it to me." He met their guarded stares, his own filling with a determination that unnerved Morgan. "I am going to need it to free him and stop this God."

Morgan's phone buzzed in the stilted hush. He slipped his cell out of his jeans and frowned when he saw the caller ID. He tapped the answer button.

"Bostrof?" He straightened as he listened to the Lucifugous demon, his pulse quickening. "Where?"

26

"Boreas is in the Sixth Hell?" Lines wrinkled Strickland's brow. He sat behind his desk, chin propped on steepled hands. "Are you certain?"

Morgan dipped his head curtly. "That's what Bostrof believes."

Reuben studied the Aerial with a probing gaze. "I thought the Khimer was found in the Third Hell."

"He was." Morgan shrugged. "That doesn't necessarily imply that Boreas and the Reaper God are there too."

Jasper narrowed his eyes. "What makes Bostrof so sure Boreas is in the Sixth Hell?"

"Because one of the Nephilim was sighted at its borders," Cassius said quietly. "Bostrof's spy came across Atropos, a Fate who fled the Spirit Realm. She told the demon she'd seen a Nephil when she'd ventured into the Sixth Hell."

He became the focus of cautious stares.

It was an hour since he'd woken up and Bostrof had contacted Morgan. Victor had convened an emergency meeting of all the bureau directors at Argonaut so they could share what had happened to Cassius and what Bostrof had learned from his spies in the Nine Hells.

Unease darkened Brianna's eyes. "Nephilim? Aren't they those giant beings from the bible? The ones that once ravaged the world of man?"

"Yes," Victor replied. "Although most of us haven't seen one in forever. They were confined to the same place as the war demons." His face hardened. "And they are even deadlier than a horde of those monsters."

A muscle twitched in Jasper's jawline as he stole a look at the bone ring on Cassius's hand. The flames had died away, Cassius managing to quench them as he'd gained a measure of control over the weapon. To his surprise, he'd found it as easy to wield as the Eternity Key.

Tightness still lingered in his gut at the memory of the nightmare he'd had while under the influence of the ring. He suspected it possessed the ability to show someone their darkest, deepest fears, just like humans occasionally reported seeing their life flash before their eyes when they had a close encounter with death.

He hadn't told Morgan and Victor about the name the God of Darkness had called him or given them more details concerning the angel with the dark hair and blue eyes whom the God had claimed Cassius had killed. The one the monster had dubbed the South Star.

Cassius traced his forehead with light fingers. He could still feel the heat of the angel's kiss and the love and absolution the stranger had bestowed upon him as he'd slowly vanished before his eyes. A shiver raced down his spine when he recalled the blood and ash that had covered his wings.

It was just a nightmare, right?

Cassius realized Victor was calling his name. He looked up, startled. "Sorry."

The demon frowned. "Are you okay?"

Cassius's throat constricted at his expression. He could tell from the rigid set of Victor's jaw that he was still worried about him, just as Morgan was.

"Yeah, I'm fine."

Victor looked unconvinced. "Brianna was asking about the ring."

Cassius met the witch's uneasy stare.

"Is that truly the Reaper God's weapon?" the Hexa director asked stiffly.

"Yes. He asked me to use it to free him."

Brianna paled. "He asked you to?"

Cassius rubbed the back of his neck awkwardly. "Yeah. I heard his voice when the ring resonated with me." He looked over at Pan. "It's not just him he wants me to free though. He means for me to save Boreas and probably Demetrius too."

The God straightened where he'd been leaning against the wall, his pupils flaring with divine light.

Morgan fisted his hands. "He told you to save Boreas and Demetrius?"

"Not in so many words." Cassius hesitated. "He said 'us.' Since I've already rescued Pan, I can't think whom else he would mean beside himself, Boreas, and Demetrius." He met Pan's gaze steadily. "We know the God of Winter is involved in this, somehow. I can't help but feel that his nephew must be too. It would explain why this God of Darkness wanted Pan out of the way."

Pan opened his mouth. A shrill ring interrupted the deity.

Strickland glowered at his desk phone and stabbed a button. "I said we weren't to be disturbed, Timothy."

His secretary's strained voice came through the speaker.

"I'm sorry, sir, but it's urgent. I have the heads of Argonaut, Hexa, and the Orden of Rosen requesting a video conference."

Strickland stilled. Victor straightened where he leaned a hip against his desk.

"Connect them," the Argonaut director said gruffly.

The monitor on the wall flickered into life. Unease prickled Cassius's skin at the somber faces of the two women and the man who appeared on the screen from where they sat in their respective offices around the world.

Now what?

Recognition flashed in their eyes when they saw him. It was replaced by wariness. They studied the other bureau directors in Strickland's office with faint frowns and visibly stiffened when they spotted Pan.

Strickland had told them about the God.

"Looks like you're already having a meeting." Henrik Viken, the angel who commanded the Order of Rosen, turned his piercing gaze on Victor. "It's good that you're here too."

Strickland addressed a petite Pakistani woman with fierce eyes and a headful of gray hair. "This is unexpected. We only spoke three hours ago."

"A lot can happen in three hours," Amal Kazmi stated in a hard voice. The mage in charge of Argonaut drummed her fingers on her desk. "I just got off the phone with the

U.S. Secretary of Defense. Their satellites have confirmed what our agents are starting to see on the ground. The fractures are shifting. Expanding even."

Cassius's stomach rolled. He exchanged a tense look with Morgan. Their worst fears were coming true.

Victor clenched his jaw. "Any sign of war demons?"

Ren Guiying, the witch who headed Hexa, shook her head. "No. Not so far." She chewed her lip. "NATO reported the same thing."

The color had drained from Brianna's face. "Are you certain?"

"Yes," Guiying said crisply. "And I've seen it with my own eyes. The fault line close to Seattle is different from how it looked yesterday."

"I spoke to CSTO half an hour ago and they've corroborated what all the defense alliances are saying." Viken's gaze locked on Victor. "It seems your theory about the ley line was spot on."

"It was Cassius's theory, not mine," Victor said flatly.

Guiying and Viken looked distinctly uncomfortable. Morgan ground his teeth.

Kazmi cleared her throat discreetly. "What happens if they all open at once?" She waved a vague hand at their stares. "Say no war demons appear and assuming Black's supposition is indeed correct, what are we looking at if all these faults open on a ley line? Of course, I expect there to be extensive local damage, but what's the worst-case scenario?"

"*Your world will be ruined beyond repair, your cities destroyed, and your people killed by the resulting quakes and ocean surges,*" Pan said in a deadly voice. "*Not only that, but the humans who survive the cataclysm will forever lose the ability to wield magic.*"

There was a sharp intake of air around the office.

The bureau heads paled on the monitor.

Cassius swallowed, his mouth dry. He hadn't realized the destruction of the ley line would have such an impact on Earth's magic users. After all, there were other ley lines on the planet.

Pan answered his question before he could voice it. *"That ley line is what we Gods refer to as a nexus. It is the original source of magic on Earth and gave birth to all other ley lines that exist on this planet. It is the same for the nexuses in other realms where magic exists."* The God's lips pressed into a flat line. *"Destroying a nexus can technically open doorways between the realms, just like the Fall did."* His brow furrowed as he met Cassius's wide-eyed stare. *"And not just the realms of the living. I am beginning to wonder about the intentions of this God."*

"What do you mean?" Victor asked tensely.

"I think he is trying to open a doorway directly to the Abyss."

"Fuck," Jasper mumbled in the stunned silence.

Cassius's heart thudded heavily against his ribs. The Abyss was a realm none had ever returned from, for good reason. He dug his nails into his palms, frustration and fury rushing through him in a hot tide that prickled his skin.

Is that what this God of Darkness wants? To destroy everything?!

Kazmi raked her hair with shaky fingers and blew out a heavy sigh. "Well, now that everyone wants to throw up, any developments at your end?"

27

"I can't believe you're not letting us come with you," Adrianne grumbled.

The sorceress observed Morgan and Cassius with a scowl.

They were in Pioneer Park, on Telegraph Hill. Coit Tower loomed against the dark skies behind them, concrete walls bright under the glare of spotlights. This late at night, the place was deserted.

Cassius made a face. "It's one of the Hells, Adrianne. Humans don't belong there."

"He's right," Julia muttered.

Adrianne's jaw jutted forward. "But there are Dark Alchemists in the Shadow Empire. Isn't that place like the Hells?"

"Not quite," Morgan said. "The air in the Shadow Empire is breathable to humans. That is not the case for the Hells." His eyebrows drew together. "You will suffocate within ten steps, your organs will shrivel and liquefy in the next ten, and I'm not even going to tell you what will happen to your bones."

Charlie paled. Bailey wrinkled his nose.

Adrianne narrowed her eyes. "How about if we erect a shield around us?"

Bailey patted her on the shoulder. "Look, babe, I know you want to help, but these guys are right. We do not belong there. Even Julia and Zach are staying back in San Francisco."

Adrianne scowled at the 'babe.'

"Yeah, I'd rather not visit the Hells." Zach shuddered. "Those realms are depressing as fuck."

Julia grimaced. "Same. And there's enough to keep us busy on Earth. War demons could appear at any moment. We'll be of more use up here than over there."

Adrianne looked like she was about to argue some more, faltered, and visibly deflated. Footsteps rose in the darkness. Morgan looked around.

Victor and Bostrof emerged from the shadows behind them.

"We're clear," Victor said.

Considering what they were about to do could technically get them kicked out of the country, they needed to be doubly sure there were no witnesses around. Irritation tightened Morgan's muscles as he observed the Fiery.

Still, I really wish he wasn't coming with us.

He knew all too well what Cassius would say if he were to voice that opinion. Although Morgan knew Cassius would never cheat on him, it didn't detract from the fact that the Empyreal still cared deeply for Victor and valued his opinions and his battle skills above any protests Morgan might make.

Morgan was conscious deep down inside that Cassius was right to think that way. He'd witnessed Victor's abilities himself during the battle a couple of days ago.

It didn't mean the Fiery's presence had stopped irking him though.

The look Victor gave Morgan told him the same thought had gone through the demon's mind and that he was wishing Morgan would kindly get the fuck out of his way and let him win over Cassius.

The air sizzled as the two of them stared each other down. Cassius pinched the bridge of his nose and muttered something rude under his breath.

"Are they going to be okay?" Charlie whispered to Zach.

"It depends," the demon grunted.

"Depends on what?"

Julia narrowed her eyes. "On whether they stop thinking with their dicks."

Bostrof squatted and lifted the manhole cover they were standing around. An inky shaft appeared.

"Man, I still can't believe the way to get to the Sixth Hell is through a sewer on Telegraph Hill," Bailey muttered.

"It's not the only portal on the West Coast," Bostrof grunted. "There are others." The demon hesitated. "Truth be told, this is not the most stable of portals." He glanced at Cassius. "But this matter seemed too urgent for us to travel to one of the other locations."

Morgan's stomach hardened. There was a safer and more reliable way to get to the Sixth Hell. Using a Reaper's portal would deliver them there without having to worry about the integrity of one of the more volatile doorways that had opened with the Fall.

Though the process would have challenged Morgan and Victor, Cassius had been confident in his ability to grant them safe passage using the Ring of Death.

Unfortunately, Benjamin couldn't travel to the Sixth Hell anymore. The Reaper had uncovered this disturbing fact an hour ago, when he'd tried to open a doorway for them to use.

"There is some kind of disturbance in that realm." Benjamin's orbits had glowed with a dismayed light as he'd studied the tiny pool of shadows fluttering beneath his scythe, Mortis hovering anxiously beside him. "One that is stopping a doorway from fully forming."

The portal had kept closing however many times he'd tried to open it. To Cassius's frustration, even the Ring of Death had been unable to open it, the weapon failing to pierce an entry point into the inky puddle.

Pan had cursed under his breath. *"It looks like Bostrof was right. Something must be happening in that realm for that God to have messed with Reapers' portals."*

The Wild God had chosen to stay in San Francisco. Since he was a target their enemy wanted to get rid of, it didn't make sense for him to waltz straight back into the lion's den. Morgan couldn't deny the relief he'd felt when Pan had readily agreed to Cassius's suggestion not to travel to the Sixth Hell. Although he knew his presence and that of Cassius and Victor were necessary for this mission to succeed, Morgan was concerned that they would be leaving the city, and the world, unprotected for however long they were in the Sixth Hell.

It was a thought Strickland appeared to have had too.

"Whatever happens over there, make sure you come back safe and sound," the director had told Morgan in a low voice after the meeting at Argonaut broke up. "Abandon this mission if you must. I'd rather have you fighting this battle on Earth than in that godforsaken place." He'd glanced at Pan and pursed his lips. "I know he's going to stick around, but I don't trust that God as far as I can throw him."

Still, Morgan was glad Pan was staying back. Having the God in San Francisco was better than nothing and he was certain the otherwordly in the city would be grateful for the deity's presence if a crisis were to unfold.

Pan wasn't called the Wild God for nothing.

Bostrof headed down the shaft first. Darkness swallowed Cassius as he followed, metal reverberating under his boots as he descended into the pit. Morgan and Victor climbed down after him.

Julia waited until all four of them reached the bottom of the eighty-foot ladder before pulling the manhole cover back in place. She paused halfway, her frowning face a pale disk against the night sky.

"Don't die down there. We'll never hear the end of it from Adrianne."

The last of the light faded with a metallic clang and the sorceress's faint protest.

They headed north with Bostrof, their preternatural vision piercing the gloom with ease. The sewers soon gave way to a labyrinth of tunnels. Bostrof negotiated them with a sure-footedness that indicated he'd done this many times before.

The air grew heavy and cold.

Cassius eyed the glistening ceiling a while later. "Are we under the bay?"

"Yes."

Morgan glanced uneasily at the rock walls around them. His skin prickled a moment later. He could feel a distortion in the air up ahead. One that put his teeth on edge.

Cassius and Victor tensed.

The portal finally appeared, a warped anomaly that cleaved the passage in two and reeked of dry, dead air. Tendrils of darkness seeped and bubbled from it, the wisps dissipating with faint hisses as they touched Earth's atmosphere.

Bostrof rocked to an abrupt halt.

Morgan's stomach knotted. He peered past the Lucifugous demon, hand dropping to his dagger and Dryad magic fluttering from his core. He froze, eyes rounding.

Lilaia had appeared from a side passage to the left. She was holding a broadsword in her hand, the weapon looking surprisingly light in her grip. The Nymph brightened when she saw her husband.

"My love!" Bostrof gasped. He closed the distance to her swiftly. "What are you doing here?!"

Lilaia let him take her in his arms and hugged him tightly, her eyes squeezing shut.

"You didn't think I'd let you leave without saying goodbye?" she said in a tremulous voice.

Bostrof stiffened. "How did you—?"

Lilaia pulled back and caressed his face lovingly, a faint smile on her lips. "I'm your wife." Her smile slipped and her brows drew together. "Which is why I'm pissed you didn't tell me about your plans, husband."

She pinched his cheek and tugged.

"Ow," Bostrof mumbled.

Suspicion darkened Cassius's face. "Bostrof, what is Lilaia talking about?"

Metal clanged in the shadows behind the Nymph. Akamon emerged from the gloom. The Lucifugous demon was carrying a heavy suit of armor and a battle axe.

Morgan stared. *Oh.*

"I'm sorry, Master," Akamon mumbled in the face of Bostrof's irate scowl. "I tried to stop Mistress from coming."

"You should have tried harder!" Bostrof growled.

Lilaia's lips thinned. "Don't shout at Mon. It's not his fault his master is an ass."

Bostrof sagged. "My love."

Cassius clenched his fists and jutted his chin. "Please tell me you're not planning to come with us?"

Bostrof turned and met his angry stare steadily. "You do not know your way around the Sixth Hell."

Victor frowned. "I realize it's been a while since we've been there, but still, we should be able to manage between the three of us."

He indicated Cassius and Morgan.

Bostrof started putting on his armor. "Trust me, that place is way different from what you recall."

"I won't have it!" Cassius stormed up to the Lucifugous and grabbed him by the front of his metal suit. "I'm not putting your life on the line for this!"

Bostrof's face hardened. "It is not your life to control or your decision to make, Guardian."

"Oh yeah?" Cassius snapped. He indicated Lilaia. "What about your wife and the baby she is carrying? Don't you care about them?!"

Lilaia flinched. A stilted silence ensued.

"It is precisely because I care for them that I'm doing this," Bostrof ground out. "If this God of Darkness succeeds in opening one of those rifts, I will lose every-thing I cherish." His eyes grew flinty. "You cannot stop me, Cassius. I am coming with you. I will not stand on the side-lines and watch this battle unfold when I know I can help you."

Cassius turned a beseeching gaze to Lilaia.

Her expression softened. "If I were not pregnant, I would be coming too."

Cassius deflated.

Lilaia patted his back cheerfully. "Now, now, just accept your defeat graciously. And take care of this big lump for me." She kissed Bostrof. "He may be a stubborn asshole, but he's mine."

The demon and the Nymph gazed adoringly into each other's eyes, oblivious to all.

Victor sighed. Morgan cleared his throat.

Bostrof blinked, ears flushing. He let go of Lilaia, hefted the broadsword and battle axe into the harness on his back, and narrowed his eyes at the portal.

"Let's go."

"Good luck," Lilaia murmured wistfully as she watched them step inside the distorted doorway.

28

It didn't take long for Cassius to realize that something wasn't quite right.

Darkness roared around them, the drafts from the currents making up the walls of the rift tugging angrily at their hair and armor. He could sense a vast, hungry emptiness beyond it, one that threatened to swallow them whole and spit out their bones. Cassius's skin prickled unpleasantly.

It hadn't been that way the last time he'd traveled through a door between the realms. *Is this the work of that God?*

"Shouldn't we be out of this by now?" Morgan yelled above the howling winds.

Victor's frown indicated he was thinking the same.

Cassius's gaze found the Lucifugous battling the storm ahead of them. *Morgan's right. It's been ten minutes. We should be past the rift by now!*

He closed the distance to the demon, the dry wind biting into his face. "Bostrof?"

The Lucifugous glanced sideways at him, a muscle jumping in his jawline. "I cannot fathom where the exit is. It has shifted."

Tension knotted Cassius's shoulders. "We can't afford to lose time in here. It might be too late for Boreas if we do."

The shadows around them shuddered and writhed. He flinched. Inky tendrils arced out of the walls of the rift. They multiplied and arrowed toward him.

Cassius recoiled.

Blasts of Hell Fire and Dryad magic clashed with the dark threads. They hissed and retreated under Victor and Morgan's attack. The pair scowled at the portal as they joined Cassius and Bostrof.

"Are we lost?" Victor asked Bostrof stiffly.

"For the moment, yes." The Lucifugous eyed the agitated currents around them. "But that's not what I'm most worried about right now."

Morgan's brow furrowed. "What do you mean?"

"I think the portal is reacting to Cassius's voice."

Cassius blinked. "What?!"

His heart constricted as the walls started closing in on them, confirming the Lucifugous demon's suspicion. He shifted into his demigod form and released a controlled pulse of divine light, dread tightening his limbs. The portal recoiled.

Shit! Is this thing alive?!

One thing was for certain. This wasn't like the Reaper God's attempts to communicate with him. Cassius could sense a clear, evil intent in the dark threads that had tried to touch him. A wave of anger brought a rush of heat to his body and quelled his fear. He was beyond furious at the God of Darkness who had brought them here.

Cassius fisted his hands and glared at the storm. "*I will not let you win!*"

The rift responded violently, the tempest intensifying to the point the updrafts dragged them across the ground. Cassius dug his nails into his palms and took a deep breath.

Morgan's eyed widened when he registered his intent. "Cassius! No!"

He grabbed Cassius's arm just as he was about to let loose his powers.

"Morgan's right!" Victor said in a strained voice. "Calm down, Cassius! You don't know what will happen if you expose your powers here!"

Cassius gnashed his teeth. He was about to shake off Morgan's hand when he froze in his tracks. He'd just sensed something behind them. A soul core where none should be.

He whirled around, his Stark Steel blade bright with Heaven's Light and the Reaper God's scythe in hand. Morgan, Victor, and Bostrof unsheathed their swords and widened their stances, their wary gazes locked on the spot Cassius was staring at.

The portal growled and screeched. A pale glow appeared amidst the squirming, inky streams. It shimmered for a moment, flickering in and out of sight. A familiar, blurry shape took form as it solidified and grew closer.

Cassius's heart lurched. "*Loki?!*"

The demon cat walked out of the shadows, feline body aglow with a golden light that throbbed from deep within him.

Cassius had returned the Eternity Key to the imp before leaving Earth. They couldn't afford to let it fall into the wrong hands if something were to go wrong during their mission to the Sixth Hell.

Loki shook himself out into his imp form, the power of the artifact he guarded shrinking to a throbbing pulse in his belly. He shuddered and rubbed his arms briskly as he eyed the walls of the storm, his wings tucked close to his back.

"God, I hate this place."

Cassius closed and opened his mouth soundlessly.

"What are you doing here?!" he finally blurted out.

Loki's tail twitched in irritation. "What am I doing here? I'm getting you out of the hellhole that foolish Lucifugous has dumped you in!"

Bostrof startled guiltily. "You know a way out of here?"

Loki's lips curled. "I am an imp who has traveled the Hells. I can sniff out realms with my eyes closed."

"Is it me or is Pan rubbing off on him?" Victor murmured to Morgan.

"They sure sneer the same way," Morgan grunted.

Relief made Cassius dizzy.

He walked over to Loki, crouched, and hugged the imp tightly. "Thanks for coming to find us!"

Loki went rigid before relaxing in his arms, a happy sound rumbling out of him. His hands clenched on Cassius's back and he burrowed his face in the angel's chest.

"This doesn't mean I'm not upset with you too, mind," Cassius mumbled into his fur. "It was foolhardy of you to bring the Eternity Key here."

"I know."

"Loki?" Morgan said between gritted teeth.

"Yeah?"

"Either step away from Cassius or turn back into your damn cat form!"

The imp grumbled and shifted back to his feline shape.

"Where to?" Cassius asked tersely.

Loki stared into the darkness for a moment before heading into the storm, his steps confident.

29

VICTOR SHIVERED WHEN HE EXITED THE PORTAL, THE wind clawing at his body fading as it lost its strength. The thought of being lost in that place of eternal shadows made his stomach roll. The imp had guided them safely through the worst of it, the glow of the Eternity Key a beacon that pulsed steadily from his body in the howling maelstrom.

The familiar stench of sulfur burned his nostrils and stung his eyes as he emerged under a red sky. He rocked to a stop and stared, the others similarly frozen at his side.

"Well, this place sure seems different from my memories," Morgan muttered.

A barren landscape of towering rock formations, treacherous canyons, and dead forests stretched out before them, the mountains and treetops looming out of the smoke curling up from smoldering fire pits and lava swamps. A permanent rain of ash darkened the air.

Bostrof's grip tightened on his battle axe, his cautious gaze scanning the deserted terrain. "Where is everyone?"

Victor shared the Lucifugous king's unease. Though not

exactly teeming with life, the Sixth Hell still harbored a decent population of lesser demons and monsters. Most would be attracted to an opening portal and they'd expected to have an audience waiting for them upon entering the hellish realm. Yet, the place appeared devoid of life, the silence around them deafening but for the hiss and spit of Hell Fire.

"Loki?" Cassius said in a low voice. "Stay close to me."

The demon cat curled around his legs, tail stiff and ears flattened against his skull. Cassius turned left and started walking, the imp brushing nervously against him.

Victor shared a guarded glance with Morgan and Bostrof before following, apprehension a tight knot in his belly. "Where are we going?"

"To find Boreas," Cassius replied grimly. "I can feel his soul core somewhere over there."

He jerked his head at a distant plain visible between two mountains.

Victor's pulse quickened. It never ceased to surprise him how accurate Cassius's senses were when it came to these things. He saw the possessive look Morgan cast at the Empyreal and clenched his jaw.

In many ways, he was glad he'd made the trip to San Francisco when fractures lines had started appearing all over the world. His immediate instinct had been to find and protect Cassius. What he hadn't expected was how badly seeing his former lover with a new man would affect him.

He'd known from the gossip circulating in Cabalista that Cassius and Morgan were unofficially a couple. Seeing them together had confirmed what all the rumors were saying and more, and was a punch in the gut he never saw coming.

Even a blind fool could see how infatuated the pair were with one another.

This would make his task of winning Cassius back much harder than he'd thought it would be, a challenge he readily embraced.

As far as Cassius was aware, Victor had graciously let him end their relationship before he'd left England for the States. They'd parted ways amicably, something Victor knew Cassius was grateful for as he'd always cherished their friendship.

He couldn't let the Empyreal know how much it had cost him to watch him walk away. Or how hard he'd fought his own base desires over the years they'd been a couple.

Because he'd wanted more than Cassius's love. He'd wanted to own him, body, heart, mind, and soul. He'd wanted to put him in a gilded cage and hide him from the world who'd treated him so cruelly since the Fall. He'd wanted to worship him. To treasure him. To make him blind to any other man but him.

To enslave him to his deepest, darkest cravings.

Victor knew it was wrong for him to think that way. He knew in his soul that binding Cassius would make the Empyreal lose the very light that had attracted Victor to him. That it would make the angel hate him. And worse.

Somewhere deep inside his subconscious was a warning Victor felt in the marrow of his bones. Controlling Cassius that way would only lead to agony and loss.

He'd never spoken to Cassius about the echo of feelings he'd sometimes experienced when they'd made love. The dark omen that always counseled him not to try and subjugate the Empyreal.

The truth was, Victor was acutely conscious that Cassius had never truly surrendered himself to him in all the time they'd been together. Even though he'd readily yielded his body and craved the pleasure Victor had given him, he'd kept his heart locked away behind iron walls.

Victor had told himself he didn't mind waiting for the day those walls would fall and Cassius would truly be his. After all, he was a very patient man. There was no denying that Cassius cared for him deeply and their sexual chemistry was off the charts. That he'd eventually win the Empyreal over completely had been a given and just a matter of time. And they both had plenty of that in this world. Or so he'd thought until Cassius had decided to leave him and Morgan King had appeared on the scene.

Bostrof's words brought him back to the present.

"What about the Nephil? Can you sense it?"

The Lucifugous stole a look at the gloom and fumes pressing in on them as they navigated a path across a treacherous expanse of smoldering bogs and fire pits.

Cassius shook his head. "No. Nephilim don't have soul cores, like war demons. I won't be able to detect it that way."

It wasn't long before they spotted some of the creatures who inhabited the Sixth Hell. Low-pitched clicks and sibilant sounds rose from a forest they passed, the glow of dozens of crimson eyes lighting the shadows beneath the trees as they peered out at them. Yet, the monsters never revealed themselves.

It was clear they were afraid of something.

The creatures' probing gazes followed them as they

headed for the narrow pass between the peaks. More crept out of caves and from gloom-filled crags and crevasses, their nervous chatter echoing against the dark, soaring walls making up the canyon.

Loki shivered and shrank even closer to Cassius.

The hairs lifted on the back of Victor's neck when they left the mountains behind and emerged onto a flatland of cracked dirt and ash. He could tell Cassius and the others shared his growing disquiet from the stiffness of their shoulders.

The air here was clean and fresh, the stench of the Hells fading with every step they took. Victor looked around warily.

It's as if another realm has intruded upon this place.

A pale line appeared on the horizon. It glittered and wavered strangely under the crimson light.

Bostrof's eyebrows drew together. "What the devil is that?"

Morgan squinted. "It looks like a...wall of some sort."

The air grew chillier the closer they drew to the phenomenon. Something crunched under Victor's foot some time later. He stopped and looked down. Goose-bumps broke out across his flesh.

There were chunks of ice mixed in with the dirt they were treading.

He swept the area ahead with his gaze and found more glittering shards scattered across the ground. It looked like there'd been an explosion of sorts, and recently at that.

"We're getting close," Cassius warned.

Somehow, the Empyreal didn't seem in the least bit surprised by the strangeness around them. If anything, he appeared to be expecting it.

Victor frowned. *What is he sensing, exactly?*

The ash falling from the sky soon turned to sleet and snow. It coated their armor and hair in grimy streaks and trickled unpleasantly down their necks and backs. Victor's breath misted in front of his face as the temperature continued to plummet.

"It seems Hell freezing over is now a fact," Morgan muttered.

The boundary line they'd spotted from afar crystallized into a thirty-foot-tall wall of ice that stretched across half the width of the plain. The jagged barrier was heavily fractured and distorted, as if it had thawed and frozen many times over.

A web of red veins was embedded deep within it.

"Is that blood?" Bostrof said guardedly.

Cassius's eyes darkened as he traced one of the crimson cracks, the fury radiating from him hot enough to melt the ice.

"Yes. It's Boreas's. He's still fighting."

He spread his wings and rose, his demigod form bright against the dark sky and reflecting off the glistening barrier. Victor and Morgan followed, Loki and Bostrof clambering swiftly up the glacier beneath them. They reached the summit of the ridge seconds after Cassius.

The demigod had dropped into a low crouch at the top, his tense gaze locked on something beyond the icy rampart. He motioned them to do the same.

Cold fingers skittered down Victor's spine when he beheld what Cassius was staring at. The land dropped before them, forming a two-hundred-foot-deep gully in the center of the plain. The walls and floor of the chasm were sheathed in thick, glittering ice. At the bottom of it, trapped on a platform of black lava rock covered in frost, was the Winter God.

Blood oozed and dripped from the shackles of writhing darkness restraining Boreas's ankles and wrists, the crimson droplets melting the ice crystals. His head drooped where he balanced on one knee, his chest heaving with his breaths and his large frame trembling as he tugged in vain at the stone bolts to which the chains were anchored.

Something throbbed deep inside the God's body. A core of blackness that sent lines of corruption flashing through his flesh with every sickening beat.

A grim foreboding squeezed Victor's heart. He couldn't take his eyes off the phenomenon. He'd seen the dreadful monstrosity buried within Boreas somewhere else before. He was sure of it.

A memory flitted through his mind. One that was out of focus and brought a sharp stab of pain to his temples. Victor winced, hand rising to clutch his head. The blurry image faded as quickly as it had appeared, leaving a bitter aftertaste lingering in his mouth and a strange heat in his belly.

He blinked. *What the hell was that?!*

Cassius shifted beside him. Victor followed his narrow-eyed gaze and stilled.

Lining the frozen gully, their fifty-foot frames towering above Boreas as they stood watch over him, were five Nephilim.

❧ 30 ❧

Morgan slanted a look at Bostrof. "I thought you said there was only one."

The Lucifugous demon scowled. "My spies only saw the one yesterday."

The Aerial's face hardened as he studied the creatures guarding Boreas. "Dammit! Even one of them would be hard to take down."

Cassius had to concur. His heart pounded heavily against his ribs as he gazed upon their enemy.

The Nephilim were as fearful as he recalled, their shadow-wreathed bodies and wings black as night and their crimson eyes cold and inhumane. They held a stone mace each, the clubs resting loosely against the floor of the gorge.

It was the Nephilim's weapon of choice and one that made angels and demons shudder alike. The monsters could smash an entire squad of otherwordly with a single swing of the blasted thing.

Cassius was relieved to see the clubs were currently free

of blood. Whatever the God of Darkness had planned for Boreas, he did not intend for the Nephilim to kill him yet.

Something else filled him with disquiet. Something far worse than the fact they now had to deal with five of the grisly colossuses to free Boreas.

His stomach churned. "Morgan?"

"Yeah?"

"That core inside Boreas. I think it's similar to the spear Chester Moran used on me when I first took my Empyreal form."

Victor flinched beside him. Cassius's gaze shifted from the dark, pulsating mass within the Winter God's body to the Fiery's pale face.

Alarm quickened his pulse. "Are you okay?"

"Yeah," Victor mumbled.

Morgan's brow furrowed. "Can I destroy that thing the same way I did the spear?"

"I don't think so." Cassius looked at the bone ring on his left ring finger and flexed his hand. "That's why the Reaper God didn't let the God of Darkness get his hands on this. He must have known it would be the only thing that could free Boreas."

Surprise widened Morgan's pupils.

Bostrof cursed under his breath. "They know we're here!"

Cassius's head snapped around. The Nephilim had turned to stare in their direction.

Wait! Can they sense us?!

A low sound left Loki. The imp was trembling where he pressed against Cassius's leg, his eyes glazed with fear. The Eternity Key fluttered agitatedly inside him, the golden light flickering with his racing heartbeat.

No. It's not us. It's the Eternity Key!

A tremor ran through the ridge as the Nephilim started to move.

"Loki, get inside my armor!" Cassius ordered hastily.

The demon cat froze for an instant before bolting up onto his shoulder and slinking down his back, his body a soft, warm weight where he settled between Cassius's shoulder blades.

The Nephilim approached the gully walls, their ponderous pace picking up.

Bostrof unsheathed his sword and axe, his nervous gaze locked on their enemy. "Anyone got a plan?"

The Ring of Death exploded into life on Cassius's left hand. He grasped the Reaper God's scythe and his divine blade with white-knuckled fists.

"Yes! Distract the Nephilim so Morgan and I can get to Boreas!" He exchanged a tense glance with Morgan. "You have to cut those shackles!"

Morgan bobbed his head jerkily. He unleashed the Sword of Wind and assumed his demigod form, his crown of oak forming seamlessly on his head as he called upon his Dryad magic.

Hell Fire bloomed around Victor. He rose, his eyes flashing crimson and his flame-wreathed, Stark Steel blade in hand. Whatever it was that had been troubling him seemed to have gone away for the time being.

Cassius shot up next to the Fiery, Morgan at his side. They folded their wings and dropped just as Bostrof jumped from the ridge, an ululating war cry leaving his throat.

Slipstreams ripped the air as the Nephilim swung their weapons.

Bostrof missed a mace by a whisper, carved a cut down one of the monster's thighs with his sword, and landed on the ground with an explosive boom. The Nephil staggered above him before regaining his balance. He raised a foot to stamp on the Lucifugous, his dreadful face devoid of emotion.

Bostrof vanished in a cloud of shadows.

Morgan blasted a colossus in the face with a sphere of black wind and Dryad magic, sliced across the monster's shoulder with his blade, and shot out of the way of his fist.

Cassius darted around a Nephil and arrowed toward Boreas.

The shadow of a club engulfed him a couple of seconds later.

Victor blocked the weapon with his sword and a shield of Hell Fire.

"*Go!*" the Fiery yelled.

Cassius swerved around the monster Victor had engaged, narrowly avoided another mace, and reached the platform. Boreas lifted his head weakly when he landed a few feet from him. Surprise brightened the God's eyes. His pupils flashed gold, his gaze regaining some focus.

"*Awakener?!*"

"Conserve your strength! You're going to need it!"

Understanding dawned on Boreas's face. He dipped his chin.

Cassius scanned the gully for Morgan, his chest tight. *Where is he?!*

The fight with the Nephilim was so fierce the ice covering the gully was collapsing in giant slabs that crashed onto the ground and filled the air with deadly shards and a veil of powdery crystals.

The hairs rose on Cassius's nape. He dove to the side and rolled.

A mace smashed into the spot where he'd been standing, splintering ice and rock. Boreas swore as black and white chunks rained down on him. Cassius gripped the Ring of Death and his Stark Steel blade, unleashed Heaven's Light, and ascended with a whoosh.

The Nephil's dead eyes tracked him as he rose up his body. The monster attacked with a swiftness that belied his size, his shadow-cloaked hand shooting forth to grab Cassius.

Cassius clenched his jaw, flashed through the monster's closing fingers with a burst of speed, and rose some fifty feet. He folded his wings and dropped, a roar on his lips.

A crimson mist bloomed as he cut the Nephil's hand clean off at the wrist, the Reaper God's scythe slicing through the monster's flesh as if it were air. A grunt left the Nephil. He looked blankly at the scarlet jet spurting from his stump, took a step back to steady his stance, and brandished his mace once more.

31

CASSIUS TWISTED SHARPLY IN THE AIR. COLD STONE brushed his wings and his back.

A frightened sound left Loki.

Cassius gritted his teeth, stabbed his Stark Steel blade into the club as it rose past him, and let the momentum carry him atop it. He landed nimbly on the weapon and moved before the Nephil realized his intent, his feet closing the distance to where the monster held the mace just as the latter blinked slowly.

Cassius sprung up his arm and onto his shoulder in a flash, somersaulted over the back of the giant's head, and sliced his neck as he let gravity take effect, his grip firm on the scythe. He touched down on the floor of the gully a second before the monster's skull smashed into the ice next to him.

The Nephil staggered blindly, stumbled into another colossus, and brought him to the ground. Violent tremors shook the gully under the impact of their fall. Blood from the dying monster's body covered the black rock and ice in a crimson gush.

"*Cassius!*"

Cassius's head snapped around.

Morgan was on the platform, his Sword of Wind halfway through carving apart the first of Boreas's shackles. Cassius's stomach knotted. Morgan was struggling to cut the dark chain.

Shit! We're going to need more time!

He darted toward his lover and the Winter God and reached them in time to block an attack, his divine blade and the scythe meeting the club that would have crushed Morgan.

Cassius's knees buckled as the Nephil tried to flatten him. Rock caved beneath his feet. Morgan stopped hacking at the Winter God's restraints, his face dark with dread.

"Keep going!" Cassius barked.

An explosion made him look sideways.

Bostrof had gone flying into a wall. He landed heavily on his back. Ice peltered him as he rolled out of the way of a Nephil's foot, his injuries leaving crimson trails in the pale crystals.

Cassius's stomach roiled at the sight of Victor struggling in the grip of another colossus beyond Bostrof, Hell Fire blasting through the gaps in the monster's fingers as he fought to free himself.

Cassius blinked. For an instant, Victor's flames looked like they'd taken on a black tinge.

Dammit! They're going to die before Morgan cuts Boreas loose!

"*Three!*"

Morgan looked up at Boreas. Cassius's gaze found the Winter God.

Boreas brought his face close to the Aerial. *"You only need to destroy three of these chains and I can break free!"*

Morgan clenched his teeth, took a deep breath, and focused everything he had on the fetter he'd been carving. Resonance throbbed through Cassius's soul core.

A storm of black currents and Dryad magic roared into life around Morgan and engulfed the Sword of Wind. His eyes flashed gold, his brow furrowing in a furious scowl. He lifted the blade above his head and bore down with all of his strength, a furious sound ripped from his throat.

The shackle shattered under his strike, the inky chain disintegrating into nothingness.

"Hurry!" Boreas barked.

Morgan dashed to the next chain.

Hope fluttered inside Cassius. He reached for the light inside him. Warmth flared on his back as Loki and the Eternity Key lent him their strength. Heat detonated deep within him, flooding his blood and his bones with a power so pure it seared his senses.

"Close your eyes!" Cassius yelled.

He bared his teeth and let loose Heaven's Light a second after shouting out the warning. Dazzling brilliance filled the gully. The Nephilim squinted and stumbled back, hands rising to block out the radiance as they were temporarily blinded.

It was all the time Victor and Bostrof needed to make their escape. They moved between the lurching Nephilim and regrouped with Cassius where he stood on the platform, the three of them forming a protective ring around Boreas and Morgan. The ground shook as the remaining four Nephilim closed in on them.

Hell Fire exploded around Victor. Shadows swarmed

Bostrof. Cassius dug his feet into the ground and braced, fingers clenched tight on his weapons. The second shackle fell just as the giants brought their clubs down upon the three of them.

The force of the strikes made Cassius's bones tremble as he countered two maces with the Reaper God's scythe and his Stark Steel sword. He glared at the Nephilim above him.

There was a blur of movement out of the corner of his eye.

"*Cassius!*" Bostrof barked.

Air locked in Cassius's lungs as one of monsters' feet connected sharply with his flank, denting his armor. He flew across the platform and took Victor to the ground.

Morgan looked up from where he was carving through the third shackle. A violent vortex bloomed around him, rage and fear amplifying his godly powers. The tempest wrapped Cassius and Victor in a protective barrier while they climbed to their feet, three Nephilim above them.

Bostrof blocked an attack from the fourth colossus.

"*Now, Awakener!*" Boreas barked.

The third chain fell, corrupt links vanishing with a hiss.

Cassius dove beneath a swinging mace, skidded on his front across the platform, and reached the Winter God. He jumped to his feet, shot above the deity, and raised the Reaper God's scythe above his head.

"Brace yourself! This is gonna hurt like a bitch!"

Boreas ground his teeth. "*Just do it!*"

Cassius's knuckles whitened on the dark handle. He swung the weapon and fractured the black core within the God with a single strike.

Boreas grunted, a rictus of pain distorting his features.

A silent detonation bloomed across the gully and through the Sixth Hell. The clouds parted violently above them at the same time the ice lining the canyon exploded in a mist of pale crystals.

Boreas's eyes blazed with divine light as he was finally freed from the evil affliction imprisoning his powers.

He ripped the fourth chain from its anchor, spun it above his head, and lassoed the legs of a Nephil together. The monster blinked and swayed ponderously before smashing into two of his companions.

A spear of ice formed in each of Boreas's hands.

He scowled at Cassius. "*Together!*"

Cassius nodded jerkily and took to the air. They moved so fast the monsters barely kept up with their attacks. Boreas felled two Nephilim in as many minutes, the spears impaling them through the eye sockets and ripping through their brains. Cassius took down a third with the Reaper God's scythe. The last of the Nephilim perished under Morgan, Victor, and Bostrof's combined efforts.

A hush fell as the battle came to an end, their heavy pants the only sounds shattering the sudden silence. Whiteness filled the gully as Boreas tipped his head back and roared, the power of winter wrapping the naked God in a blizzard that echoed his fury and pain.

32

REUBEN RAISED HIS EYEBROWS.

"You killed five Nephilim?" he said dully. "The four of you?"

Jasper looked similarly unconvinced where he stood with his arms crossed beside his lover, mouth a thin line and finger tapping impatiently against his arm.

"Are you sure they were Nephilim?" the demon grunted.

"Yeah," Cassius said tiredly where he sat on the couch in his apartment. "To be fair, there were five of us. Boreas took down two of them on his own."

He winced as Lucy applied Blossom Silver ointment to his bruised ribcage. He'd told the mage the injuries would heal on their own. She and Morgan were having none of it.

Lucy's teeth chattered as she put away the medicine. She shivered and rubbed her arms briskly. "Frick it's cold!"

All eyes turned to the God standing stiffly on Cassius's terrace, legs braced and back to them as he gazed out over San Francisco.

"If he doesn't stop soon, my feathers are going to freeze," Julia groused.

"Your feathers?" Adrianne scoffed. "My nipples are already weapons of mass destruction. I swear, I could cut through glass with my breasts."

Bailey's gaze dropped to the sorceress's chest. "She's not wrong."

Zach sighed. Charlie rolled his eyes.

Cassius and the others had returned to the city at dawn that morning. Pan, Lilaia, and the rest of Cassius and Morgan's team had been waiting for them when they'd emerged from underneath Telegraph Hill. Galliad had sent a message to Lilaia warning of their imminent return from the Sixth Hell. Regina had apparently seen the battle unfold in a vision.

Benjamin had waited until he knew they were safe before taking Mortis to the Reaper God's realm to see what they could salvage from the destruction there.

To Cassius's relief, the God of Darkness had not attacked Earth in their absence. A sour taste filled his mouth.

Although Heaven knows what he will do when he finds out we have freed Boreas.

To their surprise, the creatures who inhabited the Sixth Hell had followed them at a distance while they'd made their way back to the portal. Though they'd given Boreas and the others a wide berth and seemed wary of them, they'd appeared fascinated by Cassius, much to Loki's displeasure. Cassius had sensed that they were grateful to him for having freed their realm from the influence of the God of Darkness and the Nephilim. But there'd been more to their stares than simple gratitude.

It was as if they could see something in him no one else could.

Something that was worth their adoration.

The same could not be said for Victor. For a reason Cassius could not fathom, the lesser demons and monsters seemed petrified of the Fiery. It didn't help that Cassius himself had sensed something different about the demon since the battle. Something he couldn't put his finger on however hard he concentrated.

From the way Bostrof had stolen glances at Victor on their trek back to the portal, it seemed he had felt the same dissonance. Only Morgan, Boreas, and Loki seemed unaware of the subtle change in the demon.

Unfortunately, Boreas's arrival in San Francisco had had a side effect no one had foreseen. The bridges spanning the bay currently glittered under a thick layer of ice, as did most of the city and half the estuary. The unseasonal cold had brought the bustling metropolis to a halt and excited skaters out onto the water.

It wasn't every day San Francisco Bay froze over.

Flustered weather forecasters were putting the sudden change in the season down to a cold front that had swept in overnight from the Arctic. Only Argonaut and the other agencies governing magic users and the otherwordly knew that the city's current freezing conditions were due to the presence of one pissed-off Winter God amidst the populace.

Warmth washed over Cassius as Victor entered the apartment, Morgan and Pan in tow. Even with the central heating on full blast, the air inside the room remained chilly. The Fiery rocked to a halt, his breath pluming in front of his face.

His brow furrowed as he studied Boreas through the glass. "Is he still angry?"

"Yeah," Julia muttered. "Although, I can now feel my toes, so that's progress."

"You should go blow some fire on him," Morgan said nastily.

He started handing out the hot drinks they'd bought.

Victor narrowed his eyes at the Aerial. "I'm not a goddamn dragon."

Morgan arched an arrogant eyebrow. "So, what you're saying is, you're not powerful enough to counter his ice?"

The air sizzled with tension.

Pan rolled his eyes. *"You two should just fuck and get it over with."*

Morgan sucked in air, aghast. Victor scowled, his expression just as disgusted. An amused smile twisted Reuben's mouth.

Cassius pinched the bridge of his nose and mumbled a choice swearword under his breath. He'd thought the angel and the demon had gotten past their childish animosity after their fight in the Sixth Hell. Evidently, he'd been wrong.

"Hey, so, who d'you think would be on top if those two —you know?" Lucy whispered to Cassius out of the corner of her mouth, her brow waggling suggestively.

Julia and Adrianne leaned closer to listen in. Cassius's eyes glazed over slightly.

A condescending meow left Loki where he was parked on his lap, his yellow gaze swinging contemptuously between Morgan and Victor. The imp hadn't left his side since they'd come back to the city.

Pan headed over to the terrace door and pulled it open. *"Hey, my balls are getting blue, so dial it down and come inside!"*

Boreas looked over his shoulder. The human form he'd assumed was that of a lean man with ash-colored hair, snow-white skin, and pale blue eyes.

Said blue eyes narrowed. *"Good. I hope your dick falls off."*

Pan grimaced. *"Is that any way to treat your de facto son-in-law? And, FYI, your nephew complex does not get any more attractive with time."*

A localized blizzard formed around Boreas. His pupils flashed gold.

"I have not given my permission for your union with Demetrius!" he snarled.

"We do not need your permission," Pan countered patiently. *"Now, be a good Winter God and come try this hot chocolate."*

Boreas sniffed disdainfully, the storm abating. He stilled when he caught a whiff of the drink in Pan's hand.

"Hmm. That does smell nice."

Pan made a face. *"Like, seriously, tone it down. Dem likes my balls just as they are."*

33

BY THE TIME STRICKLAND AND BRIANNA TURNED UP FOR their impromptu meeting, the apartment was positively roasting.

"Well, the good news is the ice is starting to melt," the Argonaut director said warily as he peeled his scarf and gloves off.

Brianna's lips pressed together as she shrugged out of her coat and eyed Boreas.

"What's the matter with him?" she murmured sideways to Julia. "He looks flushed."

"Chocolate high," the Terrene angel said drily. "The guy loves the stuff. It's the only reason we still have toes to speak of and the city is not a frozen wasteland."

Boreas finished the drink and licked his lips, his eyes bright and perky. *"Can I have another one?"*

"That's your fourth hot chocolate," Morgan said sharply. "You're gonna be sick if you have more."

Boreas bristled. *"Gods do not get sick."*

"*If you stop stalling and tells us what happened in Hyperborea, I shall buy you plenty of the stuff,*" Pan grunted.

"*I am not stalling,*" Boreas protested. "*I am putting my thoughts together.*"

"Put them together faster!" Morgan snapped.

"I don't think I saw a wallet when he landed on Earth naked," Adrianne muttered to Zach. "How's he proposing to buy stuff?"

The demon shrugged. "Sexual favors?"

Pan cut his eyes to them.

Boreas grumbled for a bit before finally relating what took place in Hyperborea.

"*Four weeks ago, a rift opened in my realm and practically destroyed it. From what Pan told me this morning, it was likely the same phenomenon that manifested its presence in Ivory Peaks and here, in your city.*" The Winter God studied Cassius with a probing stare that almost had him squirming. "*The Wild God explained what you did to free us. You have my sincere gratitude for coming to our aid, Awakener.*" He jerked his head at Pan. "*And even if this stubborn fool does not say it, he is thankful too.*"

Pan made a face and fidgeted in his chair.

"It was thanks to the Reaper God's instructions that I managed to do any of it," Cassius said awkwardly where he sat between Morgan and Victor.

Boreas's eyebrows drew together. "*You do not give yourself enough credit.*" His gaze dropped to the bone ring on Cassius's hand. "*Though I must admit I was surprised to see you wield his weapon. It must be because of your status. Only the current Awakener can manifest an ability not even the Gods possess.*"

Boreas's words made Cassius's pulse quicken. *So, I was right!*

He sensed Morgan and Victor's surprise in their sudden stillness.

"*What happened to Demetrius?*" Pan asked Boreas in a harried voice. "*I looked for him everywhere, but could not find any trace of him.*"

A chill blasted from the Winter God. He fisted his hands. "*I do not know. But wherever he is, I suspect he is being forced to wield the Frost Crown.*"

There was a sharp intake of breath around the apartment. Cassius's mouth went dry. Strickland and the other bureau directors traded worried looks.

Pan's face tightened with fury.

"Who is this God of Darkness and what is he trying to do?" Cassius asked before the Wild God could interject.

Boreas propped his elbows on his thighs and scowled at the floor for a moment.

"*I do not know his name,*" he said finally. "*But he smelled like a Primordial.*"

The hair lifted on the back of Cassius's neck. Morgan and Victor flinched beside him.

"*A Primordial?!*" Pan bared his teeth. "*Are you certain?!*"

"*Yes.*" Boreas raised his head and met their shocked stares, his own dark with dread. "*As for his purpose, now that I know what else happened while I was trapped in the Sixth Hell, it is simple enough to deduce. I believe he intends to use the power of Life and Death to tear apart the barriers between the realms and open them up to the Abyss.*"

Horror drenched Cassius in a cold sweat. "What?!" He jumped to his feet, jaw clenched so tight his face ached. "That's—"

"Insane," Victor ground out.

Pan rose and started pacing the floor, his hands fisting and unfisting at his sides. "*So, this God really wants to free Chaos? I mean, does this asshole not realize what will happen if he does that?!*" He waved his arms wildly. "*Everything will be destroyed! All the realms! The otherworldly and humans! The universe will return to nothingness!*"

"*He may seem mad to us, but I am sure he knows full well the outcome of his ambitions should he achieve them, Pan,*" Boreas said gravely. "*He seemed pretty lucid when we spoke.*"

Pan whirled around, his pupils flashing gold. "*Do not tell me you agree with his plans?!*"

Boreas's tone was calm when he replied. "*I never said that. I just feel that we should understand his way of thinking if we are to defeat him.*"

"Can we defeat him?" Brianna asked in a brittle voice. Her tone soared, high and thin with dread. "Is that even possible when he's managed to imprison not just one, but three Gods?!"

"*Yes,*" Boreas said.

Morgan ran a hand through his hair, his face ashen. "I don't understand. How does wielding the power of Life and Death enable him to open the Abyss?"

"*Because Chaos is the beginning and the end of everything, as are Life and Death,*" Boreas explained calmly. "*They are four sides of the same coin. I can fathom two ways for him to achieve his aim and hence for us to stop him. One is to gain control over a God of Life. Zephyrus is a God of Spring and a powerful one at that. Since none knows his whereabouts since the Fall, his son Demetrius would make a good replacement, even if he is but a demigod. He has the seed of a God within him after all.*" The God frowned. "*And he would be easier to subjugate.*"

Cassius swallowed heavily. "And Death? Is he controlling the Reaper God the same way?"

Boreas met his stiff gaze. *"I believe the object the Khimer saw in his master's chest was a shard of the Frost Crown. That artifact is more than just a weapon. It has the power to bend minds and wills."* His mouth flattened. *"It must be how those who helped capture Chaos and trap him in the Abyss managed to defeat him all those millennia past."*

A stunned silence fell across the apartment.

"We are so fucked," Bailey said hoarsely.

"How do we stop him?" Pan said between gritted teeth. *"If we locate where the Reaper God and Demetrius are, we should be able to—"*

"No." Boreas shook his head. *"You will not find the Reaper God so easily, my friend. I believe our enemy is using him to power those war demons, so he will be heavily guarded and quite likely inside one of those rifts. There is only one way to defeat this God of Darkness and save both the Reaper God and my nephew."*

A bolt of intuition flashed through Cassius. His heart stuttered.

"The Frost Crown," he mumbled.

Adrianne blinked slowly, her puzzled gaze swinging between Cassius and Boreas. "What?"

The Winter God met Cassius's dazed stare steadily. *"Yes. We have to regain control of the Frost Crown. And only you can do that, Awakener."*

34

CASSIUS SPLASHED WATER ON HIS FACE AND STARED AT HIS reflection in the bathroom mirror.

Boreas's words echoed through his mind, just as they had done all afternoon. They'd reconvened at Argonaut to catch up on the latest developments concerning the faults that had appeared all over the world. The situation remained unchanged; the fracture lines were still shifting and expanding, adding to increasing panic. The governments of the affected countries had started evacuating cities en masse to calm the bubbling hysteria.

Cassius and Morgan had touched base with Bostrof to see if he had gleaned any clues as to Demetrius's possible whereabouts. The Lucifugous demon's contacts had come up empty so far.

Cassius heard the front door open and close as he exited the bathroom. Morgan had had a replacement installed while they'd been out.

The Aerial appeared a moment later, two whiskey

tumblers in hand. Cassius's throat constricted when he saw his lover's face.

Morgan looked as exhausted as he felt.

"Are they settling in okay?" Cassius murmured.

"Yeah." Morgan grimaced. "Loki is showing them how to play Gin Rummy."

Boreas was staying with Pan in Morgan's apartment. They'd all agreed the two Gods should remain close by while they hunted for Demetrius's location.

Cassius accepted the drink Morgan offered with a grateful sigh and sat on the edge of the bed with him. He took a sip of the whiskey and welcomed the bitter burn as it slipped down his throat.

"What a fucking awful week," Morgan mumbled.

Cassius leaned against him. "At least we made it out of the Sixth Hell alive."

A low chuckle shook Morgan. "I can always count on you to remind me that it could have been a lot worse."

Cassius smiled despite the tension roiling his stomach, Morgan's shoulder warm against his cheek. "I aim to please."

A comfortable silence stretched between them.

"What are you thinking about?" Morgan said after a while.

Cassius chewed his lip. He straightened, downed his drink, and stared into the bottom of the glass. "I'm thinking that Boreas is wrong. How the hell can I do what he's expecting me to do when I'm scared out of my mind?"

Morgan stiffened at his stilted words. He took the empty glass from him and placed both tumblers on the nightstand. Cassius shuddered as the angel took him in his arms. He closed his eyes and pressed his face into Morgan's chest, seeking his comforting heat.

"You're amazing, you know that, right?" Morgan murmured into his hair.

Cassius froze in Morgan's hold.

"I don't know why you're still doubting yourself, Cassius. You have three Gods relying on you to save their collective ass. Be more confident in your abilities."

Morgan tipped up Cassius's chin with a knuckle and dropped a kiss on his nose. Cassius's heart fluttered at the undying trust and love in Morgan's radiant eyes.

"What did I ever do to deserve you?" he whispered tremulously.

He cradled Morgan's face in his hands and pressed their mouths together gently, emotion choking his throat. Morgan's arms tightened around him. Heat flared between their soul cores.

Cassius shivered, an ache building inside him.

Morgan brushed their lips together before probing his mouth open and deepening the kiss. Desire flashed in Cassius's veins when their tongues met.

Morgan twisted and tumbled him down onto the bed, his movements growing urgent and his turquoise eyes glinting with passion. They shifted up the mattress, their hands frantic as they started undressing one another, their mouths meeting in hungry kisses.

It felt like ages since they'd made love. Cassius couldn't wait to experience the dizzying heights of ecstasy only Morgan could bring him to. He flipped Morgan onto his back and straddled him boldly.

Morgan caught his lip sexily between his teeth and ran hot hands up and down Cassius's naked thighs, the muscles in his arms bunching powerfully. "Hmm, why do I feel like I'm about to be ravished?"

Cassius cursed and arched as Morgan traced his stiff cock with a light finger. He leaned down and kissed the Aerial hard.

"That's because you are!" he growled.

Morgan chuckled at his aggressive tone. His laughter turned into a hiss of pleasure as Cassius's lips swept down his throat, clever teeth nipping at the pulse beating wildly at the base of his neck.

Cassius worshipped Morgan with his mouth and his fingers as he moved down his body, his dick aching where it brushed against Morgan's scalding skin. He wanted nothing more than to rub himself and find his release. But it wasn't often Morgan let him take the lead like this and he was determined to pleasure the Aerial just as much as he was regularly pleasured at his hands.

A husky groan left Morgan when Cassius settled between his thighs and took him in his mouth. Cassius squirmed as he sucked and licked Morgan's steely shaft, the angel's tantalizing scent filling his nostrils and making his ass twitch. Morgan grabbed the sheets and let out a lustful sound as Cassius swallowed him to the back of his throat. He fisted a hand in Cassius's hair, fixed his head, and punched his hips up.

Cassius grunted, the motion lodging Morgan deeper inside his mouth. He hollowed his cheeks and worked his jaw in strong pulls that soon had Morgan cursing and writhing beneath him.

Morgan's balls spasmed and contracted as he neared his climax. He came on a guttural shout, hips thrusting jerkily, fucking Cassius's mouth for all he was worth. Cassius swallowed and lapped at Morgan's throbbing dick until he was bone dry, his body tingling and his skin so sensitive even the sheets made him shiver.

Morgan collapsed down on the bed, his face and chest flushed and glistening with sweat, aftershocks of pleasure rippling through his twitching limbs.

Cassius straightened from where he'd been lying on his front, his heart pounding and his dick close to bursting. He took the lube from the nightstand and uncapped it hurriedly. Morgan's eyes blazed as he finally focused on what Cassius was doing.

Cassius poured the scented liquid into his hand and sat astride him.

Morgan's hands found his waist, his fingers biting into his flesh with possessive strength. "Are you gonna finger yourself?"

His gravelly voice and the hunger darkening his eyes almost made Cassius come. Morgan's sultry gaze dropped to Cassius's cock and the shadowy space beneath his quivering balls.

Cassius swallowed and nodded jerkily, his body burning and his passage aching. He wanted Morgan inside him so bad he was ready to beg.

"Good," Morgan growled. "I want to see."

Cassius shuddered, so turned on he thought he'd pass out. He spread his thighs wide open and angled his hips forward. Heat sparked between their soul cores as Morgan finally got a view of the place his dick would soon be plundering. Cassius trembled under his heated stare, precum oozing and dripping onto Morgan's belly.

Morgan dragged a finger through the sticky fluid and

licked it clean before Cassius could utter a protest. He smacked his lips and grinned.

"Sweet like honey." His expression grew fierce again. "Now, touch yourself."

The command had Cassius's belly hardening with delicious tension. He dropped a hand to his cock, gave himself a few slick strokes, and danced his fingers farther south. He bit his lip and closed his eyes when his fingertips found his entrance. His cheeks grew hot as he stroked and rubbed the tight folds guarding his opening.

He couldn't believe he was acting so wantonly.

Hot sparks spread from Cassius's sensitive flesh all the way through his passage and to his core. He moaned, his hips moving of their own volition. A rough sound left Morgan when Cassius slipped a finger inside.

Cassius blinked his eyes open and gasped at the savage expression on Morgan's face. Their gazes stayed locked as he worked himself until he was soft and ready. He pushed another digit inside and cursed with pleasure as he withdrew and pressed back in.

"Jesus, that's hot!" Morgan ground out.

He licked his lips, his hungry gaze on Cassius's slow, thrusting fingers. He was hard again, dick flushed and glistening where it rose proudly from his trimmed pubes.

Cassius pressed a hand back on the mattress and tilted his lower body forward, giving Morgan a better view. He scissored his digits and fucked himself hard and fast until he grew dizzy, the bolts of pleasure shooting through his body from his passage making his dick jerk and leak. Tension wound down his spine and tightened his limbs, heralding his orgasm.

He slipped his fingers out, grabbed Morgan's cock, and

mounted him. They both groaned lustily as Cassius impaled himself inch by slow inch, his passage contracting and relaxing, welcoming the thick intruder.

Their heavy pants filled the room when Morgan was finally seated inside his body. Cassius spent a breathless moment appreciating just how fully Morgan filled him before pressing his palms on Morgan's chest and lifting off.

Morgan cursed and gripped his ass as Cassius started dancing up and down his shaft, the bed rocking rhythmically beneath them. Cassius dropped his head forward and closed his eyes. He lost himself in the wildness of their mating, his body slick with sweat, his mouth open on throaty cries, his pulse thumping in his ears.

Flashes of light lit the backs of his eyelids as Morgan's cock rubbed and kneaded his pleasure spot. Cassius lowered a hand to his groin and started rubbing himself, aching to come.

Morgan rolled and punched his hips, matching his descent beat for beat, giving him what he wanted and more. Their flesh met with wet smacks that made Cassius bite his lip hard and squeeze his passage harder.

A buzzing filled his ears. His belly knotted, a ball of pleasure growing deep inside him, so hard and hot it hurt.

Cassius came on a loud shout, his body convulsing with sweet violence as he ejaculated all over Morgan's belly and chest, his breath catching repeatedly. Morgan grabbed hold of him, flipped him onto his back, and kept pumping his hips through his climax, his mouth finding Cassius's lips with a bone-deep hunger that made him shudder. He locked Cassius's legs around his hips, pinned his hands above his head, and rose, thrusting hard and deep.

Cassius's heart throbbed at the sight of Morgan's face,

his passage spasming with aftershocks of ecstasy even as Morgan continued fucking him. The demigod's expression was feral and his pupils flashed gold amidst a sea of cobalt every time he plunged in and out of Cassius's body, his movements feverish with need.

Cassius lifted his head off the bed and sought Morgan's mouth. Morgan obliged with a growl and took his lips in a searing kiss full of promise. Cassius gripped his fingers tight and embraced it all, their soul cores throbbing in tandem as they made love with passionate strength.

I will never tire of this. And I will never leave this man!

35

A FAINT SOUND WOKE MORGAN UP SHORTLY AFTER dawn. He blinked his eyes open. Soft light painted the sky in shades of purple and red beyond the windows of Cassius's bedroom. The Empyreal lay in his arms, his back to Morgan's chest. His rib cage rose and fell slowly with his breaths and his handsome face was relaxed in sleep.

Guilt twisted Morgan's heart when he observed the faint shadows under Cassius's eyes. *I should have let him sleep more.*

He was about to press an apologetic kiss to Cassius's shoulder when the sound came again. It was a scratching at the door.

Morgan frowned, lifted his arm carefully from around Cassius, and rolled out of bed. He opened the bedroom door and found Loki sitting on the threshold in his demon cat form, tail stiff and pupils wide in a rim of yellow.

Morgan tensed. "What's the matter?"

Loki transformed.

"Pan!" he blurted out. "Something is wrong with him!"

Cassius stirred behind Morgan.

"Loki?" he mumbled sleepily.

He stiffened and sat up at the sight of the imp's distressed expression.

By the time they got dressed and rushed inside Morgan's apartment, pulses of divine power were making the air tremble and sending tremors through the walls of the building.

Morgan's stomach lurched.

Pan lay on his couch, face drenched with sweat and mouth distorted in a rictus of pain. He was groaning and clawing at his stomach.

Boreas crouched beside him, his hands fisted helplessly at his sides. He twisted and met their alarmed gazes, his own full of woe.

"Please, help him! I do not know what ails him so!"

They crossed the floor to the couch. Cassius knelt next to Pan. Morgan hovered beside him, his heart racing with trepidation. The Empyreal hesitated before placing a hand atop the Wild God's belly. He closed his eyes and focused.

"Shit!" Cassius's eyes snapped open, his face growing tight with dread. "His soul core!"

Boreas grasped his shoulder in a white-knuckled grip. *"What is the matter with his soul?!"*

"It's—it's twisted." Cassius shook his head dazedly. "It feels like something is tearing it apart from the inside out!"

Boreas's eyes lit up with a flash of fury. A cold wind erupted around him. *"It must be the work of that blasted God of Darkness!"*

Cassius's eyebrows drew together. "But why now? If he intended to do this all along, he could have done so ages ago!"

Pan grabbed his hand. Cassius flinched. Morgan stared, equally shocked. The Wild God's eyes were open. He looked at them blindly, his pupils smoldering gold.

"*Take me...to the Spirit Realm!*" Pan stopped and swallowed, his voice full of agony. "*It is about to be destroyed!*"

Boreas recoiled. "*What?!*"

Morgan clenched his jaw. *Dammit! What the hell is going on?*

"That must be it!" Cassius jumped to his feet, his expression clearing. "That's why his soul core is becoming unstable. It's linked to the Spirit Realm!" He met Boreas and Morgan's stares, his own growing determined. "I think Demetrius is there. And he's being forced to rip his own kingdom apart!"

Boreas cursed, a chill radiating from him.

Frustration knotted Morgan's shoulders. "How do we get there? Pan said the doorway between the Spirit Realm and Earth was destroyed!"

Cassius stiffened, his eyes rounding.

"Ivory Peaks," he mumbled. He met Morgan's startled gaze. "The one in Ivory Peaks is damaged but wasn't destroyed!" He turned to Loki, his eyes bright with hope. "Do you think you can find a way to the Spirit Realm through a broken gate? Like you did for the Sixth Hell?!"

Loki chewed his lip and hesitated, his tail flicking agitatedly. He stared at Pan. His face hardened.

He bobbed his head. "I can try."

Morgan's ears throbbed when the pressure in the room plummeted. Dryad magic and black wind bloomed on his fingertips as he whirled around, searching for the source of the threat.

The scent of camphor filled the apartment.

"I will help."

Benjamin was in the kitchen with Mortis, the pool of darkness they'd appeared from fading beneath them. The Khimer looked positively haggard where he stood swaying by the Reaper, as if he had witnessed things he wished to unsee.

Benjamin's orbits flared crimson under his cowl, his rage a cold aura that almost matched Boreas's.

"I will help," he repeated grimly.

☙❧

"I CANNOT LET YOU DO THAT!" STRICKLAND SNAPPED, HIS alarmed voice loud through Victor's cell speaker. "We can't afford to lose any of you to this battle, let alone *all* of you!"

"We have no choice, Francis," Victor retorted. "If the Spirit Realm is destroyed, Earth will be next!"

The Fiery frowned as he watched Cassius pour Heaven's Light into Pan. It was the only thing he'd been able to think of to stabilize the God's soul core until they reached the Sprit Realm.

It seemed to be working. Some color had returned to Pan's face and he didn't appear to be in as much pain as before. Boreas sat stiffly on the other side of the Wild God, his face tense as he stared unblinkingly at Cassius's glowing hands pressed to Pan's belly.

Loki's fingers warmed Cassius's back, power throbbing from the Eternity Key and the imp to augment Cassius's own strength. Benjamin watched on curiously, crimson smoldering in the depths of his orbits.

Amal Kazmi's voice came over the speaker, her tone hard. "Are you certain you can win?"

The heads of the other three agencies were on the emergency conference call with Strickland.

Cassius saw Victor and Morgan glance at him out of the corner of his eye. He knew Kazmi's question was directed at him.

He clenched his teeth. "I can't promise you that. But if we don't try, Earth *will* fall."

Something that looked like regret flashed on Morgan's face. Victor's expression grew shuttered. Cassius knew what they were thinking. They resented that the world that so loathed him was relying on him once more.

Morgan squared his shoulders. "I know Cassius is too softhearted to ask this of you, but I want something in return for what we're about to do."

Cassius raised his head and stared at Morgan, his pulse quickening. Lines furrowed Victor's brow.

"Are you blackmailing us?" Viken said icily.

"No," Morgan retorted. "I am asking you to be honest."

"What are your demands?" Kazmi asked brusquely.

"I want you to make everything Cassius has done to protect this world public after we return to Earth." Morgan's voice echoed with a deep undertone of resentment as he spoke. "Every single mission. Every filthy, little secret. Every accolade you and your people have taken credit for that was rightly his. I want all of it to be attributed to him."

Victor drew a sharp breath. Something black flared from him for an instant.

Cassius blinked rapidly. *Wait. Did I just imagine that?*

"I do not understand," Loki said, confused. "What do you mean?"

Morgan ignored the imp and turned a hooded gaze

upon the Fiery. "You know I'm right. This should have happened years ago." He addressed Strickland and the other agency heads, a muscle jumping in his jawline. "I will not have Cassius carry on doing your dirty work while you all bask in glory and his reputation continues to be dragged through the mud through no fault of his own."

Loki gasped. "What?!"

Boreas blinked. Benjamin's orbits flared.

"Morgan," Cassius whispered.

Pain squeezed his heart at the hurt and anger blazing in the Aerial's sapphire eyes. He hadn't realized how badly Morgan felt about the injustice with which the world had treated him all these centuries.

"And if we refuse?" Guiying challenged, the witch's voice bereft of emotion.

Morgan met Cassius's frozen stare, his own full of resolve. "I am a direct descendant of Queen Atlanteia and the rightful heir to the Dryad kingdom." Magic fluttered around his fingers, a sparkling, green haze that smelled of the forest and a scent that made Cassius's soul throb with yearning. "I will leave Earth, take my throne in Ivory Peaks, and make Cassius my consort."

His pupils blazed as he gazed at Cassius.

Cassius went weak at the knees. He couldn't believe Morgan had even entertained such a crazy notion. A stunned silence descended around them.

Victor had gone pale where he stood next to Morgan.

"You would leave Earth?" Strickland asked in a strained voice.

Guilt darkened Morgan's eyes for an instant at the hurt underscoring the director's question.

He clenched his fists, his jaw set in a hard line. "In a

heartbeat. This world does not deserve Cassius if it continues to reject him."

Cassius swallowed. *Would I go? If he did that, would I really leave this world?*

A shudder shook him. He closed his eyes.

He knew the answer already.

He would travel to the ends of the Nine Hells to be with Morgan.

36

IT WAS NIGHTTIME IN IVORY PEAKS WHEN THEY EXITED the Reaper portal Benjamin had created to travel to the Dryad kingdom. It was the fastest way to reach the realm aside from the official gateway in Yosemite National Park. Even though Pan's condition had improved in the past couple of hours, Cassius hadn't wanted to take the risk of making the Wild God travel farther than was necessary.

Besides, the faster we get him to the Spirit Realm, the better!

Pan leaned heavily on Cassius and Boreas as they emerged under a dazzling, starlit sky ahead of Morgan and the others. Cassius stiffened and stopped.

Hildur and Regina were waiting for them in the clearing where the doorway had opened, close to the palace.

"Regina had a vision of your arrival," Hildur explained at his surprised expression. Her face tightened when she observed the Reaper and the Gods. "I didn't want to believe her when she told me who was coming."

"I didn't want to believe it myself," Regina muttered.

Boreas dipped his head. *"Thank you for granting us safe passage through your realm, Queen."*

Hildur bowed, Regina curtsying beside her. "You are too kind, God of Winter. But it is not truly my domain to rule anymore." She straightened and cast a rueful smile at Morgan. "Atlanteia's child is its rightful heir."

"I told you I have no intention of claiming your throne," Morgan muttered.

"That's not what you just told the heads of the agencies," Victor said frostily.

"Oh." Hildur arched an eyebrow. "Did something happen?"

"The Aerial threatened the human leaders. He claimed he would take the Empyreal and abandon Earth if they continue to mistreat him," Benjamin said solemnly.

Hildur narrowed her eyes. "Mistreat him?"

Loki bobbed his head, tail swinging agitatedly. "Yes. I did not know either, but apparently those fools have no appreciation for what he has done for them!" He squinted at Cassius. "I hope you were not thinking of leaving me on Earth if you relocate to Ivory Peaks. I am coming with you."

"Who said I'd let you into my kingdom?!" Morgan snapped.

Cassius sighed as Morgan and Loki entered into a full-blown argument about whom he belonged to.

Hildur stared. "Who's the imp?"

Victor's mouth pressed into a thin line. "He's the Keeper of the Eternity Key."

Hildur sucked in air.

"Isn't he supposed to be a demon cat?" Regina said suspiciously.

"This is his true form." Cassius met Hildur and Regina's surprised gazes, his tone growing urgent. "Can you take us to the gate to the Spirit Realm?"

Hildur lowered her brows. "What's going on, Cassius?"

He brought the Dryad queen and the seer up to speed with what had happened in the past few days.

Hildur paled. "The Spirit Realm is under attack?!"

"Yes," Cassius said grimly. "This is the real deal. I think the rifts that opened here and on Earth were trials the God of Darkness carried out to test what it would take to destroy a realm."

Boreas startled at his words. Morgan and Victor stared at Cassius, equally surprised.

Benjamin's pupils constricted to tiny, red dots. "That would make sense."

Hildur took a shaky breath and dipped her head jerkily. "Follow me. We will help the best we can."

She and Regina turned and led them through the forest.

"Where are Roald and the princes?" Morgan asked when they came out into the royal gardens.

"They are taking care of the damage the rift caused in the cities and villages in the realm. Galliad is with them."

They navigated a path lined with trees and flowers that led to the rear of the palace. The stables housing the royal stallions and the open-aired aviary where the giant eagles roosted came into view. The birds lifted their heads curiously when they passed, their golden eyes focusing eerily on Cassius.

An ancient woodland appeared, the trees crowding the skyline rising to merge with the forest that draped the flanks of the snow-tipped peaks above the capital. Hildur and Regina led the way into the shadows beneath the canopy.

Cassius's skin prickled at the silence that dropped down around them like a curtain. The calls of nightbirds and the noises of woodland creatures had stopped. Even the wind had died down, leaving the branches and leaves motionless. The only sounds that reached his ears were the thrumming of his heartbeat and their footsteps on the forest floor.

It was as if time had stopped in this corner of Ivory Peaks.

Moss-covered flagstones appeared amidst the grass. They formed a footpath that led to a glade. Cassius's pulse quickened.

A giant elm soared to the skies at the far end of the clearing. Sitting in its shadow was a marble pavilion bathed in the soft glow of antiquated lanterns. His eyes widened.

A cracked dais holding a life-size statue of Pan's original God form stood in the middle of the structure, the flames casting a flickering, orange light upon the polished, veiny surface.

"*Wow, they even got the proportions of his dick right,*" Boreas muttered.

Morgan rolled his eyes.

"*This sure brings back memories,*" Pan said.

Cassius looked at the Wild God. Relief brought a sudden lightness to his limbs. Pan's color was back to normal and his eyes had regained their luster.

"Bringing you here was the right thing to do."

Boreas's brows drew together. "*What do you mean?*"

"Pan is a God of Fertility and Spring," Cassius explained. "The divine energy in Ivory Peaks matches the frequency of his godly core. I thought the trip here would help heal the damage to his soul."

Pan's pupils flashed gold. He gnashed his teeth.

"*Oh, blast it all to the Nine Hells!*" he blurted out. "*Why do you have to be so goddamn nice, you stupid Awakener? It makes it that much harder to hate you!*" He shrugged Cassius's arm off and jabbed a finger in his chest. "*No wonder that God manipulated you! Be more on your guard, you kindhearted fool!*"

Cassius blinked, startled.

Boreas tsk-tsked at Pan. "*You are still clinging on to that old grudge? You told me yourself the Awakener was a victim of the foul schemes of that God of Darkness, as were many others.*"

Cassius's pulse quickened. He recalled what Chester Moran's master had told him under the cathedral and the agonizing guilt and sorrow he'd experienced at the time. The same guilt and sorrow he'd relived in his dream of the Fall, when he'd stammered an apology to the angel with the dark hair and sapphire eyes. The one whose death he was responsible for. The brother in arms he could not remember.

Is that what that was about? When I told him I never intended for him to come to harm? Did I realize I had acted on lies?!

Heat flushed through his body at the thought of the deity who'd stolen the South Star's form and stabbed him with the spear of light. Cassius fisted his hands.

I swear on everything that I am. I will find that God and make him pay!

"*Come, we must make haste.*" Pan's curt words jolted Cassius into the present. The Wild God's eyes burned as he looked at him. "*The next time you face that God, do not fall for his machinations, you hear?*"

"I won't," Cassius promised wholeheartedly.

Pan sniffed. *"Good. Otherwise I shall kick your ass myself."*

Benjamin turned to Loki. "Are you ready, imp?"

Loki clenched his jaw and nodded. The two of them stepped up to the statue. Broken circles of light appeared on the floor of the pavilion as Hildur and Regina poured their Dryad magic into what remained of the original runes around the portal.

Cassius and Morgan shifted to their demigod forms. Victor snapped his wings open, Hell Fire blooming on his feathers and Stark Steel blade.

A pale, green mist rose from the ground, the radiance flickering as the fragmented magic winked on and off. A hum filled the pavilion. It rose to a tortured whine that made Cassius's ears throb.

The ground started to shake.

"This is all we have been able to do since the Fall!" Hildur shouted, her face strained. "We could not get it to open beyond this!"

"It is enough," Loki said, his sing-song voice hard.

He took a deep breath and touched the statue. Golden light bloomed from deep inside his body. It shot down his arm and out his fingers. The imp's wings fluttered as he focused the power of the Eternity Key on unlocking the gate.

A bright circle flashed into existence around Pan's effigy. Benjamin stabbed the end of his scythe into the edge of it and pulled, his orbits blooming a bright vermilion. The circle slowly expanded under the combined efforts of the imp and the Reaper.

Hope fluttered inside Cassius. His stomach dropped as

the circle contracted again, the whine rising to a high-pitched scream as the gateway protested.

No!

Pan strode past him. The Wild God squatted between Loki and Benjamin, his face set in determined lines. His figure swelled as he let go of his human shape, his clothes vanishing to reveal his divine appearance.

Pan slammed his hands inside the circle, his pupils flaring gold and his hair fluttering with godly energy. "*I am coming, Demetrius!*"

A column of white light exploded into existence where the statue stood, the force of the silent detonation forcing Cassius and the others back several steps. Only Pan remained unmoving, the God's shout of fury echoing the holy power throbbing from his soul core.

The doorway to the Spirit Realm opened with a thunderous roar, bringing with it a flurry of snow.

37

A BLAST OF FRIGID AIR NUMBED CASSIUS'S FACE WHEN HE stepped out of the dazzling portal. Grass crunched under his feet, the once green blades coated with a heavy layer of ice. He stopped beside Morgan, his heart thumping against his ribs.

"What the hell?!"

Morgan's words were swept away by the glacial winds battering them.

Winter had come to the land of the Gods. Even Pan looked stunned by the white landscape around them and the violent maelstrom raging through his once verdant kingdom.

The gateway flickered and winked out behind them.

Loki shivered and stepped close to Cassius, teeth chattering.

Victor squinted at the white flurries spiraling down from the overcast night sky, the snowflakes sizzling and melting as they touched his flames. "Where are we?!"

Cassius spotted enormous trees rising out of the blizzard.

Boreas swore, recognition flaring across his face. "*Wait. Is this—?!*"

"*We are in Tal'Valan,*" Pan spat out. "*It is a sacred forest at the very edge of the Spirit Realm. It gave rise to this land and is the source of its nexus.*"

Cassius's stomach twisted with dread. *Shit!*

Victor frowned heavily. "So that God is doing what he intends to do to Earth? He is going to destroy the Spirit Realm's nexus?!"

"*Yes.*" Pan stiffened. "*I can feel Demetrius!*" His eyes widened. "*He is hurt!*"

He ran out into the storm.

"Hey! Stop!" Morgan barked. "We should figure out what—"

A sharp downdraft ruffled Cassius's hair. Shadows swooped above them and arrowed toward the Wild God's disappearing form.

Cassius's pulse stuttered. *War demons!*

"*Pan!*" Boreas shouted.

"Find somewhere safe and protect Loki!" Cassius snapped at Benjamin.

He spread his wings and rose before the Reaper could reply, Heaven's Light blossoming around his body and his Stark Steel blade. The Reaper God's scythe whined as he unleashed it, the weapon as hungry for blood as he was.

Cassius narrowed his eyes, his preternatural sight piercing the wintry squalls. He spotted the Wild God and dove, Morgan and Victor on his tail and Boreas pounding the ground beneath them in his God form.

Pan roared as he smashed aside the war demons

swarming him with a sapling he'd wrenched from the ground, the air around him bright with divine power. Cassius dropped amidst the dark-winged creatures and released a burst of Heaven's Light.

The monsters screeched and retreated. His stomach lurched. The fading brilliance revealed what had been hidden by the storm.

The forest was swarming with war demons, their ranks so thick they obliterated the sky.

Something else caught his eye. A radiance where none should be. There was a glow coming from the middle of the forest.

"That must be where Demetrius is!"

Pan followed his gaze and started in that direction. Cassius blocked the God's path.

"Will you use your goddamn brains for a minute?!" he snarled. "You can't just barge over there and smash your way through to him. You may be a deity, but these are war demons and they will tear you to shreds before you get within a hundred feet of Demetrius!"

Pan flinched.

"*But he is in pain!*" he protested, his expression crumbling.

Cassius's chest twisted at the agony darkening the God's eyes. He would be in the same state if this were Morgan they were talking about.

"I know." He took a shuddering breath. "And I promise. I *will* free him. But we need to do this together!"

Pan ground his teeth. Boreas placed a comforting hand on the God's shoulder. The dry rustling of thousands of leathery wings came from above them. Cassius's gaze rose to the sky. His pulse quickened.

The war demons were congregating over their position.

"This storm is too thick for Heaven's Light to penetrate!" He looked over at Boreas, his stomach roiling. "Can you clear it?!"

Boreas bobbed his head, his brow locking in a scowl. *"Demetrius may wield the Frost Crown, but I am still a God of Winter!"*

Cassius turned to Morgan and Victor. "Keep them off my back!"

The angel and the demon dipped their chins, their eyes hard. The three of them shot up in the air. Pan and Boreas shrunk as the ground dropped rapidly beneath them.

Cassius finally got a grasp of the size of Tal'Valan as they cleared the treetops. The ancient forest stretched for hundreds of miles in every direction to a distant rim of dark peaks that ringed the horizon.

The war demons screeched when they detected Cassius's presence. They came at him in a solid wave, their crimson eyes full of hate and their numbers legion.

Hell Fire and black wind bolstered with Dryad magic blasted into them. Victor and Morgan's figures blurred as they charged the front line, faces alive with bloodlust and blades carving through the enemy with deadly strikes.

Cassius cut down the monsters who broke past their defense, his Stark Steel sword and Death's scythe humming in his hands. A powerful slipstream buffeted his wings. He looked down.

The blizzard swarming the forest wavered as a storm of pure wind crashed into it. Golden light blazed from Boreas's eyes as he let loose, the currents swirling around him keeping the war demons who threatened to attack him and Pan at bay.

The winds shifted. The snow cleared.

Now!

Cassius inhaled and reached for the source of all his powers. Heat flared deep inside him. Light exploded around his body. It washed the forest in blinding radiance and destroyed hundreds of war demons in a single flash. He clenched his jaw as the monsters' remains filled the air with cinders and ash.

More! I need to keep doing this until I kill all of them!

Cassius closed his eyes, focused on his breathing, and released burst after burst of light. His bones trembled and his blood heated as power swarmed his veins in never-ending waves. His soul core throbbed what felt like a lifetime later, a familiar wave of resonance jolting him back to the present.

Morgan shouted his name. Cassius opened his eyes, the radiance around him fading. His pulse stuttered. The war demons were all but gone.

A boom tore across the valley, so loud it made his teeth vibrate. Cassius's head snapped up. Bile flooded the back of his throat.

The sky was rippling, what was visible of the stars warping as if they no longer belonged to this dimension. The Spirit Realm was starting to tear. Soon, more war demons would appear and the Reaper God would make his presence felt.

Instinct had Cassius's gaze dropping to the ancient forest. There was a glade at the very center of Tal'Valan. It was hidden by a storm of ice and snow. He could sense the soul core of a demigod within it.

One that didn't feel right.

Demetrius!

38

VICTOR SWOOPED AFTER CASSIUS AS HE DOVE TOWARD Tal'Valan, the bitter wind searing the air washing harmlessly across his heated skin. The sick feeling twisting his stomach worsened as he glanced at the sky.

He could feel the corruption pulsing from the rift forming above them. It was bringing back echoes of memories. Memories his instincts told him he should never recall.

Whatever was ripping open the Spirit Realm was doing something to him. Just like that time in the Sixth Hell, when he'd felt that strange heat in his belly after seeing the black core that had imprisoned Boreas's powers.

There was a darkness growing inside him. One that was hot and twisted and made him feverish. It felt alien, yet achingly familiar at the same time. It was as if a wealth of knowledge and power had slumbered inside him for untold centuries, locked behind the iron doors of his will until this very moment.

He blinked at that sudden thought. *Wait. What was I—?!*

"*Victor!*"

Victor startled, awareness returning with a cold blast of snow.

Four war demons were closing in on him.

Cassius intercepted them, the Reaper God's scythe and his Stark Steel sword singing in his hands as he felled the monsters. Morgan cursed and winged his way back toward their position.

Cassius drifted in front of Victor, his gray eyes dark with worry. "Are you okay?!"

Victor swallowed convulsively, his heart slamming against his ribs. *Shit! I can't believe I got distracted in the middle of a battle!*

"Yeah, I'm fine! Thanks for—"

Cassius flinched. He recoiled in the next instant, his wings driving him back some dozen feet.

Victor's stomach dropped. "Cassius?"

"Your flames," Cassius mumbled, ashen faced. He stared at Victor's body before meeting his stupefied gaze, his own full of fear. "Victor, *your flames!*"

Victor looked at his hand. Ice filled his veins.

The Hell Fire dancing on his fingertips and across his armor had started to darken. A voice rippled through his mind. One that was full of madness and came from a past he had long forgotten. It made him shudder and want to throw up.

You should let loose, Coraos. The one you covet is right there, in front of you. Defeat the Dryad demigod and he will be yours once more.

The name the voice addressed him by sent pain stabbing through Victor's skull. He gripped his head, an agony he never wished to revisit surging through him once more, threatening to tear apart his soul and his sanity.

"*NOOOO!*" he screamed. "*I will not betray him again! I swore I never would!*"

※

CASSIUS'S HEART THROBBED WRETCHEDLY AS VICTOR'S shout ripped through the air, the torment in his voice so raw he wanted nothing more than to rush over to the demon and take him in his arms to alleviate his suffering.

Morgan seemed to have foreseen his intent and was blocking his path, the demigod holding the Sword of Wind in a defensive stance as he observed the Fiery with a heavy frown. "What's wrong with him?!"

"I—I don't know!" Cassius shook his head dazedly. "I've never seen him like this!" He made to move. "I should go to—"

"Don't!" Morgan snapped. "It's too dangerous! He's—"

His words ended on a gasp. He bent over and grunted, the color draining from his face as he clutched his belly.

"*Morgan!*" Cassius screamed.

Fire seared his soul core before he could reach the demigod. Something shattered inside him. Cassius's breath froze.

He knew instinctively it was a part of the spell that had erased his past.

Images flickered before his mind's eye, just like that time when the Ring of Death had first resonated with him. Cassius stared blindly at memories that shifted through his mind, too fast for him to grasp their meaning. He waited for the pain that would crush his skull. Except this time, it did not come.

Instead, he heard a voice. One he had not heard in a while.

Remember...

Cassius shuddered, the voice of the demigod he had once been echoing sweetly in his ears. The flash of memories slowed. His eyes widened.

Remember what happened...

A battle took shape before him. One that was being fought by an army of Gods, angels, demons, and spirits against a legion of other Gods, war demons, Nephilim, and monsters, in a realm of darkness he had always feared. A realm that he'd always assumed he abhorred because everyone else did.

The Nether.

Except it wasn't what he'd thought it was.

The images shifted dizzyingly, bringing him past hundreds upon thousands of clashing figures, their movements so infinitesimal they appeared frozen in time, their mouths open on silent screams and their bloodied weapons all but motionless in their grip. The still snapshots accelerated, closing in on the center of the war.

And there, hovering at the forefront of one faction, his long, fair hair and his armored body blazing bright with divine power, his sword brimming with Heaven's Light, was the demigod he knew himself to be.

At his side were four others. Three more figures who wore the same armor as him but for their distinctive colors, among them the angel with the black hair and blue eyes he had seen in his dream. Cassius blinked.

The South Star was holding the spear of light the God of Darkness had pierced him with in his hand.

His heart stuttered when he saw the fourth figure.

It was Morgan. Or rather, Ivmir.

The demigod hovered in all his wrathful splendor beside Cassius, his crown atop his head and the Sword of Wind trembling with tremendous power in his armored hands, dark currents swarming with Dryad magic wrapping him in a mantle of black and green.

The South Star turned his head and looked past Cassius's former demigod form to the Cassius who observed the battle as if through a looking glass. He smiled once more, the same smile of affection and absolution he'd shown Cassius in the dream. He opened his mouth and pointed at something across the way.

Remember what they did...

Cassius followed the direction he indicated. Horror curdled his blood.

The God of Darkness floated at the head of the enemy faction, body wreathed in ominous, eldritch shadows, eyes a bottomless abyss full of hate.

A silent scream of denial worked its way up Cassius's throat.

Because there, hovering next to the enemy God, black flames swarming his dark wings and broadsword, his crimson eyes full of a zealous light Cassius did not recognize, was a demigod who looked a lot like Victor. One who had once pledged to always stand by his side.

Movement caught Cassius's petrified gaze. He turned and met the eyes of the demigod he had once been. Seraphic light lit the pupils of the Awakener, his expression pure fire and fierceness.

Remember who we are...Icarus...

"*Icarus?!*"

Morgan's tortured voice jolted Cassius out of his trance. He gasped and straightened, air flooding his starving lungs in a cold rush. Sight returned. He blinked and looked around jerkily, expecting to see war demons arrowing in on their position.

The sky was empty but for a few of the monsters swirling above the forest.

Cassius's heart thumped heavily as he met Morgan's dazed stare.

"Icarus?" the demigod repeated, his voice breaking.

Tears filled his eyes and fell down his cheeks. He wiped them hastily and came to him.

Cassius shuddered as Morgan wrapped him in his arms and repeated his true name over and over, like a prayer he'd resolved never to forget.

"Icarus, my Icarus!"

He rained soft kisses all over Cassius's face, his voice searing Cassius's mind and heart and making his soul rejoice. A sob left Cassius's throat. He clung to Morgan, feeling whole for the first time in five hundred years.

He was Icarus, the Awakener.

The demigod who had led a war in the Nether.

The being the God of Darkness loathed above all else.

Cassius stiffened. He lifted his head off Morgan's shoulder and looked past him. His stomach twisted.

Watching them from a distance, black tears dripping down his tortured face, his body and the broadsword he now wielded wreathed in inky flames, was the dark-winged demigod who went by the name of Victor Sloan.

39

MORGAN'S PULSE RACED AS HE BEHELD VICTOR'S NEWLY
revealed form. He could feel the immense power
emanating from the demigod. He'd expected the flames
around him to reek of corruption. Except they didn't.

Just like the black wind he possessed, the fire around
Victor seemed to be an extension of his divine abilities
rather than a manifestation of evil. The memories Morgan
had just experienced rushed through him once more.

Was it all a dream?!

He clenched his fists.

No. It was real. Cassius's name is Icarus!

He could feel the tremors still quaking through
Cassius's soul core not just at that revelation, but at what
they'd witnessed in that timeless moment of remembrance.
The war in the Nether they had led.

Cassius stared unblinkingly at Victor, his eyes full of
sorrow and trepidation. Morgan frowned. It was no coinci-
dence that they'd both caught a glimpse of their past at the
exact same moment.

Why part of the spell that had long held back their memories had cracked now, he wasn't sure. But there was no denying the truth echoing deep in Morgan's gut as he gazed upon the dark demigod watching them with a miserable look on his face.

The three of them were connected by a twisted thread of fate that extended way back into the past, to the forgotten times before the Fall.

Tal'Valan trembled beneath them.

Morgan's gaze snapped to the forest. His stomach lurched. The ice storm in the center was growing, the ferocious maelstrom expanding even as Boreas struggled to contain it with his own winter tempest. The bellow of the Wild God came from the darkness below.

Another crack reverberated across the valley, making the air vibrate unpleasantly. The rift in the sky throbbed above them. Morgan's breath stuttered as a giant skeletal finger slipped through the tear in the Spirit Realm.

The Reaper God was here.

"We need to go!" Cassius said urgently.

Morgan met his gaze and bobbed his head. Cassius turned to Victor. He hesitated before closing the distance to the dark demigod. Morgan stiffened.

"Come with us," Cassius said, his tone steady.

Victor flinched. "I—I can't." He swallowed, his eyes glistening with unshed tears. "I betrayed you!"

Cassius's brows drew together. "You were as much a victim of his machinations as I was. I may not remember everything that happened, but I know you did not deceive me of your own free will."

He took Victor's hand.

Victor gasped and tried to wrench his fingers free, his

flames flaring agitatedly. Morgan clenched his teeth and prepared to attack, black wind and Dryad magic swirling around him.

"Stop, Cassius!" Victor cried out. "I don't want to—"

"You won't hurt me, Victor."

Victor recoiled, his black wings freezing before sagging. Cassius's face softened. Dark tears were trailing down Victor's face once more, the crimson in his pupils swathed in grief and blackness.

Cassius brushed away the wet trails with his fingers. "We'll talk, after this. Let's finish what we came here to do."

Victor took a shuddering breath and nodded.

☙❦❧

WIND TORE AT CASSIUS'S WINGS AS THEY DROPPED TO the center of Tal'Valan. He squinted through the snow and ice numbing his face and spotted Boreas and Pan at the east edge of the storm.

They landed next to the Gods with dull thuds.

Boreas recoiled at the sight of Victor's demigod form, his powers faltering for a moment.

"*So, this is who you truly are!*" Pan spat.

"We don't have time for that right now!" Cassius snapped. "Demetrius's soul core is about to shatter!"

Pan paled. "*What?!*"

Cassius turned and gazed at the sheer white wall before them. "I'm going to cut through this!"

The screech of war demons came from high above. A sour taste filled his mouth as he searched the sky with his gaze. A fresh wave of monsters was pouring out of the opening rift. The Reaper God's right hand was almost completely visible.

Blood pounded in Cassius's ears.

He sheathed his Stark Steel sword and tightened his grip on the Ring of Death. Heaven's Light bloomed around him. He raised the scythe and swung it at the storm with a roar. The weapon sliced through the barrier, creating a doorway.

"Watch my back!" Cassius yelled as wind roared and battered them.

He entered Demetrius's tempest.

The power of the Frost Crown dropped on him like a dead weight, driving his feet into the ground and locking the air in his lungs. He saw Morgan and Victor buckle out of the corner of his eye. Boreas and Pan managed to withstand the pressure through their sheer, godly strength.

Cassius willed his legs to move. Frost crept across his armor and the Reaper God's scythe as he made for the center of the clearing, slowly deadening his limbs and his fingers. Black flames washed over him in a warm wave, melting away the ice.

He turned his head and met Victor's gaze.

"Together!" Victor shouted, his jaw set in a hard line.

Cassius nodded and forged ahead, the demigods who loved him at his side.

The war demons' shrieks rose from the sky. He looked up and caught a faint glimpse of leathery wings and crimson eyes far above the forest. Relief flashed through Cassius. He wasn't sure if it was luck or oversight, but the monsters seemed helpless in the face of the ice storm.

His soul core throbbed, startling him.

A voice sounded in his head, faint and weak. *My heart...
you must destroy the shard in my heart...*

Cassius stiffened. *Demetrius?!*

Understanding dawned as the demigod's tormented
words sank in. His eyes widened.

*The Frost Crown! There must be a shard of the Frost Crown
in Demetrius's heart, too, just like there is one in the Reaper God!*

"I think I know how to save Demetrius!" Cassius yelled
above the wintry squall.

Boreas and Pan closed in on him.

"*How?!*" Pan shouted.

"There's a shard of the Frost Crown in his heart! I need
to destroy it!"

"*What?!*" Horror filled Pan's face. His eyes flashed gold.
"*NOOO! I am not letting you do that! He will die!*"

Cassius clenched his jaw. "He won't! Just trust me,
okay?!"

Pan shook his head, fear robbing him of his senses.

Cassius's heart twisted. "Morgan! Victor! Hold him
back! Boreas, help me!"

The Winter God hesitated before nodding. Pan
screamed and cursed as Morgan and Victor grabbed his
arms and forced him still. Cassius ignored the raging deity
and kept moving.

The violent forces pulsing from the Frost Crown
swirled around and against him, trying to freeze the air in
his lungs and turn his body to ice. He gritted his teeth,
drew on Heaven's Light, and lifted one foot after the other.

Morgan's soul resonated strongly with his own while he
fought to keep Pan restrained, the black wind and Dryad
magic roaring from his core making a sound that matched
the tempest.

The storm flickered ahead of Cassius. A shape loomed out of the thick veil of ice and snow.

It was a giant oak tree.

Standing frozen beneath it, his body swathed in dazzling brilliance, was Demetrius. The demigod's eyes were white and blind and his beautiful face bereft of emotion. The Frost Crown blazed atop his head, savage and potent with fury.

Cassius looked up at the sky. The rift was tearing it apart.

His stomach plummeted as the ground cracked beneath him. The air rippled, magic leaking from the nexus at the heart of the Spirit Realm.

Shit!

A shape bolted out of the white haze. Boreas closed in behind his nephew and locked his arms around his body.

Demetrius's brow furrowed.

The war demons screamed and dropped toward them. Their wings tore and their bodies were ripped to pieces under the devastating force of the Frost Crown. Still they came, bound by the master who controlled them and the Reaper God who powered their wretched existence.

Cassius's heart thumped as he gazed at the senseless demigod. Something glinted on Demetrius's chest. A point of brightness centered over his heart.

"*Now, Awakener!*" Boreas roared.

Cassius ground his teeth, approached Demetrius, and stabbed his heart with the Ring of Death. The shard shattered with the sound of a breaking world.

The demigod froze, body going rigid.

Pan bellowed at the other end of the clearing, his scream of fury and anguish making the air vibrate.

Demetrius gasped, awareness returning to his face. Cassius met his dazed stare, yanked the Reaper God's scythe from his chest, and grabbed the Frost Crown.

The weapon seared his flesh and numbed his bones.

Cassius roared, Heaven's Light detonating around him. He wrenched the Frost Crown from Demetrius's head and lobbed it at Boreas. The Winter God snatched the weapon from the air and pressed it atop his head.

A shriek of pure rage tore across the Spirit Realm.

Cassius caught Demetrius in his arms as he fell and looked up jerkily, his heart thundering against his ribs.

The Reaper God was emerging from the rift. He raised his leg. A giant skeletal foot appeared from beneath his robe of shadows and descended toward the center of Tal'-Valan, aiming to crush them.

Cassius's eyes widened.

Peering out of the rift behind the Reaper God, the inky mantle around him rippling with wrath, was the God of Darkness.

"*I WILL DESTROY YOU ALL!*"

Boreas scowled. His eyes flashed gold. "*You can fuck off back to where you belong, asshole!*"

Divine power exploded around him.

Cassius cursed and shielded Demetrius with his body as they were thrown across the frozen ground. The essence of winter shot from Boreas's hands as he raised them to the sky, forming a spire of ice some fifty feet wide. It ascended rapidly, clearing Tal'Valan in the blink of an eye.

The Reaper God's orbits bloomed crimson and gold. He leaned forward.

Boreas roared and directed the spike straight into the Death God's chest, impaling him with the weapon. It smashed through his rib cage and shattered the shard in his heart.

The Reaper God's figure quivered violently before exploding in a rain of bones and black mist.

The light in the war demons' eyes blinked out. They grew limp and fell, their dying bodies raining down onto the ancient forest amidst the remains of the skeletal God. Ice exploded as they crashed violently into branches and upon the frozen ground.

The rift closed with a noise that put Cassius's teeth on edge. The crevasse where the Spirit Realm nexus had been stretched to breaking point shook violently and shrank as it healed.

The God of Darkness's howl faded to nothingness.

Silence fell over Tal'Valan.

With it came the end of winter.

✦ 40 ✦

BLOOD THRUMMED IN CASSIUS'S VEINS AS HE GAZED AT the clearing sky. The stars were slowly winking back into life.

"Is it—is it over?!" someone mumbled.

Cassius startled and met the dazed stare of the demigod in his arms. He lowered Demetrius to the ground and carefully pulled aside his bloodied robe. Relief made him weak.

Demetrius's wound was already healing.

"Thank God!" Cassius whispered shakily.

Demetrius looked past him to the bright spots of light dotting the inky firmament. Gold trembled in his pupils as his powers slowly returned. Tears darkened the haunting green in his irises.

"Is it really over?" he said brokenly.

Cassius took his frozen hand, his own chest tightening with emotion. "Yes, it's over."

"*Demetrius!*"

Pan's shout tore across the clearing. The ground trembled as he dashed toward them, Morgan and Victor striding rapidly in his wake.

Boreas helped Cassius bring Demetrius to his feet. "You did well, nephew."

The Winter God gently squeezed Demetrius's shoulder.

Demetrius sniffed and bobbed his head. He wiped his face and turned, a dazzling smile lighting his features as he looked upon the God who stumbled to a stop a short distance away.

"*Demetrius*," Pan murmured numbly, ashen faced.

Ice and snow melted in an expanding circle around Demetrius as he stepped into his lover's arms and kissed him. The power of spring washed over Tal'Valan in a warm, fresh wave that painted the landscape in a sea of green.

Cassius's heart lightened as he gazed at the couple. He couldn't believe it was really over. His pulse quickened. He looked over at Victor.

The Fiery had returned to his normal appearance, his face shuttered and his blue eyes dead. He met Cassius's stare and flinched. A sound came from the forest's edge before Cassius could utter words of comfort to him.

A tall, thin, naked man with snow-white skin and long, flowing, black hair was stumbling out of the shadows beneath the trees. Boreas swore and headed over to him.

Morgan stopped beside Cassius, his expression guarded. "Who's that?"

The Ring of Death trembled on Cassius's finger. *Oh.*

Boreas returned, his arm around the stranger's waist. Cassius swallowed. He removed the ring from his hand and passed it to its rightful owner. The man accepted it wordlessly, the ice-cold flesh of his fingers brushing against Cassius's palm. He shuddered as he slipped the weapon on.

Red and gold flared in the Reaper God's eyes. A robe of shadows trembled into existence around him, his body flickering to bone for an instant. Morgan stiffened as he finally registered the stranger's identity.

"*Thank you, Awakener*," the Reaper God murmured.

Cassius nodded, unsure what to say.

"Master!" Benjamin emerged from the forest, Loki at his side. The Reaper rushed over to his God and dropped before him on one knee, head bowed. "I am glad to see you well, Master."

"*Stand, Benjamin.*" The Reaper God's pupils shrank to tiny circles. "*What of Mortis?*"

"He is safe. He is with friends, on Earth."

The Reaper God sagged, eyes flaring with evident relief. "*Good.*"

Loki's wary gaze shifted from the Reaper God to the couple embracing passionately. "How long are they going to kiss for?" The imp paused and squinted. "Wait. Is he groping his bottom?"

Demetrius flushed, wrenched his mouth free, and pushed Pan away.

"I can't believe you!" he snapped, rubbing his behind gingerly. "We're in company!"

"*I have not seen you in weeks, my precious lamb,*" Pan protested. "*Surely, you know that kiss is not enough to quench my thirst for thee.*"

Demetrius's face grew pinched. "Your thirst is never-ending!"

Boreas muttered something under his breath. Pan sighed, despondent.

"Don't give me that puppy-eyed look," his lover said sharply. "Your dick doesn't look in the least bit repentant!"

Loki's gaze dropped. He recoiled, nose wrinkling. "*Eeew!*"

⚜

A PALE LIGHT WAS CREEPING ACROSS THE SKY WHEN THEY stepped out of the pavilion in Ivory Peaks.

Morgan's breath shuddered out of his lungs, the Dryad magic steeped into the bones of the kingdom rushing over him with a clean, green scent that reenergized him from the inside out.

Cassius's fingers brushed against his hand.

Morgan turned and gazed into the bright, gray eyes of the demigod he loved. He twisted, hands rising to cradle Cassius's face and kiss him.

A giant golden wing dropped between them.

Asteria snatched Cassius from his grasp and pulled him close to her body. The eagle crooned urgently, her large beak rubbing up and down the Empyreal as she started grooming him. Cassius chuckled.

"Hey!" Morgan turned to the prince watching on morosely. "I thought I told you to keep your eagle away from what's mine!"

"I'm not exactly happy about it either," Leiv muttered where he stood next to his father and mother.

Loki came out of the portal. He rocked to a stop next to Morgan, eyes rounding and ears flickering. "What is that giant bird doing to Cassius?"

Roald and Leiv stiffened when Boreas exited the gateway to the Spirit Realm. Pan and Demetrius followed, the Reaper God and Benjamin in their wake. Victor emerged last.

"Well, this is something," Regina mumbled weakly as she stared at the Reaper God.

It was clear the seer recognized Benjamin's master.

Cassius finally managed to escape Asteria's clutches and joined Morgan.

"You won," Hildur said quietly.

Cassius dipped his head. "Yes."

A muscle jumped in Roald's jawline. "Is it truly over?"

Cassius hesitated. Morgan took his hand. Cassius's fingers tightened reflexively around his.

"It is for now."

The Dryad royals looked at one another, relief bringing color to their pale faces.

"*You have our gratitude again, subjects of Atlanteia,*" Boreas said solemnly. "*This battle might have had a different outcome if not for your assistance.*"

The Dryad royals bowed.

"*Yeah, thanks,*" Pan murmured.

Demetrius elbowed him viciously in the ribs.

Pan grimaced, cleared his throat, and dipped his head formally at the Dryads. "*Thank you.*"

"Isn't there something else you wish to say?" Demetrius whispered out of the corner of his mouth.

He indicated Morgan and Cassius with a not-so-subtle jerk of his head.

"*Oh.*"

Pan squared his shoulders and turned to face them. Cassius tensed next to Morgan. Morgan squeezed his hand gently.

"*First off, that was a shitty thing to do.*" Pan jabbed a finger at Cassius. "*I thought I was going to have a heart attack when you skewered Dem with that damn scythe!*"

"That is not what we discussed!" Demetrius hissed. "I *told* him to stab me in the heart!"

Loki's mouth curled.

"You are such a fool," he told Pan haughtily.

"Are you sure that's the Keeper of the Eternity Key?" Roald whispered nervously to Hildur.

The queen sighed.

260

PAN SCRATCHED HIS HEAD AND FLASHED AN AWKWARD look at the Dryad royal family and Regina.

"*You guys sure you want to do this here? In front of all these witnesses?*"

Cassius glanced at Morgan. Morgan shrugged.

"We don't have any objections," Cassius murmured. "I trust everyone present here. They will keep this a secret if we so wish."

Morgan nodded. "I agree."

Hildur traded a puzzled look with the other Dryads. "What's going on?"

"*We made a deal,*" Pan explained. "*I told them I would reveal what I know of their past if they helped me save Demetrius.*"

Regina inhaled sharply. Hildur and Roald stared, surprise widening their eyes.

Pan turned to Victor. "*What about you? You stand to lose the most out of this.*"

Victor fisted his hands, his face darkening. "It is time for me to face the consequences of my actions."

Cassius's belly twisted. "Victor."

Morgan's brows drew together. Cassius knew the Aerial was upset that he still cared for the other man, regardless of his past deeds.

Pan blew out a heavy sigh. "*Seriously, you fuckers make me want to weep.*" He narrowed his eyes at Cassius and Victor. "*Know this before I tell you the truth. You were both victims of the machinations of that Primordial. The only one who always distrusted that God was this dumbass here.*"

He cocked a thumb at Morgan.

Morgan blinked, his face clearing. "Really?"

"*Yeah,*" Pan muttered. "*It was like some kind of creepy sixth sense. Elios hated you for it. He wanted to get rid of you because he knew you would one day figure out his intentions.*"

Morgan froze. Victor's pupils flashed crimson. Cassius's heartbeat thundered in his ears.

"Elios?" he repeated hoarsely.

Pan nodded grimly. "*That is the name of that God of Darkness.*"

Boreas gaped.

"*You remembered it too?!*" he blurted out. "*I thought I was the only one. It all came to me during that battle!*"

Pan rubbed the back of his neck. "*It is because part of the spell that was used to obliterate those memories broke when Victor awakened.*"

"What?" Hildur mumbled. Her confused gaze swung between Pan and the Fiery. "What do you mean?!"

"*Victor is a demigod, like Cassius and Morgan,*" Pan said guardedly. "*His powers manifested in the Spirit Realm, just now.*"

The Dryads paled and stared at the Fiery.

"My name is—" Victor faltered. He swallowed, his nails digging into his palms. He lifted his chin and met Cassius's gaze head on. "My name is Coraos."

His words echoed loudly in the hush that befell them.

"*You are the son of Nyx, the Primordial Goddess of the Night,*" Pan said matter-of-factly. "*Your father was Nimexis, a demigod of Darkness and Shadows. Elios is your half-brother.*" He glanced at Morgan. "*As is Ivmir.*"

Shock drained the color from Victor's face. He swayed, as if all the strength had left his body.

A buzzing sounded in Cassius's ears. He could feel Morgan's pulse thundering against his fingertips where they held hands.

Pan turned to them.

"*Your mother was Nyx,*" he told Morgan. "*She bequeathed you her greatest treasure, the Sword of Wind, before she passed. It was the weapon she wielded to banish her father Chaos to the Abyss. As for your Dryad origins, your sire was none other than Isdar, the demigod son of Queen Atlanteia. It is from him that you inherited the crown of oak that denotes your lineage.*"

Morgan drew a sharp breath. Hildur gasped. Regina leaned heavily on her staff, her expression stunned.

Pan's gaze shifted to Cassius. "*Out of the three of you, your origins are the most mysterious. You are rumored to be the son of Aether, the Primordial God of Light. As for your mother, her identity remains an enigma to this day.*"

Cassius's limbs went weak.

"Is that why the Lucifugous and the Nymphs call me the Guardian of Light?!" he mumbled.

Pan's face tightened. "*Yes. But there is more to it than that. You see, you are not just a demigod or the current Awakener. You are one of four Guardians tasked with keeping watch over the Nether."*

Heat flared through Cassius's belly from Morgan's soul core. He could tell the demigod was as dumbfounded by this revelation as he was.

"A Guardian of the Nether?" Cassius repeated numbly.

Pan dipped his head solemnly. *"You are Icarus, the North Star. Your brothers are Archon, the West Star, and Nildar, the East Star."* He paused. *"As for the South Star, he is no more. He perished when the Nether tore open and the Fall happened."*

Cassius's breath hitched. He squeezed his eyes shut.

He could feel his heart breaking with every word Pan uttered.

Morgan grasped his hand so tightly he would have broken his bones had he been human.

"The war in the Nether." Cassius's vision blurred with tears as he opened his eyes once more and gazed at Pan. "Was it instigated by Elios?!"

"Yes," Boreas said.

Cassius's head twisted jerkily to the Winter God.

"We know now that it must have been his first scheme to bring about the return of the Primordial he always worshipped and looked upon as the rightful ruler of all that exists. His grandfather, Chaos."

"Elios is the son of two Primordial Gods, Nyx and Erebus," Pan added in the shocked silence. *"His twin is Hypnos. Hypnos disappeared after the Fall. Those of us able to recall our past suspect he is the reason the memories of the Fallen were erased."*

Blood rushed in Cassius's ears, a pounding storm that tore at his soul.

"What was his name?" he whispered, his gaze locked

unblinkingly on Pan. "The South Star. Tell me his name. Please."

Something that looked a lot like pity flared in the depths of the Wild God's eyes. *"Rohengar. His name was Rohengar."*

The tears spilled over and dripped down Cassius's cheeks. The face of the angel with the slate-blue armor and the smile that could light up the sky swam before his eyes.

He wasn't aware of his sobs until Morgan took him in his arms and crushed him to his chest. Cassius buried his face against the demigod's heart and prayed for forgiveness.

But he knew it would never come. Not after what he had done. His hands were forever drenched in the blood of his fallen brother and his sins would follow him to the end of his days.

❧ 42 ❦

ONE WEEK LATER

"What is this, some kind of sick tradition?" Suzie Myers asked suspiciously.

Morgan made a face and paid for his order. "I don't know what you mean."

The witch scowled and indicated the table in the middle of the *Occulta* where his team had gathered. "What I mean is you guys always end up gathering here like a flock of unwanted crows after one of your missions and drink me out of a bar."

"We're paying customers, Suz," Julia said in a hurt voice as she picked up a tray brimming with beers and cocktails.

"*You* can come every night," Suzie grunted. "We make twice as much money as a holiday weekend whenever you turn up."

Morgan easily believed that claim. *Occulta* was the most popular hangout amongst the otherwordly and magic users in San Francisco.

Julia arched an eyebrow. "Are you pimping out your friend?"

"You know I am," the witch said shamelessly. She glanced over at their table and frowned. "By the way, I don't see Charlie."

Morgan's mood darkened. "He's with Reuben and Jasper."

Suzie stared. "What's with that look? And what's he doing with Snow White and Grumpy?"

Morgan smirked at the nicknames the witch had given the angel and the demon.

Julia put the tray back down and leaned over the counter.

"The operative word in that sentence is 'doing,'" she whispered conspiratorially.

Suzie blinked. "Huh?"

Julia sighed. "Join the dots, Suz."

Suzie frowned. Her face cleared. She inhaled sharply.

"*Get out!*" She grabbed her chest in a pearl-clutching move and slapped Julia on the arm. "No way is that cutie pie being done by those two?!"

Julia winced. "Easy there, Muhammad Ali." She grinned. "And he is. Charlie is probably jammed between that angel and that demon like a sandwich filling right now."

Morgan made a gagging noise.

"Who's jammed between whom like what now?" someone said dully.

Suzie whirled around. Zach had come out of the back room. He was filling in for a bartender who'd called in sick for the night. He narrowed his eyes at his girlfriend.

"We're not doing a threesome." The demon's gaze

flicked to Julia and Morgan. "And definitely not with either of those two."

"Hey!" Julia protested.

"What's wrong with us?" Morgan grumbled.

Zach pointed accusingly at Morgan. "*You* are high maintenance." His finger moved to Julia. "And *you* will get us stabbed in the back by your stalkers."

Morgan bristled. Julia smiled, pleased.

"You're right," Suzie said with a shrewd nod. "Not that I wanted a threesome." She waved a hand vaguely. "We were talking about Charlie and his two beaus." She stared at their table and chewed her lip. "By the way, who are those guys with you? And is that kid of legal age to be here?"

Morgan followed her gaze.

"They are uninvited guests," he said nastily. "Feel free to kick them out."

Julia rolled her eyes. "No, they're not. They're our...friends."

Suzie's brow furrowed. "What was with that pause?"

৩৩

"*I* THINK YOU SHOULD STOP DRINKING," PAN TOLD Demetrius, his tone fairly harassed.

Demetrius pouted, the flush of color staining his cheeks a clear indication that he was well on his way to getting totally drunk. "And I think you should stop being a party pooper." He leaned sideways and nudged Mortis's shoulder. "Isn't that right, Mort?"

The Khimer clutched his non-alcoholic cocktail and

stole a nervous glance at the silent figure beside him. "Hmm, sure."

The Reaper God popped some peanuts in his mouth and crunched slowly, his dark gaze sweeping the crowded bar as if he were tallying how many souls he would be harvesting tonight.

Cassius sighed. They were the center of attention and not necessarily for the right reasons. The otherwordly and magic users in the city were used to all kinds of weirdness. But even they could tell that half the people seated at their table didn't really belong in this realm.

For one thing, the Gods were dressed like gangsters, a state of affairs Cassius blamed entirely on Pan. The only ones in attire appropriate for the venue were Demetrius, Mortis, and Loki, and this only because Julia and Adrianne had taken them shopping earlier that day.

Demetrius's stunningly good looks weren't helping matters, a fact Pan seemed to be regretting since it had been his idea to meet up tonight.

As for Mortis, Pan and Boreas had granted him a human body so he could navigate the Earth freely for the day and accompany his master. The guise they'd given him matched Demetrius's handsomeness, his warm, honey flesh and rich brown eyes contrasting sharply with the pale-skinned Reaper God next to him.

"Can they really do that?" Morgan had asked skeptically when Benjamin had arrived with the message from Pan. "Give him a human body?"

The Reaper had shrugged. "They are Gods of Life."

"By the way, why are you carrying messages for Pan?" Cassius had said curiously.

Benjamin's orbits had flared for an instant.

"Master and the Wild God have become good friends," he'd replied, mildly puzzled. "They spend a lot of time talking these days. I am unsure of the subject matter, but Master seems very intrigued by what the God has been telling him."

Loki had huffed at that, his cat tail swinging with disdain.

The imp was currently seated next to Cassius, his curious gaze roaming the bar. He had taken on a teenage human form thanks to some help from Boreas, the only hint of his otherworldliness his yellow eyes and the tiny horns hidden under his beanie hat.

Cassius caught Pan glancing at him. For some strange reason, he thought the Wild God had arranged this meeting to try and cheer him up. Considering his mood lately, this wasn't exactly a bad thing.

He and Morgan still hadn't told Strickland and their team about what had been revealed to them following the battle in the Spirit Realm, nor had they confessed their true identities. Victor had left for London almost immediately after their return to Earth and Cassius hadn't heard from the Fiery since.

He knew the demon needed time to come to terms with what he'd done. Still, Cassius wished they could talk, like they used to in the past.

His heart twisted painfully at that thought. He knew there would be no going back to the old days. Not after everything they'd learned from Pan.

When he wasn't being miserable and wallowing in silence, he and Morgan had spoken for hours on end after they'd come back to San Francisco. They'd pooled together every bit of information they'd gleaned from that moment in the Spirit Realm when they'd recalled who Cassius was and what had happened in the Nether, to see if it would help them elucidate the mystery of the Fall itself.

So far, they hadn't gotten any closer to the truth.

Still, Cassius knew the day would come when they would finally uncover what had happened during that war and how Rohengar had died.

One good thing that had come out of the fight to save Pan's kingdom was that the fracture lines on Earth had all but disappeared. It was because the Reaper God was no longer being controlled by the Frost Crown.

"This is weird, right?" Adrianne hissed to Cassius out of the corner of her mouth.

Boreas stirred the ice in his drink and gave her a winsome smile from where he sat opposite her.

Bailey swallowed. "Like, totally weird, right?"

Morgan and Julia returned with their trays of drinks before Cassius could say comforting words to the sorceress and the wizard. Loki reached for a beer.

Cassius batted his hand away from the bottle.

"You're sticking to soda," he told the imp firmly. "I don't want Suzie losing her license. Besides, you know what happened the last time I gave you beer."

"I only have a low alcohol tolerance in my cat form," the imp protested.

"It's soda or nothing."

Loki released a sigh worthy of an Oscar.

Demetrius propped his chin on his steepled hands and observed Cassius with a heated stare. "By the way, did I tell you I used to have a crush on you?"

Morgan spat out his whiskey. Cassius opened and closed his mouth soundlessly.

"*I knew this would happen*," Pan grumbled.

"Wait." Morgan looked up from where he was dabbing his shirt with a napkin, suspicion darkening his eyes. "Does this mean you were being a complete douchebag to Cassius because your boyfriend had a crush on him?!"

"What?" Demetrius scowled at Pan. "Were you nasty to my sweet boo?!"

"*No, my lamb*," Pan said hastily. He glared at Morgan. "*And you! That is the pot calling the kettle black, is it not? I mean, you got jealous of a goddamn eagle!*"

Boreas tittered. The Winter God's ears had gone a rich red. Cassius cut his eyes to his drink.

"What's in that glass?" he asked Morgan and Julia suspiciously.

"A double vodka," they said simultaneously.

Everyone froze before slowly staring at the Winter God.

Adrianne's mouth pressed into a thin line. "So, that's a quad vodka?"

Morgan swore. "Fuck, he's drunk, isn't he?"

Loki's haughty gaze swung between Demetrius and Boreas. "I see the two of them share the same awful alcohol tolerance."

Cassius decided not to remind the imp that his wasn't any better. A hot hand landed on the back of his knuckles, startling him. Demetrius leaned across the table, a pout on his striking face as he danced a finger teasingly up and down Cassius's flesh.

"Now, now, Cass, don't ignore me. It's not every day I get to see my favorite hottie in all his glory."

Adrianne's elbow slipped off the table. Bailey choked on his beer. Julia looked at Morgan and grinned.

The Reaper God leaned sideways.

"*Is this what they call flirting?*" he asked Boreas.

The Winter God nodded, beaming. He was evidently a happy drunk. The Reaper God straightened and eyed Mortis with a faint frown.

"Is something wrong, Master?" the Khimer said anxiously.

"*I like the way you call me master,*" the Reaper God said solemnly.

"Ah." Mortis bit his lip. "Okay."

Cassius stared. *Wait. Are those two—?*

"Cassius," Demetrius crooned.

"Hey, jerk face, control your boyfriend!" Morgan snapped at Pan.

The Reaper God rose abruptly. "*Come, Mortis.*" He offered his hand to the Khimer. "*It is time.*"

Something that looked like disappointment flashed in Mortis's eyes. "Oh." He took the Reaper God's hand and let him pull him to his feet. "Yes, we must return." A brittle smile stretched his mouth as he glanced around the table. "Goodbye, everyone. It was nice to see you again." He looked at the Reaper God. "If you give me but a moment, Master, I shall dispose of this body and return to my—"

"*Whatever for?*" the Reaper God interrupted blankly.

Mortis blinked. "Huh?"

"*I have an agreement with Pan and Boreas,*" the Reaper God said. "*This body is yours to do with as you wish. And you shall be needing it for what we are about to do. Now, off to the hotel we go. Pan has booked us the best suite in town.*"

Julia's eyes rounded. Adrianne blinked, confused. Her face cleared. She gasped and covered her mouth with a hand.

"What?" Bailey said, puzzled.

Pan smirked like he'd played the best joke in the world.

Cassius made a face. *So, that's what he was teaching the Reaper God?*

"What—what do you mean, Master?" Mortis stammered as the Reaper God led him away. "What hotel? What are we going to *do?!*"

The Reaper God stopped abruptly, his pupils flaring crimson and gold. He brought his face close to Mortis.

"*Why, I thought that would be evident. We are going to consummate our relationship, of course. Pan has given me some careful instructions and a book on the subject. It is called the Kama Sutra. I made notes.*" He bobbed his head, his expression confident. "*We are going to try all the positions.*"

"*Ma—master!*" Mortis squeaked, face flushing beetroot red.

"*That Khimer doth protest too much,*" Pan chuckled as the Reaper God exited the bar with his blushing and clearly eager bride.

"Did you know?" Morgan grunted.

"*What, that they had the hots for one another?*" Pan shrugged. "*Mortis is the Right Hand of the Reaper God and his closest companion. That foolish God was bound to fall for one of his Khimers one day. I am just glad it's this kid. He is guileless and has a pure heart. And I know he returns his master's affections.*"

A warm feeling fluttered through Cassius's chest. He was happy for Mortis. He gasped as he was suddenly yanked across the table by the neck of his shirt.

"Bad Cassius." Demetrius shook a finger under Cassius's nose and hiccupped. "You deserve a punishment for shrugging me off."

Cassius froze as the demigod smacked their mouths

together in a wet, sloppy kiss. Morgan made a horrified sound. Loki sucked in air.

The noise level in *Occulta* dropped.

"Holy crap!" Suzie squealed from behind the bar.

Julia slapped the table and wheezed, tears streaming down her face. Gold flashed in Pan's eyes.

He glared at Cassius, incensed. "*You damn Jezebel!*"

Cassius and Morgan's adventures continue in Oathbreaker.

WANT A FREE PREQUEL STORY?

Sign up to Ava's newsletter to get Unbound, as well as new release alerts, sneak peeks, giveaways, and more.

AFTERWORD

I hope you enjoyed Edge Lines, the third book in Fallen
Messengers. This book is a turning point in the series, with
more shocking revelations about Cassius and Morgan's
pasts and the introduction of Victor Sloan as one of the
main secondary protagonists. A lot of this story is set in
other realms only alluded to in the previous books and I
had a lot of fun bringing those to life for you, especially the
world of the Dryads. I would love it if you could leave a
review of Edge Lines on Amazon or Goodreads. Reviews
help readers like you find my books and I truly appreciate
your honest opinions about my stories. Make sure to stay
signed up to my newsletter to get more free stories in the
Fallen Messengers universe!

BOOKS BY AVA MARIE SALINGER

FALLEN MESSENGERS

Fractured Souls - 1

Spellbound - 2

Edge Lines - 3

Oathbreaker - 4

CONTEMPORARY ROMANCE WRITTEN AS A.M. SALINGER

Nights Series

Twilight Falls Series

ABOUT THE AUTHOR

Ava Marie Salinger is the pen name of an Amazon bestselling author who has always wanted to write MM urban fantasy. FALLEN MESSENGERS is her first MM urban fantasy romance series. When she's not dreaming up hotties to write about, you'll find Ava creating kickass music playlists to write to, spying on the wildlife in her garden, drooling over gadgets, and eating Chinese. She also writes contemporary romance as A.M. Salinger.

Discover where you can connect with Ava:

https://linktr.ee/avamariesalingerauthor

Ingram Content Group UK Ltd.
Milton Keynes UK
UKHW021113030523
421135UK00017B/145/J